# THE
# DEVIL
## AND THE
# MUSE

# THE
# DEVIL
## AND THE
# MUSE

MANDY JACKSON-BEVERLY

CRICKET PUBLISHING / U.S.A.

Copyright © 2017 by Mandy Jackson-Beverly

All rights reserved. Published by Cricket Publishing, established 2015.

**Author's Note**

This novel is a work of the author's imagination, and all names and descriptions of the characters, including the Congressman called Ross Thorton, are entirely fictional. Any similarity between fictional characters and real people is strictly coincidental. Real businesses, events and locations that are mentioned in the narrative are used fictitiously.

Jackson-Beverly, Mandy.
The Devil And The Muse / by Mandy Jackson-Beverly. — 1st ed.

Paperback edition
978-0-9965088-4-1 1. Dark Fantasy —Fiction. 2. Vampire —
Fiction. 3. Occult — Fiction. 4. Supernatural Thriller — Fiction.

*To Birdie,*
*with love.*

# THE MOTTO OF THE ALLEGIANCE
## SINE VIRTVTE OMNIA SVNT PERDITA
(Without courage, all is lost.)

**The Allegiance:** An ancient organization that protects art and Creatives, and gives sanctuary to those threatened by religious zealots.

**Creatives:** Artists who paint truths within paintings, secrets only visible to a few; their images share the gift of prophecy. All Creatives have amethyst-colored eyes.

### *Key Members of the Allegiance*

**The Lady and the Rose:** Goddess, and protector of the Allegiance.

**Hakon:** Nordic fae prince, creator of the Allegiance, father of Prudence, and married to Sonja.

**Sonja:** Ancient immortal Nordic seer.

**Prudence:** Italian immortal seer, head of the Allegiance, married to Stefan, mother of Gabriel.

**Stefan:** Serbian vampire, warrior, poet, member of the Allegiance.

**Gabriel:** Italian, half-vampire, half-warlock, second-in-command of the Allegiance.

**Alessandro:** Italian vampire, warrior, member of the Allegiance, married to Chantal, father of Christopher and Coco.

**Chantal:** American vampire and Creative, mother of Christopher and Coco.

**Christopher:** American, half-vampire, half-human, lawyer for the Allegiance, engaged to Layla.

**Coco (Colombina):** American half-vampire, half-human, Creative, member of the Allegiance, and UCLA art professor.

**Kishu:** American, father of Chantal, grandfather to Christopher and Coco, and member of the Allegiance.

**Antonia:** Italian human with a touch of fae blood, mother of Layla, mediator for the Allegiance.

**Layla:** Italian human with a touch of fae blood, psychoanalytic therapist, engaged to Christopher, member of the Allegiance, and Coco's best friend.

**Sabine:** Ancient Italian vampire, warrior, doctor, and member of the Allegiance.

**Pelayo:** El Salvadoran vampire, Gabriel's protégé.

**Maria:** Italian, human, member of the Allegiance, and café owner.

**Frederico:** Italian vampire, warrior, member of the Allegiance.

**Eduardo:** Italian art professor, and human member of the Allegiance. Husband to Caprecia, father of Louisa.

**Caprecia:** Portuguese vampire, member of the Allegiance.

**Louisa:** Human, Italian artist, protected by the Allegiance, Ignacio's former lover. .

## *Other Characters*

**Ignacio:** English, lone vampire.

**Jeremy:** American law student, twin to Arianna, son of Katja (human) and Elion (fae). Protected by the Allegiance.

**Arianna:** American, student, adoptive parents are Isabel and Steven. Protected by the Allegiance.

**Isabel:** American, protected by the Allegiance.

**Jason:** American, human, accountant for the Federal Department in Washington, D.C., longtime friend of Christopher.

**Kenan:** Italian vampire, determined to destroy all Creatives and the Allegiance.

**Domenico:** Italian vampire, and Kenan's maker.

**Freyja:** Nordic goddess of the Underworld.

Hidden in the midst of the Dolomite Mountains of Northern Italy, stands *Casa della Pietra*, the stronghold of the Allegiance. The rise of her tall towers burst through clouds of darkened gray, she is a titan of a fortress, a protector of all who enter her walls.

If you listen, you might hear the ancient seer, Prudence, speaking words of reassurance to those new to this place. For Arianna, Jeremy, and Isabel have entered a world where immortals live with unparalleled purpose, and great love.

There has been no whisper of Kenan's whereabouts, but evil creeps with silent steps, and lurks behind its prey, waiting for a shimmer of weakness to appear in one's humanity.

As the Creative, Coco awakens, and she is drawn to a painting. Pigments of paint pull at her fingertips, and a hidden image appears. She glimpses the nuance of darkness lingering in the decrepit minds of the wicked.

Enter into this world,
but cast aside old ideas.
Step carefully,
but step with deliberation,
For there is no room for indecision
when the devil lies waiting...

# 1

*A TEENAGE GIRL walks briskly along a street. She passes a row of vacant weatherboard homes marred with boarded windows. A rusted chain-linked fence separates the decay of urban life from the cracked and potholed cement sidewalk. A streetlight flickers once, twice, and then sputters its last breath. The neighborhood is cloaked in darkness. A wind that comes from nowhere pushes the girl along with scatterings of trash. She trips and falls, spilling books from her bag. Thunder cracks and rain pelts down. She pushes her long black hair back from her eyes and searches for her belongings.*

*As she reaches for a textbook, a heavy black boot crushes her hand to the sidewalk. She cries out and gasps for breath, shaking uncontrollably. A pale hand grabs her by the throat, drags her into a nearby alley, and throws her onto the ground. A tall man in dark clothing stands over her. In one swift movement he rips her jeans apart and tears away her panties. He stares at an area just below her right hip and spits on her skin.*

*"Whore!"*

*He pulls her up by her hair and holds her firmly against the wall. She screams. He pushes her torn panties into her mouth and then undoes the zipper of his jeans. He shoves her legs apart, runs a hand over her pubic hair and this time her scream is muffled when he thrusts into her. A mocking smile crosses his face.*

*"A virgin whore!"*

*He thrusts deeper and faster. His smile reveals his extended fangs. The girl's eyes widen in horror. A flash of lightning crosses the sky. The attacker leans his head back and runs his tongue over his bloodstained lips. He hoists the unconscious girl into a fireman's carry, and flees into the darkness. A rivulet of blood fades into a memory, washed away by drops of rain.*

Pigments of paint return to the canvas. Coco drops her hand and stares at the image she has painted of Christopher's D.C. townhouse. Lightning floods the studio and a deluge of wind and snow swirls around *Casa della Pietra*. A familiar meow beckons Coco back to real time. She picks up Thalia, her thirteen-pound cat, grateful for the familiar feline form.

# 2

*Washington, D.C.*

JASON SANDBERG PONDERED the figures on the computer screen. He leaned back in his chair, gazed around his office, and drummed his fingers on his desk in time to AC/DC's "Highway to Hell" blasting through his headphones. His dark hair fell in disorganized curls over his forehead and onto a pair of rectangular, black-rimmed glasses.

He had repeatedly analyzed the documents from the appropriations subcommittee on Labor, Health and Human Services, and Education, and followed the routes where specific funding had been allocated over the past few years, but something just didn't add up.

The issue lay not in the departments where the funding had been allocated, but further down the line to the actual writing of checks, specifically in education. In defense of the accountants, this was an easy oversight. The school in question looked like any other inner-city school: the majority of students from single-family homes, mostly Latino and African American, with a high dropout rate, nothing out of the ordinary there.

But Jason knew better than to ignore the niggling in his gut. Unbalanced budgets never sat well with him, and money missing from an already strained public school system pissed him off royally. He remembered where he had heard of Todos los Santos Community High School. A friend of his had taught science there until a lack of funds forced the few members of the Parent-Teacher Administration to decide whether to keep science or physical education. They chose the latter. Shortly after, the school had changed its status to a religious charter school, and was overseen by a conservative branch of the Catholic church.

Jason ran the numbers one more time while he waited for statistics on graduating students to come through via his secretary. This was the problem area where the figures didn't correlate. From what he could tell, the daily amount funded for each student didn't equal the number of physical bodies in the classrooms. This might never have come to his attention, had he not seen a Missing Person flyer stuck to a wall while attending a recent PTA funding meeting. The curled edges and faded tape showed the flyer had been up for some time.

The girl in the photograph had been missing for two years, and she had attended Todos los Santos. As much as it pained him, Jason could see how one absent teenager could get lost in the ever-widening cracks of the social system, but the number of missing students over a two-year period in Ward 8 alone had reached double digits. Delving further, he had discovered more similarities: the missing students were all female, and came from Catholic families.

He looked up and pushed off his headphones when his secretary entered and placed a file on his desk. "Here's the list of high schools in the areas you requested, along with the entering and exiting student lists."

"Thanks," Jason said. "Any word from Chris's office?"

"Not yet, but I'll let you know as soon as Michelle calls." She set a mug of coffee and a bagel and cream cheese on a paper plate next to the file.

Jason looked up. "Thanks."

"Figured you'd missed breakfast…again," she said, on her way out the door.

He slid his headphones back over his ears, took a swig of coffee followed by a bite of the bagel, and then opened the file. What he saw confirmed his initial thoughts. Things were not kosher at Todos los Santos Community High School. When the first few bars of Warren Zevon's "Lawyers, Guns and Money" started playing, he pushed up the sleeves of his denim shirt, took out his phone and checked the time. It would be 7:00 a.m. in L.A.

He placed his headphones around his neck, pushed a pre-programmed number on his phone, and left his friend another message.

"Where the fuck are you, Chris? Call me—it's urgent."

# 3

PERCHED ON THE rooftop of an affluent Georgetown, D.C. residence, the vampire cast his gaze along the street to an approaching SUV. His dark, shoulder-length hair, framed his angular Latino face that was fixed in an austere expression. He rubbed a hand over his dark stubble, and then raised himself to his full height. Flurries of snowflakes twirled and swayed as they were picked up by a fierce wind howling over the city.

A set of iron gates opened inward at the far end of the street. The black Cadillac Escalade slipped through and into the high-walled property. The vampire waited until the clang of metal told him the gates had closed. He leaped thirty feet to the ground, and ran at breakneck speed toward the high walls. He came to an abrupt halt; his immortal body showing no signs of fatigue, no gasping for breath or rapid heartbeat. He tilted his head and listened, hoping to hear a hint of speech before the garage door closed.

For weeks he had observed many dark-windowed vehicles drive in and out of this place. Public records revealed a European investment group recently bought the property; cash sale, all furniture included, no questions asked. When the vehicles left these grounds, they headed to a warehouse near Ward 8, owned by the same investment group.

The vampire was aware of the dark magic bordering the properties, having been burned many times by the curses that reached out to intruders. He climbed the closest tree, hoping for a better view of the garage. But as soon as his feet landed on the first limb, a strand of silver spread out from the bark and wormed its way over his boots. He winced as the metal ate through the leather into his skin.

A car door opened and a girl's voice cried out *"Ayuda!"* The vampire lashed at the twisting silver vine with a knife and freed himself. The wounds would heal, but he would hear the young girl's scream for help forever. Pelayo had first heard about the missing Latinas from friends who lived in D.C. He had tracked the girls for months, and from what he could tell, their journeys ended here. Tonight, the girl's plea for help was the information he needed. As much as her situation gnawed at him, he knew better than to go in without backup.

Moments later he unlocked a nondescript door in an alley, slipped inside and closed the door behind him. Prudence, head of the Allegiance, had asked him to pick up items from Christopher's D.C. office. He walked over to the mahogany desk. A sticky note with the word "urgent" written in bold letters graced a large yellow envelope, and there were numerous memos attached to thick files, each with a note from Michelle, Christopher's secretary, asking that he call her as soon as possible.

A computer bag sat next to the files. Pelayo reached for the strap and yanked it over his shoulder. A wave of nostalgia washed over him, and his eyes pricked with tears. The essence of familiarity rushed up his fingers and a spark of joy he had dared not seek touched his heart. He placed everything inside the computer bag, took one more look around the office, and exited.

# 4

*Casa della Pietra, Northern Italy*

THE VISION OF the girl's rape flashed across Coco's mind. She eased herself onto a chair and practiced the controlled breathing exercises her grandfather, Kishu, had taught her. Gradually, her mind calmed, and she mentally replayed the image she had seen behind her painting. This time she endeavored to separate the emotional context, to see beyond the trauma and look for clues.

Coco closed her eyes and tapped into the basic observational skills her artistic profession demanded. *A run-down area...urban.* She sniffed and caught the smell of diesel fuel. She listened to the wind and rain, and then heard another sound, not a car, something bigger. *A bus.* She pushed her imaginary pause button and stared at the young girl's face. *Dark straight long hair, brown eyes, thin plucked eyebrows, no jewelry. Latina.* The scene continued, but Coco froze on the image of the man. *Pale skin, thin lips, and sinister expression...not human.* Coco searched for more clues. The vampire held the girl against a wall. *A red-bricked wall. A dead-end alley. Trash on the ground.*

The scene disappeared and she snapped back to the present. Coco shivered, feeling somewhat faint from the intensity of the assault. Moments later, Gabriel's arms encircled her. She clung to him and breathed in his scent, that oddly reassuring smell of sandalwood and berries.

"Behind the painting," she said. "You need to see the images."

"Do you want to go into another room?" Gabriel asked.

Coco shook her head. The sound of his velvety deep voice, tinged with an Italian accent, had calmed her. The shift in his embrace told her that his arm was extended to the painting. She closed her eyes and prepared herself for the sounds of horror. When the scene had finished replaying itself, Gabriel picked her up, and sat with her in his arms on a plush club chair by the fireplace.

Coco gazed into his golden eyes. "Can you find her?" she asked.

"I hope so," Gabriel said. He lifted her chin, and kissed her.

"I love you so much," she whispered.

"*Ti amo,* Colombina. *Mia bella musa.*"

# 5

CHRISTOPHER SAT ON a sofa in front of a dwindling fire, with his beloved fiancée, Layla, curled up beside him. His strong body had healed from the near-fatal gunshot wound he had received, while helping to rescue his mother, Chantal, from the heinous vampire, Kenan. This time, the vampire genes Christopher had inherited from his father, Alessandro, had saved his life.

He flipped through a slew of emails, and then listened to the messages from Jason. They had been friends for years, having first met when they were both freshmen at UCLA. During their first year they had been roommates, and later went on to share an apartment in Westwood Village. After graduating, Jason relocated to D.C. where he gained his Masters in Public Policy from Georgetown University. For the past four years he had worked for the Federal Department where his job required him to disperse discretionary funding for education. Jason loved numbers and hated the politically corrupt. Christopher tapped on Jason's number. His friend picked up on the first ring.

"Chris, where the hell have you been?"

"Family emergency. I'm in Italy. What's up?"

"I need your advice," Jason said.

"Legal, or as a friend?"

"Both. I've found some discrepancies in funding. My research has led me to one of the big boys, and it's dirty. This isn't just about money. I think there's some kind of correlation between where funds were allocated and a bunch of missing female high school students."

Christopher leaned forward.

The line was silent.

"Chris, are you there?"

"I'm here, just taking in what you said. How many others know about this?"

"Anyone with access to this information wouldn't notice anything off. I look for anomalies. Most of the employees around here just want to get home for dinner at a reasonable time. But there are four of us with access codes, including my secretary. The only reason I found this was because I happened to be at a PTA meeting at one of the local public schools and saw a poster for a missing girl. Her name rang a bell, and when I got back to the office I remembered why. She was listed as attending one of the schools to which my department allocates funds. Which, by the way, is a charter school, a Catholic charter school, so they receive funding. According to the files, this young girl was only listed as "absent" for a few weeks and then went back on the books as "present." Thing is, she's been missing for two years. And she's not the only one, there are others and it runs into double figures. The Department of Education has been paying out funds for students who have been missing for years."

"So you're suggesting one of the four people with access to this information is committing fraud," Christopher said.

"Yes."

"What would this person gain from this act?" Christopher asked.

"I'll take a wild guess and say he's being blackmailed."

"He?"

"Yeah," Jason answered, "as far as I know there's only one person out of the four of us with a closet full of sordid lies, and it isn't my secretary."

"Is everything in the file you left with Michelle?" Christopher asked.

"Yeah, it's all there."

"I'll take a look and get back to you, but for now, please keep this to yourself."

"Chris, this is D.C. We've got vice chairs in bed with the NRA, a bunch of fucking morons who don't believe in global warming, and others who use religion as an excuse for their bigotry. If any of those assholes are in any way responsible for missing kids and misused funds, I want to help take them down. But yes, I'll keep this to myself for now."

Christopher sent a text to Gabriel from his iPad: WE NEED TO TALK, URGENT!

Gabriel's response was immediate: On my way.

Christopher continued his conversation with Jason. "Are you owed any time off?"

"A shitload, why?" Jason replied.

"Best if you come here. If you're correct about this, then I need to get your smart ass out of D.C."

"I am right about this, Chris. I'll see what I can do about a flight."

"No need. Do you remember my buddy Gabriel?"

"The Italian guy?" Jason asked. "The one who looks like he stepped out of a GQ magazine?"

"Yeah," Christopher said. "That's him. Pack your bags. He'll be at your apartment shortly. Come with an open mind, okay? Oh, and Layla's pregnant."

"You're one lucky bastard. I'll hug her when I get there."

# 6

CONGRESSMAN ROSS THORTON picked up his briefcase and a manila envelope, and made his way from his office to the basement of the Capitol Building. He breathed easier when he saw that the private underground subway system was almost deserted, just a few interns running errands, and the conductor. The sterile-looking area with its white walls and gray cement floor spoke of cleanliness, almost antiseptic, something he appreciated. He stepped into the first compartment of the open-air tram and slid across the red vinyl seating.

The tram took less than a minute to reach the Russell Senate Office Building. When the car pulled to a stop, the fluorescent lighting flickered. Thorton looked up at the conductor, who frowned, and shrugged his shoulders. A slight sheen appeared on Thorton's forehead, and his palms became damp with sweat. He ran his hands down his pant legs, eyed the empty platform, and rose. The only item he carried was his briefcase. With his eye on the exit, he put in his ear buds and allowed Bach's Concerto for two violins in D minor to soothe his frazzled nerves.

The vampire assassin had caught the scent of fear in Thorton's blood as he'd leaned in to pick up what he'd come for. He watched him walk toward the exit, take the steps two at a time, and then disappear. In a blur the vampire was out on the street. He slid a bloodstained fingernail under the seal of the manila envelope and read the list of names and addresses. He smoothed his greasy black hair off his face, sneered through thin lips, and ran his tongue over yellowed teeth. He folded the paper, tucked it in a pocket, and tossed the envelope into a nearby trash can. Four names. Tonight, three would die.

O

Jason flicked on the TV to catch the latest news, while he stuffed clothes into a canvas duffle. He placed his laptop, multiple hard drives, power cords and papers inside his messenger bag, and then took one last look around to make sure he had everything he needed. As he picked up the remote, he heard a familiar name. He froze. His heart raced as the newscaster confirmed the information that went with the video clip. The scene showed police cars surrounding a taped outline of a body on the ground. The victim worked as an accountant at the Federal Offices. Before the story ended, Jason pushed a saved number on his phone and waited for his secretary to answer.

O

Just across town, four women walked out of a trendy Georgetown restaurant. Two hailed cabs, the other two walked in the direction of a parking lot, pulling their coats tight to ward off the chilling wind. They chatted about dinner and the lack of significant others in their lives as they handed the valet their tickets and waited. A few minutes later the valet pulled up, the two women said goodnight to each other, and the Prius owner waved as she drove out of the lot and onto the street.

The valet jangled a set of keys. "I'll be right back," he said, and ran down the ramp to retrieve the woman's car.

"Thanks," the woman said. She hugged herself and shivered as a gust of wind flitted past. She thought she heard footsteps and turned around but saw nothing. She jumped when her phone suddenly vibrated. She unzipped her purse just as it was ripped out of her hands. A sharp intake of breath, and then she stood perfectly still. Her eyes darted from side to side, she desperately wanted to scream, but fear claimed her voice.

Another sudden rush of cold air blew around her. She prayed silently. *Please, help me...* A man appeared in front of her. His pale skin reminded her of the candles she kept on her dining room table, and the burnished luster of dripping wax. Her gaze drifted over his cheeks and nose to his eyes. *Eyes without a soul...*

He reached a hand toward her and traced the curve of her high cheekbones with a bloodstained finger, over her lips, her chin and down her neck. *So cold...* He moved closer, and now his cold hand was tightly clasped over her mouth, his other tugged open her coat.

A sharp stabbing pain struck her stomach. A blade sliced upward and across. Something warm oozed from her body. The man held a bloodied knife in front of her face, and she watched as he licked the blood from the blade. Her knees gave way but he yanked her up. Two narrow shots of pain struck her neck, and then fire bolted through her veins. He let her go, and she fell to the ground. The last thing she heard was a car approaching.

The valet parked the car at the top of the ramp. He opened the door and looked around. A single high-heeled shoe lay on the pavement, by his feet. Strewn close by were a lipstick case and a woman's purse. He noted the dim light of a mobile phone pulsing. He saw splatters of blood, a woman's lifeless face, her mouth open and her eyes staring up at him. He leaned over and vomited. When he'd emptied his stomach, he pulled out his phone and hit 911. The still night erupted into a barrage of sirens and uniformed officers.

In response to an urgent text from Gabriel, with instructions to find Jason's secretary, Pelayo now found himself tracking down her murderer. He skirted around multiple police cars and an ambulance parked on the street at the entrance to the parking lot. He watched from a distance as two men loaded a stretcher that held the body of Jason's secretary into the back of a coroner's van. Pelayo inhaled. He searched past the woman's blood for the scent of the vampire responsible for her murder. When he found what he needed, he bounded off in pursuit at immortal speed.

Heading west along G Street, he cut through the George Washington University grounds, where he stopped for a moment and searched for a visual on his prey. The sharpness of his own vampire vision allowed him to see past normal human eye constraints, and in the distance he spotted him making his way across the Potomac Parkway. From the direction the vampire was headed, Pelayo had no doubt he was on his way to Jason's home on 27th Street.

When he hit Jason's neighborhood, Pelayo leapt up onto the roof of a row of brownstone buildings, and raced along the rooftops. He quickly narrowed the distance between the vampire and himself. He jumped down onto the road, and leapt over a gate at the side of Jason's townhome. A dog next door began barking loudly. Pelayo saw the vampire assassin at Jason's backdoor, just as he was reaching for the doorknob. Seconds later, Pelayo had his prey on the ground, and a machete at his throat.

Pelayo sensed the familiar presence of his maker. He glanced up to see Gabriel suddenly materialize, and then stride across the courtyard toward him. "Snowing here, too," Gabriel observed, brushing snowflakes from his shoulders.

"Been a bitch of a winter," Pelayo replied. The serious tone of his voice was softened by his Spanish accent.

Gabriel knelt on one knee, and spoke to the vampire in Pelayo's grasp. "Who are you working for?"

Silence.

Pelayo's machete sunk further into the vampire's neck, while Gabriel searched his pockets. He found a folded piece of paper, read it, and then retrieved a phone from the vampire's jacket. He scrolled through the list of messages and recent calls.

Gabriel stood. "Who ordered the woman killed?"

"Fuck you!" the assassin said.

Gabriel tossed a rune into the air. The aged stone hovered above the vampire's greasy hair for a moment, before Gabriel snatched it out of the air. He gave a quick nod to Pelayo. The machete flashed, and the assassin's severed head rolled to one side, disintegrating into ashes along with the rest of his body.

"He was following orders," Gabriel said, "but he's killed two innocent people. No doubt, Jason was next in line. I couldn't see any relation to either the missing girls or the Georgetown property you've been watching." He unfolded the piece of paper he had found in the vampire's pocket, and ran it under his nose. "Written by a human," he said. "A list of four names, two of these people are dead." He snapped a photo of the names and addresses. "I'll have Christopher call."

Pelayo looked at the list and shook his head. "*Mierda.* I'd better get over there." He returned the machete to its sheath.

"And I need to get Jason out of here," Gabriel said. "Alessandro and I will meet you at the Georgetown residence soon."

Pelayo handed the computer bag he had slung across his chest to Gabriel. "Prudence asked that I pick this up from Christopher's office," he said. "I'm curious, who owns this bag?"

"A young man named Jeremy," Gabriel said. "Why?"

Pelayo shrugged. "I sense a familiarity, something that reminds me of someone from my past."

Gabriel took the computer bag and slung it over his shoulder. "Jeremy is one of Christopher's interns. But we recently found out he has a twin sister, Arianna."

The dog next door started barking and Pelayo was glad for the distraction. "Let's talk more about this later," he said, and swiftly ascended into the night.

○

After calling his secretary numerous times, Jason had left a message, asking that she call him as soon as possible. He heard the next-door neighbor's dog barking, and jumped when his phone vibrated. He looked at the screen and answered. "Chris, did you see the fucking news?"

"Yes," Christopher said. "Stay where you are. Gabriel will be there momentarily. Do you have everything you need with you?"

Jason turned off the TV. "Yes," he said. He swung his computer bag across his chest and picked up his duffle. When he looked up, a man was standing inside his home, at the door. Startled, Jason dropped his bag. "What the fuck?"

Gabriel extended a hand. "Jason," he said. "Are you ready?"

He ignored Gabriel's hand. "How the fuck did you get in here?"

Gabriel picked up Jason's duffle. "I'll explain in a moment." He tossed a rune into the air. Moments later, the room sat empty.

# 7

## Casa della Pietra

COCO STOOD IN the doorway of her parents' suite and stared at her mother standing by the fireplace. *We have the same amethyst eyes.* Alessandro ushered her inside and closed the door.

"We look more like sisters," Coco said, "rather than mother and daughter."

"Your eyes are as I remember them," Chantal said.

Coco ignored her mother's words. "It's odd to think that in a few years, I'll appear older than you."

"Alessandro said your hair lost its color when you saw—"

"I'll die," Coco cut in, "and you'll live forever,"

Chantal shook her head and reached out to Coco. "Please, stop and listen to me," she said.

Coco's body trembled. "I'll die before all of you." She turned to leave but Alessandro blocked her way. "I feel sick," Coco said. "My latest painting...the girl's rape...finding Mom..."

"I understand," Alessandro said, "you've been through a lot in a short amount of time." He placed his hands on her shoulders. "We're working on finding the girl from your painting. As for your concerns about aging, let's discuss that later, okay?"

Coco nodded, and turned and faced her mother. She squeezed her eyes shut as she remembered Kenan's violent assault twenty-eight years ago. *The scar on his forehead, his slicked back dark hair, and Mom's blood on his lips.* When the vision passed, her eyes opened and flickered with pain. "I saw Kenan throw you through the air," she said. "Your body hit a tree and then fell to the ground. There was so much blood." She took a step forward and fell into Chantal's arms.

"I'd hoped you would not witness Kenan's cruelty," Chantal said. "Before that day, I chose to be blind to the acts of evil mankind is capable of. Now, I'm not." She kissed Coco's cheeks, squeezed her hands, and looked into her eyes. "We must work together to make sure the scales of goodness outweigh those who choose to be monsters. Kenan, and the likes of him, will know the vengeance of mothers, who for millennia have been made to suffer under the hands of madmen lusting power and greed. I'll continue my work with the Allegiance as a Creative, but now I'm also a warrior.

"You've suffered, Colombina," Chantal continued, "and for that I'm sorry. Alessandro told me of the courage you've shown over the years, and Kishu tells me that your willingness to move through the pain of rehabilitation after the car hit you was remarkable. But for now, I want to hear from you…about living in Hawaii, going to university, and finding out about your abilities as a Creative. Will you sit here with me, as mother and daughter, and share your story, please?"

At that moment, Coco realized that sitting with her mother and sharing her life's story was the only thing she wanted to do.

# 8

GABRIEL CONTEMPLATED HOW Jason might react when told of the reality of magic and immortal creatures. He did not doubt that Jason's curiosity and ability to adapt and grow in what others may see as difficult situations would enable him to initially accept the new ideas. But Jason would expect his questions to be answered, and in detail. He monitored Jason's face searching for signs of anxiety or fear, but what he sensed instead was intrigue.

"What the hell?" Jason said. He looked up and saw Christopher leaning against a sofa.

"We had to get you out of there quickly," Christopher said.

"What happened to my secretary?" Jason asked.

Christopher shook his head. "I'm sorry, Jason," he said, "she was found dead. Both her and the other accountant who worked in your department were murdered."

Jason glared at Christopher. "She was an accountant's secretary for fuck's sake."

"A secretary with access to damaging information," Gabriel said.

Jason breathed in deeply and brushed a hand across his eyes. "Shit!" He looked around the room. "Where am I?"

"Northern Italy," Gabriel said. "This villa belongs to my family."

"Did you knock me out or something?"

"No," Gabriel answered. "How you arrived here is complicated and revolves around a complex form of magic and science. In all honesty I can't give you a better answer."

"I don't know what the hell you're talking about," Jason said. He turned to Christopher. "What's really going on here?"

"You're standing in the headquarters of the Allegiance," Christopher said. "We're not affiliated with any government or any particular country. Our members are gifted in certain areas. Gabriel's strengths are varied."

"So there are others who can do this shit?" Jason asked.

"Yes," Gabriel said.

Jason raised an eyebrow.

"My mother is one such person," Gabriel added.

The door opened and a woman entered. She was the same height as Gabriel, a little over six feet, and she wore a long gown made of silver satin and trimmed with tiny handmade velvet roses. Her body seemed delicate but her serene presence filled up the room. Her sleek white hair tumbled down to her waist, and framed an angelic face, with strange eyes flecked with gold. She walked over to Jason, shadowed by a large female black jaguar, and Stefan, who towered over everyone. "Hello, Jason, my name is Prudence, Gabriel's mother, and I believe you already know my husband, Stefan."

Jason regarded the black jaguar with wide eyes.

"Algiz will not hurt you," Prudence said. "She is a gentle soul."

Stefan extended a hand to Jason. "Good to see you, again," he said.

"Gabriel's parents?" Jason asked. "I thought you were his uncle."

"A slight deviation from the truth," Stefan said.

Christopher looked to the door as Layla entered. She walked over to Jason and gave him a hug.

"Thanks, I needed that," Jason said, "and for what it's worth, I always figured you were something other than human."

"Actually," Layla said, "I'm fairly normal."

"You're anything but normal," Jason said. "You live with Chris. That, in itself, has always made me think you're some kind of extraordinary being."

Christopher ushered Jason to a sofa. "There's more you need to know."

Jason sat opposite Christopher and put his elbows on his knees. "I agreed to come here because I need help figuring out what's going on in D.C.," he said. "Young girls are missing, money is being pilfered, my secretary and another work associate have just been murdered and I want to find the person behind all of this. But I'm not sure I can do it on my own, and, let's face it, people have gone missing in D.C. for much less. I called you Chris, because I need your help. So, whatever weird family shit's going on here, I'm honestly not interested, although the science behind the nano-travel has piqued my curiosity." He shook his head. "D.C. is full of zombies and bloodsuckers, so for now just spit out whatever it is you need to say so we can move on and get the bastards responsible for murdering government workers, kidnapping the girls, and stealing government funds."

"Your analogy of bloodsuckers in Washington, D.C. is apt," Stefan said. "What was once a great capital where intelligent rhetoric was both spoken and heard, and debate encouraged, has yielded to greed and power, a shark tank where only the deadliest predators survive. And yes, my friend, I am a creature born from humanity. But I do not need to suck the life force from others because I am infinitely stronger than most. However, blood keeps me alive so that I may protect and serve those in need of protection. As you know, I am Stefan Lazarevic, husband of Prudence and father of Gabriel, member of the Allegiance, and a vampire." Stefan bowed his head and then grinned at Jason.

The room went silent for a moment and Gabriel sensed a slight surge of adrenaline throughout Jason's body. "If you have questions, Jason," Gabriel said, "then now would be a good time to ask."

Jason removed his glasses, cleaned them on the inside of his corduroy jacket, and then slipped them back on his face. "In all honesty, I can't think past the fact that my secretary and a work associate are dead. For now, I need to focus on what I do best, and that's anything to do with numbers and logic. How about you tell me more about this organization you're all a part of, and then either get me back to D.C., or let me work here."

Prudence took a seat beside Christopher. "We are an ancient organization and our work is unbounded," she said. "We protect Creatives, those who paint truths within paintings, secrets only visible to a few. And we give sanctuary to those threatened by religious zealots. We believe one such creature is responsible for the missing girls you have brought to our attention. You, Jason, are now under our protection. I am grateful for the information you have given us, and will greatly appreciate any further work you can do to assist Christopher with the legalities involved with this case. While we can remove the creatures responsible for the torture of these poor girls, it will take facts to bring down the human puppets in Washington."

Jason stood. "I'm in," he said, "but I'll need copious amounts of hot coffee and fast Wi-FI."

"Done!" Christopher said. "I'll show you to your suite, and then let's get to work."

"Sounds good," Jason said. He hesitated for a moment, and then looked at Stefan. "Do I need to carry a silver cross, or holy water…maybe a clove or two of garlic?"

"Utterly useless!" Stefan declared. "And before you ask, the whole daylight story is just that; a story made up to help humans feel safe. As for the holy water, I tend to stay away from it."

"I'll keep that in mind," Jason said, as he extended a hand to Prudence, Stefan and Gabriel, and then followed Christopher and Layla out of Gabriel's study.

"Do I need to be concerned with the ease in which Jason received our information?" Prudence asked.

"I did not sense fear or anxiety around him," Stefan said.

Gabriel shook his head. "Perhaps he mirrors the minds of others whose creativity came to life through numbers," he said. "Copernicus, Galileo, Newton, Lovelace, da Vinci, shall I go on?"

Prudence chuckled. "Point made, and he is a charming and enterprising young man," she said. "We have a strong triangle of talent in Christopher, Jeremy and Jason." She placed a hand on Gabriel's arm. "I need to show you something."

# 9

GABRIEL AND PRUDENCE stood outside the main guest suite of Gabriel's coastal villa. The door opened, and Coco and Christopher's grandfather, Kishu, greeted them with his trademark smile.

"Gabriel," he said, "how are you?"

"Somewhat confused."

"How is she?" Prudence asked.

Kishu's smile dissipated and he shook his head sadly. "Her warrior spirit is fierce, but her heart is broken."

"Enough of the games, Mother!" Gabriel said. "What's going on?"

Kishu stepped back inside the bedroom. Gabriel and Prudence followed.

The dimly lit room fluctuated with the flutter of candlelight. Gabriel's instincts brought his gaze to a woman who seemed asleep on the bed. Her lifeless body looked pale with death, but Gabriel knew better. He walked over to a chair beside the fireplace and sat down.

"Explain," he said.

Prudence sat on the bed. She ran a hand gently down the side of the woman's face and then held her hand. "In this world, Louisa seems dead. But as she drew in her final breath, her spirit was taken from her body to another world."

"Taken by whom?" Gabriel asked.

Prudence looked into his eyes. "There is only one bold enough to journey to this realm and steal a person's spirit."

"Freyja," Gabriel said. He thought for a moment. "And the ashes in the urn, I take it they're not Louisa's?"

"Stefan and I switched Louisa's body with the carcass of a stillborn calf, shortly before her incineration. Magic helped, of course."

"Does Ignacio know?" Gabriel asked.

Prudence shook her head. "He called Stefan a while ago insisting that Louisa came to him in a vision begging him to find her. We plan to meet with him shortly. I brought Caprecia here while you were in D.C., and at this time she is speaking with Eduardo and will explain what has happened."

Gabriel leaned back in the chair. "Why would Freyja do this?"

Prudence thought for a moment. "Perhaps when Ignacio chose love over completing a task for Kenan, in this case, kidnapping Colombina and delivering her to him, Freyja may have suggested the killing of Louisa as a way of exacting the perfect revenge. But Freyja, unbeknown to Kenan, swept in and stole Louisa's soul, and then waited for me to accept her invitation."

"Why would she do that?" Gabriel asked.

"To protect the one she loves," Prudence said, "or to use as collateral."

"I'd bet the latter," Gabriel said. "Do you think Kenan knows that Louisa's spirit lives?"

"I do not believe so," Prudence said, "and I can only imagine his fury at Freyja when he discovers she saved Louisa from death."

"He's using Freyja just as he uses everyone around him," Gabriel said.

"Immortals, like mortals, are blinded by love," Kishu cut in.

Gabriel let out a short breath. "I'm not sure Kenan is capable of love."

"Love, like trust, must be earned," Kishu said, "and Kenan's heart is wrapped in evil. He may need to lose the one who truly loves him, in order for him to discover love."

Gabriel stared at Louisa's still form. "How do we find Louisa's spirit, and how can you be certain that she will live in this world when her spirit is returned?"

"It is my hope that my father will offer us his help," Prudence said.

"Your father?" Gabriel asked. "Why would he come forth now?"

Prudence gazed upon her son. "My mother came to me in a dream. She handed me the rune, Raido."

A shiver ran over Gabriel's body. "When do we leave?"

"You cannot come on this journey with me, Gabriel," Prudence said. "You must stay at *Casa della Pietra*. If Kenan forces Freyja to penetrate my magic, then you will be the only hope we have of maintaining the fortress."

"Who will go with you?" Gabriel asked.

"Your father and I will take Ignacio and Caprecia."

Gabriel considered the situation. "What do you need me to do?"

"Keep Louisa's body safe. No essence of evil must touch her skin. For now, Kenan believes she is dead, but if he were to find out Louisa's life force hangs in the ether, he will most likely find a way to either destroy her, or the one who took her soul."

"You think he'd try to kill Freyja?" Gabriel asked.

Prudence pushed a lock of Louisa's hair away from her face. "Mad men are capable of anything."

"What makes you so sure that Freyja still holds Louisa's soul?" Gabriel asked.

"She left her essence on Louisa's skin," Prudence said. "She gave me nothing short of an invitation to find her."

"Why didn't I feel it?" Gabriel asked.

"I am closer to the ethereal plane."

Gabriel stared at Prudence. "Are you sure this isn't a trick?"

"I sense Freyja's love for Kenan," Prudence said. "She sees the essence of the child that he once was, and the evil that overshadowed him through his maker. She has faith in him."

Gabriel stood and turned to the fireplace, watching as the flames grew higher. "You're trusting your life to a goddess, a woman who once tried to claim your mother's soul."

"My mother has reached out for me. I must go to her," Prudence said. She rose and walked over to Gabriel. "Ask yourself, if this was you, would you not go?"

"I would not hesitate," he said.

"Take Louisa and Kishu to the inner sanctum of the fortress. Stefan and I will meet with Ignacio and bring him to Louisa," Prudence said.

Gabriel walked over to the bed. "May I tell Colombina?"

"Of course."

Gabriel lifted Louisa into his arms, and stood with Kishu and Prudence. The flames in the fireplace went out.

# 10

*San Gimignano, Italy*

WHEN STEFAN AND Prudence emerged from the shadows of the Church of Collegiata, the place was silent. The early closing hours of the winter season, along with an unusually harsh snowstorm, meant the streets of the ancient town were deserted. Prudence blew across the palm of a hand. Candles standing tall in candelabras sprang to life and shed blossoms of golden light throughout the sacred space.

"Beautiful," Stefan said.

"Yes." Prudence tilted her head and admired the striped arches that graced the interior. She had always seen this building as one of the best-kept secrets in Tuscany, for so many tourists declined to venture inside. She wondered if the steps leading to the entrance overwhelmed the weary traveler, who chose instead to view this little gem from the piazza.

They made their way to the small Chapel of Santa Fina. A bunch of violets appeared in Prudence's hands and she laid them on the ground beneath the altar; their sweet bouquet seeped into the air. She turned to Ghirlandaio's fresco, *Announcement of Death to St. Fina*, and filled her senses with the beauty of the painting.

"The gold platter in this piece always reminds me of the diadems the women of Renaissance Florence loved to wear," she observed Stefan. "Strange to think the one you bought for me was made by this same artist."

"Indeed," Stefan said, "Tommaso proudly explained to me that it was the first piece of such jewelry his son had made. Do you remember how excited Ghirlandaio was the day he saw you wearing it at the festival?"

Prudence smiled. "Yes, I do."

They returned to the main section of the Duomo. Prudence took in the detail until her gaze lingered upon the pulpit. "I hear Savonarola's voice on occasion. One cannot say he was not passionate about his cause. His congregations were certainly captivated by his rhetoric and ideas."

Stefan caught her hand in his. "Savonarola's audience listened through fear, *tesoro*. A similar audience cheered as his body dangled in the hangman's noose in Florence a few years later. The inquisition pretended to lull, but congregations knew the truth. To show interest in any cause other than that of the Catholic Church meant death."

The clicking sound of a lock being freed caught their attention. Stefan pulled out his sword and stood defensively in front of Prudence. He lowered his weapon when he saw the English vampire, Ignacio, striding up the aisle toward them. His sunken eyes and gaunt face showed he had not fed in days.

"Ignacio," Prudence gave a courteous nod.

"Certain death is correct," he said. He twisted the heavy-set gold ring on his middle finger, pushed his dark, tangled hair away from his eyes, and looked around the church. "I was made to watch while supporters of the Catholic Church tortured my loved ones. They saved me for last, and I welcomed death. I had nothing to live for. I had failed my family. The strange thing about pain is that you forget the agony. But the screams from my mother and sister while they were continually raped, tortured and then burned alive, still haunt me, even after so many centuries have passed. And if by chance I do sleep, I'm woken by the sardonic laughter of the inquisitors." He glared at Stefan until he sheathed his sword.

"You got to choose this life, Stefan. I did not. The immortal that pulled me out of that rat-infested cell also sought revenge. He saw opportunity in my pain. He made me an immortal, and then introduced me to blood tainted with opium, and later trained me as an assassin. I've killed many, and not one of those deaths has brought me the sweet revenge my maker promised. Louisa is the only one to bring joy and peace to my heart. Until her, I never thought I'd be able to love anyone, let alone find someone who loved me."

Prudence stepped forward. "Stefan told me that Louisa came to you. We believe you."

Ignacio raised his head and gazed into Prudence's eyes. "Have you seen her too?"

"Yes. Dark magic allowed one of Kenan's men to gain access to Louisa's apartment. He injected her with tainted heroin and then fled. But Louisa's spirit was taken moments before her heart stopped beating. The ashes Eduardo keeps are not hers. What you saw in your vision was her spirit."

"Where is she?" Ignacio asked.

"We have her physical body protected away from Kenan, and Kishu watches over her," Prudence said. "But in order for us to find her spirit we must gather help from those closer to that realm."

"My mother and sister died protecting pagan beliefs," Ignacio said. "Strange that in order to find Louisa, I must face the demons from my past."

"The only demon we must face," Stefan cut in, "is Kenan. He ordered Louisa killed."

"Does he know that she lingers between worlds?" Ignacio asked.

"If he does," Prudence said, "then we are all in grave danger, including the one who rescued your beloved. I know you work alone, Ignacio, but I must have your oath that for this journey you will uphold the Allegiance."

"For Louisa, I will pledge my life to the Allegiance, Prudence."

Prudence stared into the depths of his dark eyes, and then embraced him. "We are your family now, Ignacio. You will never be alone again." Sensing his uneasiness of being comforted, she stepped back.

"May I see Louisa now?" Ignacio asked.

Prudence nodded. "Of course." She waved an arm and a gust of wind swirled around the three immortals. The candles went out and moments later the church stood empty.

# 11

## Casa della Pietra

THE THREE IMMORTALS appeared on the landing at the top of an aged stone staircase. Ignacio looked around. He breathed in the smell of earth, and sensed they were underground. Without further delay, he followed Prudence as she descended the well-worn granite steps. Had it not been for the vision of Louisa calling out to him, asking him to find her, the thought of giving his entire confidence to the Allegiance would not be something he would find virtuous.

Stefan's unyielding presence permeated behind him. The Serbian vampire was a good man to have on his side, and had been the only acquaintance he had trusted with Louisa's safety. In hindsight, he realized what Prudence had told him made sense, about another vampire injecting Louisa with tainted heroin. This time their addiction had almost cost him the life of his beloved.

Prudence turned right at the next landing and came to a stop in front of a solid oak door. She turned to Ignacio, placed a hand on his shoulder, and spoke to him, although no words left her mouth. "*We will find her spirit, my dear. You have my word.*"

The door opened and they entered an inner sanctum. Ignacio's gaze went immediately to the figure laid out on a bed in front of a fireplace. Reflections of honey-colored light from the flames lit Louisa's tranquil face, and gave a reddish tinge to her wild dark hair.

"May I hold her?" he asked, not taking his eyes from her.

"Yes," Prudence said. "In fact, your touch will help strengthen her energy. I believe Louisa can hear us, but because of her present state of bound consciousness, she cannot speak or awaken."

Ignacio sensed humans in the room. He turned and saw Kishu. "I owe you, old man. Prudence says you have been watching over Louisa."

"Look forward, not back," Kishu said. "Blame and guilt are fuel for fire."

Ignacio nodded and his eyes swam with tears. He brushed a hand across his face and when his vision cleared he saw the impeccable image of the Italian art professor, Eduardo Benatti. Ignacio went to him. "To offer you an apology would be an insult. What happened to Louisa while she was with me is inexcusable. I don't expect your forgiveness, only that you will allow me to bring her back to you."

Eduardo clasped his hands onto Ignacio's shoulders and stared into his eyes. "We have all made mistakes. Find my daughter, bring her back and love her every moment of every day and every night. Promise me this, Ignacio."

"You have my word," Ignacio said.

Eduardo squeezed his shoulders before letting go. With no further words spoken, Eduardo left the room and the others followed, leaving Ignacio alone with Louisa, void of her joyous laughter and cheeky rhetoric. He eased onto the bed and kissed her lips. His nostrils flared as he searched for her. He pushed past the slightly acidic smell of chemicals and breathed in her scent of marjoram.

# 12

## *Svalbard Islands, Arctic Ocean*

THE VAMPIRE LAY still and silent. Beads of sweat gathered on his brow and slid along his nose before pooling on the sodden cotton sheet beneath his pallid face. A jolt of pain caused him to grimace. He shivered as familiar featherlike fingers traced over the many scars that paid homage to his turbulent youth.

The practiced song of the black siren cradled his emotions. He knew nothing of time, caught, as he was, in the cradle of her world. Amid the raven darkness, he could taste the gelid air, singed with death and decay. He willed his mind to extract his last memory.

A blade.

Agony.

Darkness.

The siren sang a haunting melody, and her voice guided Kenan back to a scene from his early childhood.

## *Florence, 1490*

He could tell by the gray light that dawn had arrived, and for this, he gave thanks. His fingers, cold and numb, were clasped around a frayed bible. His knees ached from kneeling on the rigid wooden board for what seemed like hours, but he dared not move. To do so, would dishonor God.

He peered up at his mother. Her stern face, furrowed by the harshness of life, remained solemn while she repeated the holy words spoken by the priest. Kenan's heart stirred in response to the choir of voices that rang out around him. The fixed melody cleansed his body, and for a moment, God touched his meager soul. Oh, how this sacred music moved him. In an effort to keep his emotions at bay, he closed his eyes tightly together while the rise and fall of the *Agnus Dei* washed over him.

"Amen," he said.

His mother shuffled him out the door and into the frigid morning. They waited, while the crowd of worshippers and members of the choir said their goodbyes and continued with their day. His mother guided him toward their stone cottage tucked behind the chapel. He looked across the valley at the eiderdown of mist floating above the city of Firenze, and thanked God for his perfect life.

Suddenly, his mother stopped walking and yanked him to her. At the side of the chapel stood two black horses hooked up to a lavish carriage. He heard an unfamiliar male voice, and could tell by the clipped intonation that the message it was delivering was of the threatening kind. His mother bent toward him. "Go to the house, finish your chores, and then continue to study," she said. Her Tuscan dialect held remnants of Latin, and like her face, was authoritarian. "I shall be along shortly."

He let go of her hand. "Yes, Mama," he said, and ran across the courtyard and into the cottage. A few hours passed and his curiosity got the better of him. He peeped through the wooden shutters of his attic bedroom window across the front courtyard to the chapel grounds. The horses and carriage were gone, and the male voice he had heard earlier had since been replaced with his mother's angry tone. She burst out of the side door, followed closely by her brother, the priest. Neither looked happy. He withdrew from the window, to the table in his room, opened his bible, and pretended to read. His ears strained to catch the angry whispers from his mother and uncle as they entered through the kitchen.

"Then why did they come here?" his mother asked. "We only seek the principles of the Catholic Church. Tell me you have nothing to do with the profaneness of that family of heretics who call themselves the guardians of this city. Swear this to me!"

Kenan heard footsteps advance up the steps. Moments later, his uncle stood before him, calm and devoid of anger. "Would you like me to read to you, Kenan?"

Kenan looked up and shook his head. "Thank you, but I want to pray now."

His uncle's eyes looked moist. He brushed his hand across Kenan's forehead. "You are a good child," he said, and then turned and walked away. Moments later, his mother entered the room, and gestured for her son to kneel beside her on the floor. They prayed together in silence.

○

Later that night, Kenan awoke and noticed a soft glow emanating from the chapel. He threw clothes over his sleeping gown and slipped quietly outside. At the chapel, he went to the window and stood on the tips of his toes and peered inside. The tall figure of his uncle sat crouched over a table, writing by the light of a candle.

Kenan watched as his uncle wiped his eyes on the sleeve of his robe, and looked up at the figure of Jesus on the cross, with his bloodied hands and feet, and his gaze lifted toward heaven. "I write of love," his uncle said, clutching the papers to his heart. "Surely to create such poetry cannot be seen as heresy."

He tucked the papers inside a book, and walked over to the wall opposite. The long dark cassock blocked Kenan's view, but he noticed that when his uncle walked away the book was gone. He ran back to the house. From his bedroom window, he watched his uncle close the chapel door and wander slowly toward the cottage. Every now and again he would stop and look up to the stars and smile. Kenan allowed himself one last peek and then buried himself under the covers.

Three weeks later, the black horses and carriage returned. Kenan slipped out of the house, concealed by the shadow of a new moon. He sank behind the stonewall surrounding the property and listened as the familiar voice of his uncle and the Catholic cardinal argued from within the chapel.

"But I have done no harm," his uncle said, "I only speak of love and devotion to Our Father. I have not uttered one word of sacrilege. Surely you must know this of me!"

"Enough!" the cardinal said. "You have shamed this family with your pathetic humanist words. Your impiety is not worthy of this sacred ground. Where are the books?"

"You may look all you wish," his uncle said, "but you will not find books of heresy here…only words of love."

Something being thrown against wood shattered the silence. "You have disgraced my family and for that you will pay."

"But I took in your child," his uncle said. "I love him as if he is my own flesh and blood. Please, do not take him away from me, I beg of you—"

"You will never speak of my son again!" the cardinal said.

Upon hearing these words, a rash of confusion took over Kenan's mind, but a sharp slapping sound, followed by a thud, quickly cleared his thoughts. He peered cautiously over the wall and watched as the cardinal strode out of the chapel and into the waiting carriage. The last image Kenan saw of this man who had confessed to being his father, was the red silk of the holy man's robe draped over his black shoes. The driver snapped the reins and steered the horses onto the narrow road and out of sight.

When the clatter of the horses' hooves had faded, Kenan thought to jump over the fence, but froze when he saw a figure dressed in dark clothing and a hooded cape suddenly enter through the chapel door. It was then that he heard the unmistakable voice of his mother. "Take him!" she said. "The thought of never having to see his face again brings joy to my heart." She stormed out of the chapel and toward the house.

Kenan's eyes widened and his breath stalled. Once his mother was out of sight, he gathered his courage, leapt over the fence and ran to the window. A moment later, cold hands grabbed his arm and dragged him across the floor of the chapel, dumping him at his uncle's feet.

"Curious boy," the hooded man said. "You shall watch me take this man to hell, where he belongs."

The hooded man's Latin was cast with a strange accent that Kenan had not heard before, and his face glistened like candlewax. Kenan's body trembled and he scrambled on his buttocks toward a wall. The man threw back his head and laughed. When his joyous reveling passed, Kenan found his voice. "That man—the one in the red robe—is he my father?"

The hooded man snorted. "Your father is an important member of the Catholic Church, and as such, his identity must be kept secret. The man lying on the floor could never be anything close to the man of God your father is." He circled around Kenan's shaking body, and stopped before him. He lifted a finger to Kenan's chin, and tilted the boy's head back so their eyes met. "But you must keep this secret. Do you understand? This is God's wish. To speak of it would not be wise."

This man had yielded complete control over Kenan's mind. Unable to speak, he nodded, and as the hooded man's finger left Kenan's chin, he noticed his yellowed fingers and filthy fingernails. He looked at his uncle, sprawled out on the floor. The man's bruised eyes opened slightly as he reached an arm out to Kenan. In a flurry of movement, the hooded man grabbed his uncle by the throat and bit into his neck. Blood overflowed from his mouth and onto the stone floor, until the body of the man Kenan had loved as a father, fell limp and empty of life.

The hooded man let go of the body, licked the blood from his lips, and turned to face Kenan. "When you see me again, it will be to make you one of my kind. I will give you eternal life. And in return you will guard all that is sacred from those who call themselves humanists." He strode toward Kenan, grabbed his arm and bit into the boy's wrist.

A searing pain raced up Kenan's arm and throughout his body. He went to scream but met the hooded man's glare and fell silent. Seconds later, his arm was hanging limply beside him, and all signs of the bite had disappeared. Kenan's vision blurred and he fought back the nausea that had gathered at the back of his throat.

"There is no escaping me now, boy," the hooded man said, "I have tasted your blood. I will find you."

The hooded man vanished and Kenan stared at what was left of his uncle. He screamed as his mother yanked him up from the ground. He stared at her in disbelief. "Come," she said, "we must dispose of the body. He can rot in unhallowed ground."

Another ripple of pain brought Kenan out of his memories. The siren brushed her fingers over his temple and the pain subsided. He deplored this feeling of helplessness, and the pain associated with his injuries. Pain reminded him of his mother and the guilt he carried for her death. He was eleven years of age…

O

Kenan stared at the gray walls of his bedroom and reflected on his pathetic life. The shutters that once hung over the windows were now barely connected and gave little shelter from the wind and rain that crept through the broken windowpanes. He could hear his mother's nasal voice calling out to him. His stomach lurched in anticipation of the fetid room that awaited him. He had come to loathe his life, and his mother. Since she had become ill, her incessant labored breathing, soiled and stained bedclothes, rotting skin and foul breath haunted his every waking moment.

He could not escape.

Perhaps if he waited before attending to her, she might drown in the thick mucus that drained down the back of her throat. Perhaps if he waited, he may never have to clean up the vomit that fell so often from her mouth. He listened, and it was at that moment he recognized something he'd not heard in months: the serenity of silence.

He closed his eyes and allowed this anomaly to wash over him, and within that peace and quiet he once more found the path to God. He begged forgiveness for his heartless wishes of death to his mother, of the constant aspiration that his life be better, and that he had a father who wanted him.

He rose from his bed and crept into his mother's bedroom. Bile caught in his throat at the sight that greeted him. His mother's balding head rested on the yellowed pillow, turned slightly toward the doorway as if begging for him to return to her side. Her shallow eyes stared directly through to his soul, cursing him for his laxity in attending to her in the moments before her death. Kenan stepped back and gripped the doorjamb, as his breathing escalated to short, quick gasps.

"God, forgive me," he whispered.

It was then that he finally allowed the tears of his childhood to slide from his soul and onto his cheeks. His tears did not come from sorrow, but from unconstrained joy. Finally, he was free of the confines of his sickly mother and regulated youth.

Walking over to the bed, he pulled a blanket over her face. "Goodbye, Mother," he said.

He turned and bolted out of the bedroom, grabbing only his tattered bible and a long coat that once belonged to his uncle, before fleeing the cottage and running down the now barely-used road to the chapel, and toward the center of the city.

For a while he enjoyed the freedom of his anonymity, but as the temperature dropped and the shredded soles of his shoes did little to protect his numbing feet, he longed for connection and family. Kenan had tired of stealing food and sleeping amongst the drunks and deranged members of society. He wanted more. Luck came to him in the year 1495. He was twelve years old.

# 13

TWO LATINA GIRLS sat huddled together on a king-sized bed. The room was decorated in tones of gray, but the white duvet and pillows were stained with blood. The girls were barely conscious, their bodies covered in deep cuts and welts. Another girl was propped up on a tufted white chaise lounge, her long, dark hair was matted with blood, and her neck and shoulders displayed dark bruises and puncture wounds. Her breath came in shallow gasps, and her arm, judging by its angle, appeared to have suffered from multiple fractures, and hung lifelessly at her side.

Still another girl, whose clothes were ripped, frantically tried the latches on the boarded-up windows, only to find them nailed shut. She heard a noise and quickly turned around, and stared at the only door, watching as the handle turned downward. Two men entered. One had dark eyes and a long face with an unusually high forehead, and chiseled cheekbones. His yellowish, platinum blond hair was pulled back, and emphasized the cruel look of his elongated face. The other man looked disheveled, and his narrow eyes had a lunatic's stare. As he walked closer, the sneer on his face turned into a crazed grin that exposed an unusually wide gap between his upper middle teeth.

The fourth girl backed up, finding herself trapped in a corner. "Get away from me!" she yelled. "What do you want?"

"Time for our boss to have a little fun," said the crazed-looking man.

She noticed that his partner held a thin strap in his hand. She glared at him, and his dark eyes seemed to bore into her mind. The crazed man grabbed her shoulders, forcing her against a wall as the blond-haired assailant yanked her right arm toward him, rolled up her sleeve, and tied the strap around her small forearm. She fought him, kicking out and twisting her body, her ear-splitting screams reverberating around the room. A sharp pain, just below the crease of her right elbow, brought a look of horror across her face. The rush of fear that flooded her mind quickly passed, and ecstasy reached out to her.

An older vampire entered the bedroom. The two men holding the girl carried her limp form over to him. He sank his fangs into her neck, and allowed just enough of his venom to seep into her blood and arouse her lust. This, he knew, mixing with the rise in the girl's dopamine levels caused by the heroin would bring her to a state of blissful euphoria. He rushed her downstairs into another bedroom, laid her on the bed, and tore off her remaining clothes.

Suddenly, he saw the tattoo above her mound, and slapped her face in anger. He grabbed her hands and tied them together at the wrists. Over his head, a large hook dangled threateningly. Lifting her without effort, he suspended her petite body by placing the rope over the hook, which was attached to a long metal chain, connected, through a series of pulleys, to a T-shaped steel pole secured into the floor. The vampire jumped off the bed, and began pulling on the chain until the girl was hoisted above the bed.

The girl whimpered, and this seemed to bring pleasure to the vampire. He kicked off his boots, stepped out of his black jeans, and stood in front of the girl on the bed. He grabbed her legs, held them tightly around his hips, and then thrust into her until she cried out in pain, and he relished in his own orgasm. A few minutes later, he bit into his wrist, held the girl's mouth open, and forced her to swallow a few drops of his blood. The girl retched, and again he slapped her, hard. He held her face close to his, and whispered. "The night has just begun."

The three vampires silently navigated the border of the 1930s Georgian-styled house that Pelayo had been monitoring. The two-story brick residence sat alone, shrouded by a forest of mature evergreen trees. A foreboding cloud floated across the moon, leaving the garden immersed in a blanket of obscurity.

Gabriel approached the inner gardens. Wisps of steam rose from a swimming pool that graced a paved and neatly landscaped yard. He knelt down and ran the palm of a hand over an area of dirt where the elegant trunk of a silver birch stood rooted firmly in the ground. He whispered a string of words in Latin, before thrusting his hand deep into the ground and retrieving an object. He blew away the dirt, and stared at the figurine.

"Another talisman," he said, "Norse in origin, and by the wear on the copper, it's ancient." He pointed to barely visible markings engraved upon the surface. "See the outline of a woman, with her right wing extended and a hand placed over her heart. How her left hand rests upon the top of her thigh?"

Alessandro and Pelayo crouched next to Gabriel.

"Freyja," Alessandro said.

The talisman sprang to life. The woman twisted and stretched out her wings as if she was awakening. Her hands reached out toward Gabriel. In one swift movement, Gabriel dropped the object to the ground and pinned it with the tip of his knife. Blood leeched out from the metal, and in seconds the talisman disappeared.

"I guess I was correct about her name," Alessandro said.

"I'll take that as an apology," Gabriel said. "A little warning would not have gone amiss."

They stood.

"Similar objects have been buried around the property, to keep other creatures away. For now, they can stay. We've enough space to enter and leave." Gabriel tossed a rune into the air. "Show me the interior of this house."

He closed his eyes and allowed the visions to materialize in his mind. Once he had the information he needed, he opened them and pulled out his phone and sent a text. He looked up at Alessandro and Pelayo.

"Five vampires inside, all male, three upstairs in the main living room feeding on three human girls. The vampires on the lower level are older, one's torturing and raping a young girl...she's maybe fifteen years of age;

he has her tied to a bed at the front of the house. The other is playing video games in a room off the kitchen."

"Did you notice anything else about the girls?" Pelayo asked.

Gabriel nodded. "They appear Latina." He noted Pelayo's corded neck, and the quickened pulse of his jugular vein. "Which one do you want to go after?" Gabriel asked.

"The one in the kitchen," Pelayo said.

Alessandro took out two knives from inside his jacket. "I'll take the bastard in the bedroom," he said.

"Remember," Gabriel said. "We need at least one alive to question."

"I'll do my best to remember that," Alessandro said.

"I've alerted Dr. Fiore," Gabriel said, "she'll meet us back at Christopher's townhouse and take care of the girls." Gabriel's nostrils flared and he turned toward the forest.

A figure emerged from the trees.

"Actually, I'm here," Dr. Fiore said. "Your description of the state of the girls sounded urgent. Prudence felt you might need reinforcements."

Ignacio appeared beside her. "I'd be delighted to help send this bunch of depravity to dust," he said. "They all stink of Kenan. He has shit-holes like this in every city."

"Do you know the locations?" Gabriel asked.

"No, but they're not difficult to find," Ignacio said. "Just follow the signs of debauchery. Personally, I keep away from such places."

"We'll discuss this later," Gabriel said. "Doctor, go with Alessandro, the young girl in the downstairs bedroom needs immediate attention. The three females upstairs are being drained. Ignacio and I will tend to them until you can get there."

Gabriel and Ignacio appeared in an upstairs bedroom. A blood-splattered carpet led a path to a grisly scene. Ignacio's mind flooded with the silence of intense focus. He yanked the nearest vampire away from his prey, his mouth gushed a stream of crimson as he struggled to find his voice. Ignacio kicked him in the back of his knees. Bone popped. He fell to the ground with a yell. Ignacio grabbed a handful of his hair and wrenched the vampire's neck to one side. A short crunching snap followed. His razor-sharp blade sliced easily through skin, muscle, and bone. Ashes of death fell to the stained carpet.

Another vampire made a break for the door. Ignacio vaulted into the air. His right foot thrust into the center of the vampire's back shattering his vertebrae. Ignacio grabbed the vampire's head and with a quick jolt ripped it from his body. Kenan's stench filled the room.

Ignacio noted the three mounds of ashes and knew Gabriel had ended the third vampire's immortality. He strode over to one of the dying girls. He knelt beside her, cut open his wrist and allowed a few drops of his blood to enter her mouth. Another girl lay wrapped up in a blanket on a sofa. Her eyes were closed and he noticed the black bruising on her face slowly fading.

Gabriel held the third girl in his arms. Her body limp, her face pale except for a smudge of Gabriel's blood on her lower lip. He held a hand above her heart with his palm facing upward. An aged stone hovered in the air. Shards of magic permeated throughout the room.

Ignacio gazed in reverence at the scene playing out before him. He had never witnessed this kind of magic. He'd heard the rumors, of course, and observed his biological mother administer potions centuries ago, but nothing compared to the essence flowing from Gabriel at that moment.

His thoughts drifted back to another time, before Louisa was taken from him. He had been watching her from a safe distance, outside the art school in San Gimignano. He overheard Coco ask Louisa why she stayed with him. Her answer washed over every part of his being. He had replayed her words repeatedly in his head.

*You know nothing of Ignacio. He's a good man—and I stay because I am in love with him.*

He looked again at Gabriel and the young girl and wondered if perhaps he was witnessing the truth of alchemy. Just as Gabriel had brought the girl from the brink of death to life, Louisa's devotion to him had transformed his heart from misery to love. And then a revelation hit him. Love is the powerful weapon of the Allegiance. He fell to his knees and allowed his silent tears to fall. All his life he had only known hatred, manipulation and abuse. This bitterness had spurred him through each lonely day and even lonelier nights. He allowed his heart to open to the threads of tenderness and healing vitality that danced around him.

Gabriel bowed his head. Flecks of energy flowed between his heart and the girl's like a river of life. A soft murmur floated from her mouth. Gabriel closed his fingers around the rune and returned it to his pocket. Ignacio stood and helped Gabriel wrap the girl in blankets.

"Do you smell it?" Ignacio asked. "Before they were tortured, these girls were injected with heroin."

"Yes," Gabriel said, "I know."

Ignacio twisted the ring on his finger. "Fuck! Was what I used to do any better? Getting women high, and then fucking them…like they were mine to do what I liked with?"

"What you did was wrong," Gabriel said, "there's no denying that. But you've been given a chance to make amends, to make sure that what Kenan's doing comes to an end."

Ignacio shook his head.

"We all have our demons, Ignacio," Gabriel continued. "Whether we choose to face them, or not, is our choice." He walked toward the door. "Stay here while I check on our comrades and the other girls." A familiar high-pitched whistle caught his attention. "Pelayo has one of the vampires alive for questioning."

Ignacio caught Gabriel's arm. "I didn't understand the Allegiance before," he said, "but I do now."

"You will find Louisa and bring her back," Gabriel said. "Of this I'm sure."

Ignacio turned his attention to Dr. Fiore as she entered the room, carrying a limp body. He gathered cushions and made a space on the floor for the girl, then covered her with a throw rug.

"She's okay," Dr. Fiore said, "but Alessandro's taking a beating. He could do with some help. That vampire is ancient."

Ignacio and Gabriel raced down the stairs and burst into the lower bedroom.

"About fucking time!" muttered Alessandro. One of his arms dangled at an odd angle and blood oozed from deep cuts on his face.

His aged opponent held a hand over a sizable gash near his heart, and did a double take when he saw a familiar figure in his peripheral vision. "You bastard, Ignacio!" he screamed. "You killed my son!"

"Your son?" Ignacio asked.

"My son killed your Tuscan whore!"

Ignacio's eyes narrowed, and Gabriel noticed his fingers twitch against the handle of his knife. Gabriel moved quickly. The old vampire suddenly clutched his chest and gazed upon a blade buried deep in his heart. Blood dribbled from the corners of his mouth and slid down his chin. Gabriel drew his sword, and Ignacio watched as the decapitated head fell to the floor. He stared at Gabriel.

"Louisa is one of ours," Gabriel said, "and therefore protected by us. You had your vengeance, now we have ours." Gabriel gazed at the bloodied sheets on the bed, and at the pulley and chains that until moments ago had been used to torture an innocent girl. He slid his sword back into the sheath tied at his thigh and turned to Alessandro. Gabriel waved a hand over his wrist and a small cut appeared. He held the wound above Alessandro's mouth and let three drops fall.

"Thanks," Alessandro said.

Gabriel put a hand on Alessandro's shoulder and gave it a quick jolt. Alessandro winced. "Pelayo has one alive and I have questions," Gabriel said. He exited the room followed by Ignacio and Alessandro.

A Micarta handle protruding out of a vampire's sprawled body on a hardwood floor caught Gabriel's attention. He did not doubt that by the time the aged immortal had realized the house was under attack, Pelayo had landed the sixteen-inch machete into his chest, pinning him to the floor. He lay perfectly still. Gabriel sensed that he dared not move for fear of the blade slicing through his superior vena cava. To make matters worse, the wound had begun to heal. He wasn't going anywhere in a hurry.

"Why these girls?" Gabriel asked.

"Get him off me!" the vampire said.

"You're in no position to bargain," Gabriel said. "Why these girls?"

The vampire's eyes strayed to Pelayo. "Ethnic cleansing," he said.

A deep growl reverberated from Pelayo's chest. Alessandro and Ignacio stood on either side, ready to stop him from attacking. Gabriel continued. "Why only females?"

"Fuck you, and fuck the Allegiance!" In an effort to end his own suffering he went to lunge. Gabriel tossed a rune into the air and the vampire froze. A look of terror flashed across his eyes. His death would be slow and painful. The blade had grazed his heart. Internal bleeding had begun. He could not move his limbs.

"Answer my question and I'll end your life in an instant," Gabriel said.

"I'm already dead," the vampire said. A corner of his mouth lifted into a sneer.

Gabriel sensed the blood flooding throughout the vampire's body. He grabbed the rune, and nodded to Alessandro and Ignacio. They released Pelayo. He branded another machete and sliced through the immortal's neck.

"*Vete al Diablo!*" Pelayo whispered.

Gabriel laid a hand on Pelayo's shoulder, and spoke quietly to him in Spanish. "Call our comrades here in D.C. and make sure the girls are returned safely to their families."

# 14

## *Casa della Pietra*

COCO WOKE UP in darkness, sweating and shaking, pulled from a nightmare where something evil had been chasing her. A flash of lightning flooded the bedroom, bringing with it a deluge of rain and wind that swirled in a tempest around the fortress. In the semi-darkness, she saw Thalia perched on the back of an armchair. The sight of her beloved cat helped to lower Coco's quickening pulse.

Thalia arched her back and cast a knowing glance in Coco's direction. She leapt from the chair and padded across the wooden floor, stopping for a moment at the slightly open door. She meowed, and then disappeared into the adjoining studio.

Coco turned on a lamp and instinctively looked at her hands. She saw the telltale drops of paint on her fingers. Thunder rumbled over the fortress, rattling windowpanes and causing Max to whimper, who lay beside her. "You're okay," Coco said, stroking the dog's head. "It's just a storm."

Intrigued to see what she had painted during her sleep, Coco eased out of bed, threw on a robe and followed Thalia into the studio. The lights flickered in response to the storm outside, and then settled a soft glow over the studio. She walked up to the easel and her most recent painting.

The scene was a favorite of hers, and the expanse of green grass, dotted with tall trees and sculptures, and groups of students in various poses brought with it a pang of nostalgia. To Coco, the sculpture garden at UCLA represented the heart of Los Angeles. As a student, and later, an art professor, she had crossed this garden at least twice a day for six years, on her way to the art department and home again.

As she lifted a hand to the canvas, the prickling sensation at the tips of her fingers reminded her of the reason she had painted this image. Shifting her focus, Coco brought her fingers slightly back from the painting. Tingles ran up her arm as the pigments of paint lifted from the canvas revealing the first of a series of scenes.

*Arianna is on a bed curled up in a ball, her body pained and trembling. She stares through tear-filled eyes at a photograph of Isabel and a man who looks to be in his early forties. The paint dissipates and settles on another scene...*

*Arianna and Jeremy are seated either side of a bed. A woman lies motionless, her head covered with a scarf of soft blues and purples. Arianna stands. "I'll be outside if you need me," she says. Jeremy grabs her hand as she walks by. "Please...don't leave," he says, "I don't want to be alone." Arianna embraces him. His body shudders as he breaks down sobbing.*

*Arianna stands in front of a mirror, staring at her reflection and the thin gold cross on a chain that hangs around her neck. She unlatches the chain, drops it in a drawer and pushes it closed.*

*Arianna enters a room. The walls are covered in framed artwork showing intricate pen and ink drawings: bleeding hearts, animals, mythological creatures, and colorful scripts. A young man greets her with a hug. His arms are covered in a labyrinth of tattoos. He guides her to a private area surrounded by black drapes. She sits, and he reclines the chair. He unfolds a white towel and hands it to her. Arianna folds up her t-shirt, undoes the zipper of her jeans, lowers them a little and tucks the towel into the top of the denim.*

The pigments slipped back onto the canvas and the image of the sculpture garden returned. Coco lowered her hand. She breathed in and out deeply as she processed the scenes she just witnessed. Thalia's body curled around her feet and eventually brought her out of her melancholia. She looked down and noticed the painting of Christopher's D.C. townhouse and cringed at the memory of the brutal rape scene it hid.

She turned to leave but froze. "The vampire...he was looking for something..." She ran into the bedroom, pulled on a pair of jeans and a sweater, and raced out of Gabriel's apartment to Christopher's rooms. She knocked, and moments later Christopher opened the door.

"What's going on?" he asked.

"I painted last night," Coco said. "You need to see this."

"Give me a moment."

Coco nodded and leaned against the wall. She could hear Christopher speaking with Layla. After a minute or so, he reappeared and walked with her back to her studio. "I think I know what the missing girls all have in common," she said.

Coco revealed the images of Arianna hidden behind the painting of the sculpture garden. "I want to show you the place where the girl was raped," Coco said. "Maybe you'll recognize it." She sat the painting of Christopher's brownstone apartment on the easel, and then held a hand toward the canvas. As the pigments dissipated, revealing the neglected street and the face of the young girl as she fell to the ground, she heard Christopher curse. A flash of lightning flooded the room, and the gruesome image receded.

"Do you know the place?" Coco asked.

Christopher nodded. "Yes, it's part of Ward 8," he said, "one of the poorest residential areas in D.C., and on its way to becoming gentrified. The demographic of the area fits with all of the other missing girls' profiles."

"Shit," Coco said, "I'm going to have to ask Arianna if she has a tattoo. She'll think I'm crazy."

Christopher shrugged. "Prudence said that after she'd finished explaining the purpose of the Allegiance and the unusual traits of most of the members, Arianna and Isabel seemed quite open to everything. The biggest skeptic was Jeremy. I'm about to wake him up, we've got work to do." He took out his phone and sent a text. He received an answer immediately, and looked up at Coco with a grin. "He'll make a good lawyer, he's already on his way to my office."

"Birds of a feather..." Coco said.

# 15

CHANTAL WAITED IN Gabriel's study for Alessandro and the others to return from D.C. She paced back and forth in front of the fireplace, arms crossed, and clutching her body as if warding off the cold. She stood still when she sensed a slight ripple in the air, and watched as the group appeared. She gasped at the sight of Alessandro's bloodied and torn clothes. Her stare met his, and the fire within her soul burned with desire for him. He strode across the room, picked her up in his arms, and fled up to their suite.

Alessandro kicked the door closed, and laid Chantal on their bed. Her mind went silent, a blank canvas waiting to be filled. A brush of lavender, the soft pink of ballet slippers, and a swirl of peach immersed her being into the *all* that is Alessandro and her divine love for him. His essence swept over her body and mind, and seeped like nectar into her spirit. She found his lips and he willingly opened them to her. Two lovers starved of each other's love.

She remembered the last time they had made love together and marveled at how strange it was that both of their bodies had not changed since that fateful morning. She thought of Alessandro's grin as he had gently placed the needle onto his favorite record before he climbed back into bed with her. How the tender melody of Rachmaninoff's Rhapsody on a Theme of Paganini, Op. 43, 18th Variation, had floated through the sweet chill of morning air. The ripple of notes that blended to form the exquisite melody echoed in the memories that had played over and over again for the past twenty-eight years. And now, once more, the same music was all around her.

She caught the familiar grin upon Alessandro's face, and how the flecks of amethyst in his eyes sparkled with joy. She kissed his forehead in thanks. She pulled at his clothes, and moments later they were both naked. The contours of his tightly defined muscles reacted to the caress of her touch as she worked her way across his athletic shoulders and arms, to the tapered tips of his long fingers. His tongue claimed her mouth, and in that moment, she transcended into the passion of the first time they had made love.

The velvet caress of his lips melted along her neck and collarbone, to her breasts. His tongue swirled around her nipples, until each one became firm and raised. He moved down her body, and slid his tongue between her thighs, darting in and out of her softness until his fangs grazed her clitoris before plunging into her femoral artery. She cried out his name. Time froze, as she released her bound emotions to her beloved through her blood. He would feel her eternal love for him.

A euphoric moan rumbled in Alessandro's throat. He moved over her body, and Chantal stared into his tear-stained eyes. He entered her, and the power of his unrestrained passion equaled her own. She pulled his head toward her and kissed him with hunger, scraping his lips with her fangs.

"Take my blood, my love," Alessandro whispered. He stroked her hair, encouraging her to drink from him. Her lips trailed along his neck and to the vein above his heart. She inhaled his scent, sank her fangs into his vein and drank in the ecstasy of everything that would forever be her beloved Alessandro.

Through the rush of blood into her mouth, she saw the years of pain Alessandro had endured without her. Their bodies moved together, Alessandro cried out. He pulled her mouth to his and savored the taste of their blood woven together, mixed with the elation of passionate sexual release. They lay together; satiated, faces damp with tears, their souls tangled in rhapsody.

# 16

COCO WALKED DOWN the stairs and along the hallway to Arianna's room. She tapped on the door, and was surprised when it opened almost immediately.

"I realize it's kind of early," Coco said, "but I need to ask you something."

"It's okay, I didn't sleep much," Arianna said. She glanced at the large German shepherd standing with Thalia, next to Coco. "I wondered what happened to Thalia, what's the dog's name?"

"Max," Coco said. "He's one of Gabriel's many dogs."

"I made coffee, you want some?"

"Sure, thanks," Coco said. She followed Arianna into her room that seemed more like a one-bedroom apartment.

"This is quite a place, your boyfriend has," Arianna said with a grin.

"It's his mother's, actually," Coco said. She took a mug of coffee from Arianna, and then wandered out to the living area, where they made themselves comfortable. "Listen, I only found out about all of this a while ago and I couldn't tell you, for obvious reasons."

"I understand," Arianna said. "It's okay."

Coco leaned forward and stared at Arianna. "Are you really okay? Your world has changed dramatically in twenty-four hours, and it's a lot to take in. One minute you're in L.A., then next you're here in Italy."

"Honestly, Coco, I'm good, thanks…just figuring it all out. In truth, I'm not looking forward to going back to my old life."

Coco took a sip of coffee. "I'm not sure any of us will be able to go back to our old lives," she said, "especially knowing what we do now. I don't think Prudence is going to throw us back there in a hurry, and I can't imagine being without this part of my life anymore, especially Gabriel."

"I doubt he's going anywhere without you," Arianna said.

Coco smiled, and looked down at the mug in her hands. "I need to ask you something," she said.

"What's up?"

Coco looked up. "I had a kind of vision of you."

Arianna sighed. "Oh jeez, already I don't like where this is going."

"You were really sad," Coco continued. "You were wearing a gold cross on a chain around your neck, and you took it off and placed it in a drawer."

Coco noticed Arianna's face flush.

"I need to know if you have a tattoo," Coco said, "somewhere around here." She pointed to the area above her right thigh.

Arianna nodded. "Yeah, I do," she said. "But honestly, it's weird that you know this about me. I mean…that stuff's private."

"I get that," Coco said, "and I'm sorry, but I think this is really important. Young girls have gone missing and if I'm right about this, then your tattoo could actually help us find them."

Arianna took a deep breath, and then sighed. "Okay," she said. "An artist friend of mine did it for me. He has a studio at Venice Beach, and he's known for his intricate work. The image I asked for is kind of a…" She put a hand to her mouth and shook her head.

"It's okay," Coco said. "I know this whole thing…this new reality, it's all too weird, and I wouldn't ask you if I didn't think this was important, Arianna. What does the tattoo mean?"

Arianna sniffed back tears and pulled down the top half of her jeans to show Coco her tattoo. "It's a symbol. It means that I've given up Catholicism. I'm an atheist. But it's more than that," she said, pulling up her jeans. "A few years ago, a young Latina girl was found dead in a dumpster in downtown L.A. She'd been raped and beaten, but her death didn't even make headline news. According to her friends she had started to question her faith…her Christianity. When she died, a few of her friends decided to get a tattoo in memory of her, but it became more than that. It's really a symbol of being free of all religion…a way of showing our support for her."

Coco pulled out her phone and handed it to Arianna. "I need a photo to show Gabriel."

"Oh shit," Arianna said, "you're kidding, right?"

Coco shook her head.

Arianna cursed under her breath. She grabbed Coco's phone, pulled down her jeans and snapped a few shots of her tattoo, and then handed the phone back to Coco. "My mother is going to freak out."

"You're an adult," Coco said, "and besides, are you sure Isabel still practices Catholicism?"

"Oh, I know she doesn't," Arianna said, "hasn't for a long time. I'm more concerned about the whole tattoo thing. If she finds out that girls have gone missing because they have the same tat, she's not going to want me to go anywhere. I want to get the letter and Katja's diaries from the bank in New York, and I'm pretty sure Isabel won't want me going anywhere if she knows about this."

"Let's take this one step at a time. Maybe Prudence can talk to her." Coco stared at the photo on her phone, typed up a note, and sent the text to Christopher and Gabriel. "By the way, this guy's a really good artist."

"Yeah, he's pretty cool," Arianna said. "I think you'd really like his artwork."

Someone knocked at the door. Arianna walked over and opened it to find Gabriel standing there with Isabel and Jeremy.

"That was quick," she said. "Come in, Coco's still here. Hi Mom, couldn't sleep either?"

"Yes and no," Isabel said, "but I'd love a cup of coffee."

"Me too," Jeremy said.

Gabriel followed Isabel and Jeremy into Arianna's suite and walked over to Coco.

"I just left Christopher," he said. "Are you alright?"

Coco nodded. "Of course I'm okay. How about you?"

"Better now I'm home and with you."

*Did you find the girl from my painting?* Coco asked him silently.

*Let's talk about that later.* Gabriel sat next to her, took hold of her hand, and waited until Isabel, Jeremy and Arianna were settled. "I understand Prudence explained about the Allegiance, what we are, how you arrived here, etcetera, but due to a recent discovery I want to confirm a few details." He turned to Jeremy. "What can you tell me about your mother and father?"

Jeremy shifted a little on the sofa, and crossed his arms over his chest. "Mom's name was Katja Lange. I asked her once why she never took our father's name, and she said that she wanted to keep her anonymity." Jeremy looked toward Arianna; she nodded and urged him to continue. "Apparently he died the night Arianna and I were born. Mom only spoke about it once...on my fifteenth birthday. She said they were out walking, something they always did in the early evenings. A car came out of nowhere and out of control. It hurtled toward them both. My father pushed Mom out of the way and that was all she could remember. She woke up in the hospital, in labor, and all alone.

"The doctor explained that her husband had died in the accident. She never saw his body. They just gave her an urn that held his remains. She had no family, limited savings and no way of keeping both of us. That's when she received a call from an adoption agency in L.A. saying they had a couple desperate for a baby girl. It broke Mom's heart to give my sister away, but in those days she didn't really have a choice."

The tears brimming in Arianna's eyes did not go unnoticed by Gabriel. Nor did the imperceptible ribbon of love connecting the twins.

Jeremy turned to Arianna. "I know she loved you."

"So Katja had her daughter and her husband taken from her in a matter of days," Arianna said. "How did she cope?"

"My guess is that she had some help with this," Gabriel cut in. "Perhaps her husband's friends and relatives."

"But Mom never mentioned anything about my father having relatives," Jeremy said.

"You mentioned that Katja left diaries. Where are they now, Jeremy?" Gabriel asked.

"In a safe deposit box at a bank in New York," Jeremy answered. "Arianna and I plan to get them next time we're in the city together."

Isabel turned to Gabriel. "Katja also told me about the diaries. She had me promise that I would follow up and make sure the twins both read them. She was adamant about it."

"Did Katja tell you the name of her husband?" Gabriel asked.

"No, just that everything is explained in her diaries, and to be sure the twins read the letters from their father," Isabel said. She looked at the twins. "We need to go to the bank and retrieve your belongings from the safe deposit box."

Gabriel nodded. "I agree, but perhaps it's best if Jeremy not leave the safety of this fortress."

"But I don't want my sister to go alone," Jeremy said.

Gabriel sat forward. "By now Kenan will have a dossier on you, Katja, and anyone else associated with the two of you," he said. "We'll discuss the best way to access the bank and go from there. I understand how confusing our world may seem to you, but for now, I ask that you accept our hospitality. There are matters of some urgency that need our attention. By no means does this make your situation any less urgent, as everything is connected, but time is of the essence." He gestured to Arianna. "I don't believe it was an accident that you and Coco met as you did and became friends. And then to find out that you have a twin brother, who happens to work for Coco's brother, in D.C.? No, this goes beyond mere coincidence."

Arianna nodded. "I agree," she said. "So what does it all mean?"

Isabel placed her coffee cup on the table beside her. She rose gracefully from the sofa, and approached a window. A thin headband held her long, dark brown hair off her face. She wore a pale blue shirt, navy blue pants, and medium heels that exemplified her dancer's body. "In many ways, Gabriel, you seem familiar to me. You see, quite a few years ago, I met a man—one of Steven's friends—my late husband." She fixed her gaze on something in the distance, and smiled. "The man I refer to was kind, and, like Steven, he worked in the field of immigration, although I'm not exactly sure in what capacity, and, to be honest, I figured it best not to ask. Some evenings when they worked late at the office, I would cook dinner and drive it over. I remember Steven's friend never seemed to eat much.

"On one such night, I stayed late and helped write up papers Steven needed the following day in court. When we were finished, I asked the man about himself. I remember he glanced up at Steven, as if seeking his approval before he continued. Steven nodded, and the man shared his story with me. I remember it as if it was just an hour ago."

"But what does this have to do with what's going on now, Mama?" Arianna asked.

Isabel turned and faced Arianna. "The gentleman I speak of had the same cool touch to his skin, and pallor of face as the two men whom we met at Coco's apartment...Stefan and Alessandro."

For a few moments the room fell silent.

"Did Dad's friend tell you anything about himself?" Arianna asked.

"Yes, he shared his life's story with me, but asked that I keep it to myself, which of course I've done. But since we arrived here, I've found myself wondering about that night in Steven's office. You see, Steven's friend told me about the man who saved his life, and that he will honor him until the day he dies. He said his savior's eyes were flecked with gold." She turned and faced Gabriel. "Is the phrase 'without courage, all is lost,' familiar to you? And if so, Gabriel, what is the name of the man I speak of?"

A shadow of a smile broke over Gabriel's face. "You speak of my comrade, Pelayo."

"Yes," Isabel said. "His name is Pelayo."

"He chose well in trusting you and Steven," Gabriel said, "and I regret I did not meet your husband. I also thank you for keeping Pelayo's story safe."

"So," Isabel said. "We are all somehow connected through fate."

"Yes," Gabriel said, "indeed we are." He stood with Coco and walked to the door. Before he exited, he spoke to Isabel. "Could you join me in the main kitchen in a few minutes, please?"

"Of course," Isabel said.

He closed the door, put an arm around Coco, and headed for the kitchen. "There's some business that needs attending," he said. "Get some rest."

"Anything to do with the tattoos?" Coco asked.

"Yes," Gabriel said.

"You're leaving again?"

He pulled her close and kissed her. "Yes," he said. "But I'll see you soon."

Coco looked into his eyes. "It's a shame you don't get mileage."

# 17

GABRIEL AND PELAYO sat at one end of a communal-styled rustic wooden table. The thick boards, worn and dimpled, held memories of loud and crowded dinners, and an abundance of food and drink. A large fireplace built into a tall wall of rock ran parallel to the table, and opposite stood a wide archway that framed an extensive modern kitchen. A fire crackled and spat, giving warmth to what Gabriel had always perceived as the heart of the fortress. He trailed a finger over a deep scratch in the wood, and listened intently as Pelayo explained more about the projects he worked on with Isabel's husband in Los Angeles.

"It wasn't until a few years after Steven's death, that I discovered a young girl who was the daughter of one of his clients had been reported as missing," Pelayo said. "Her body showed up in a dumpster in downtown L.A. The community was devastated, not only with the brutality of the crime, but for what they saw as a lack of media coverage the girl's murder received. They questioned that if the victim had been a white girl in Beverly Hills, the case would have garnered more attention from the media. Since then, the number of missing Latina girls has risen dramatically. Not just in L.A., but in neighborhoods across the country."

Gabriel pulled out his phone, and showed Pelayo the image of Arianna's tattoo. "Coco thinks this particular tattoo is somehow connected to the missing girls. Have you seen this before?"

"No," Pelayo answered, "but there's some kind of recognition. Who is this?"

"Steven and Isabel's adopted daughter, Arianna," Gabriel said. "She's the twin of—"

"Jeremy," Pelayo cut in. "The owner of the computer and bag I picked up in D.C."

"They'll be here momentarily," Gabriel said.

Pelayo shook his head. "Everything's connected, right *amigo*?"

Gabriel placed his phone in a pocket. "Isabel said the same thing."

A smile broke across Pelayo's face when he heard footsteps approaching. Both men looked up at the kitchen door as Isabel entered. She froze when she saw Pelayo.

Pelayo led her to a chair at the table. "Are you alright?" he asked.

Isabel nodded, and took out a handkerchief and dabbed her eyes. "I've thought of you often over the years. You disappeared so quickly after Steven's death."

"I apologize for my absence," Pelayo said, "at the time, it seemed best that I leave. It was important that I continued with the work Steven and I had begun."

Isabel rested a hand over Pelayo's. "It's good to see you."

Gabriel set a glass of water on the table in front of her. She took a sip just as the door opened, and Arianna and Jeremy entered. Gabriel pulled out two chairs, and motioned for the twins to be seated either side of Isabel.

Isabel clasped Arianna's hand. "Jeremy and Arianna, this is Pelayo," she said. "The gentleman I spoke of earlier."

The twins stared across the table at Pelayo. Arianna accepted his outstretched hand. "You knew my dad."

"Yes," Pelayo said, "he was a good man."

Isabel tucked her handkerchief up a sleeve. "I trust Pelayo implicitly," she said.

Jeremy shook Pelayo's hand. "So you're like Stefan?" he asked.

Pelayo looked to Gabriel for approval. He dipped his head and returned to his seat at the head of the table. "Yes," Pelayo answered. "But not as old. You've entered a world where secrecy is an integral part of our lives and crucial to our existence. I'm happy to share my story with you, but I must ask that you do not share it with others."

"*Tu secreto está a salvo conmigo*," Arianna said.

Pelayo nodded. "*Gracias.*" He turned toward Jeremy.

Arianna couldn't help but notice a slight change in Jeremy's demeanor since meeting Pelayo. He seemed less anxious, more relaxed. She studied him while Pelayo waited for Jeremy's reply. Pelayo's dark eyes seemed sad, and the shadow of a beard and moustache gave him the appearance of a man whose work took precedence over his personal attributes. But this did not fool Arianna. She saw Pelayo's rugged allure. He looked to be in his late thirties or early forties, although in retrospect she had no idea how long he had been this age. He stood about five foot ten, with a broad chest and, she gathered, a muscular body. She found herself drawn to the deep, rich timbre of his voice, and his heavy Spanish accent. But she sensed something that others may not notice at first glance. For now, she thought it best to keep this to herself.

"You have my word," Jeremy said.

"You're the owner of the computer bag?" Pelayo asked.

A smile broke across Jeremy's face. "Yes, thanks, I'd given up on ever seeing the bag or my computer again."

"*De nada*," Pelayo said. "So, my story…I was born in El Salvador during a time of civil unrest. As a little boy I would walk to school. It was not unusual to see dead bodies on the side of the road… some were burned, some were mutilated. This was how I grew up, and it was normal to me. I never knew life to be any different. When I turned sixteen, I aspired to become a teacher. I wanted to educate others in the hopes that this might help bring peace to my community."

Pelayo shook his head. "The El Salvador of my youth was an angry country. Farmers were forced to give up their properties and work for the greedy men who took what had once belonged to them. People were hungry. People were disheartened. In my early twenties, I joined the military, and after my training, I was approached by an English-speaking stranger. He had a translator, and through him, he offered to train me in the Special Forces. He promised that I would be paid well, but, more importantly, that my family would be protected. I remember my mother's tears as she hugged me goodbye. She begged me not to leave, but I wanted to give her a life better than the one she was living. I hated seeing my family starve, having to beg for food."

Pelayo crossed his arms, and leaned forward on the table. "When I boarded the plane headed for the United States, I began to understand the true meaning of what I'd signed up for," he said, "which turned out to be fighting for the same greedy people that stole from my family and friends. Later, in the midst of combat, I'd wonder what I was fighting for and whom I was fighting against. Years passed, and when I finally found the way back to my home and family, there was nothing left. Everything I knew had been destroyed. Even the green card I had been promised was a lie."

Jeremy frowned. "So what did you do?"

Pelayo looked at him. "I made my way across the desert of eastern Arizona."

"*El Camino del Diablo...*" Arianna whispered, "the Devil's Highway."

"I didn't see the devil," Pelayo said, "only men desperate to return to loved ones. I was luckier than most. I survived. But I returned to the United States an angry man. I headed east, and waited in the shadows for the right time to destroy the man who enlisted me and taunted me with his promises of hope.

"The night of my revenge, when blood was once again on my hands, I whispered prayers to God for forgiveness before turning the knife on myself. I wanted to be with my family again, but instead I woke up in a warm bed. A gentle man with a friendly smile was changing a dressing on my chest. I begged him to let me die, and went to strike him, but I was too weak, and the gentle man was quick and strong. Weeks passed, and then one evening another man appeared at the house.

"He seemed familiar. He told me about a group who protected those who work for social justice, and others called Creatives. When I heard his story, I knew I'd found a true brother. I was sick of the brutality of war, of hatred and greed. I chose instead to protect those who had the slightest chance of bringing peace to an angry society."

Pelayo looked up and saw tears on Arianna's cheeks. "Cry for my beautiful country and the people of El Salvador, Arianna, but not for me.

My life is now rich with friendship, and my heart has found peace. I have purpose in my life."

Jeremy looked across the table at Gabriel. "So it was you who saved Pelayo?"

Gabriel nodded. "Yes, but it was Christopher and Colombina's grandfather who brought Pelayo back to health. His name is Kishu, and you'll meet him soon." Gabriel pushed out his chair and stood. "Pelayo is now your guardian. But until we know more of Kenan's whereabouts and those who follow him, you will all need to stay here."

"But I start law school soon," Jeremy said.

"I understand your concerns," Gabriel said. "Talk to Christopher about this. For now, I suggest you join him in his office. I have a feeling he's going to need your help with a case he's working on." He turned to Isabel. "There's something Pelayo and I need to attend to, we'll catch up with you later."

A woman wearing an apron that hugged her generous waistline, entered from the opposite end of the room. "No one is going anywhere until you've eaten," she said, her English drenched in an Italian accent. "I'm Maria, you must be Isabel, Arianna, and Jeremy."

"Yes," Isabel said. "Is this your kitchen?"

Maria chuckled. "For now, yes. Do you like to cook?"

"Yes, I do," Isabel said, "and I'm happy to help you with anything."

"I'd like that," Maria said. "Why don't we start by giving you a guided tour of the pantry, and don't worry, I don't bite!"

18

### Venice Beach, California

THE STEADY BEAT of drums paired with a booming bass pounded through an open window. Moments later, a melodic-sounding woman's voice purred over a microphone, voicing opinionated lyrics into her own distinct form of poetry. A chorus of out-of-tune and slurred voices, and a skunk-like scent in the air, suggested a party was in progress at the Ocean Front rooftop apartment.

A few doors down, a car door slammed, followed by giggling and groans of sexual pleasure. As Gabriel and Pelayo walked closer to the corner where the alley met Ocean Avenue, the stench of urine mixed with salt air began to dissipate. The ghostly image of a leafless tree, painted in shades of gray, black, and white, spread over the tiled walls of a building. On the footpath, where stark black tree roots met cement, two men sat on the ground, drinking coffee from a nearby twenty-four hour coffee house. One checked his phone, and the other slurped his drink.

Gabriel and Pelayo crossed the road and then disappeared up a flight of stairs. Arianna's description of her friend's tattoo studio mirrored to perfection the actuality of the place. The front door seemed more in keeping with a private detective novel set in a dingy building in San Francisco, than a tattoo studio in Los Angeles. Written on the window in nondescript font were the words Art Studio. A blind had been pulled down over the glass to avoid anyone peeping in.

The two men listened at the door for sounds of anyone inside. Pelayo shook his head, and Gabriel pulled out a rune, and tossed it in the air where it hovered for a moment. A short click indicated the door was no longer locked. Gabriel snatched back the rune, slid it back in his pocket, and entered the studio with Pelayo.

A wall of windows opposite the entrance beckoned the world of night to enter. Neon signs lit up the room, throwing twisted shadows across the floor and walls. An easel stood in one corner, and on the ledge sat a piece of Masonite with an intricate pen and ink drawing done on matte white Bristol Board and framed in blue tape. The image showed an open book with a tree growing out from the pages, and symbols describing a theme of heartbreak grew from the branches.

Gabriel held a hand over the image, and watched as a drawing of a woman's face drenched in heartache looked up and smiled at him. He returned her smile, then dropped his hand and the woman returned to her pose. Gabriel observed the rest of the studio. A corner of the room had been curtained off with black drapes.

"This is as good a time as any to practice some magic," Gabriel said. He smiled at Pelayo. "How's that going for you?"

Pelayo shook his head. "Your blood may run through my veins, *amigo*, but I'm not sure the magic exists in me."

"Well, you're my only prodigy," Gabriel said. "So I expect you to keep practicing. Come on, let's see what you can do." He pointed to the drapes. "Pull them back."

Pelayo stood, feet apart, and with a look of determination waved a hand in front of the drapes. Nothing happened. "Like I said, I lack your abilities."

Gabriel raised an eyebrow. "Remind me when we get back to the fortress to give you some lessons." He stared at the drapes and they opened, accompanied by a string of Spanish curses muttered by Pelayo.

A modern reclining chair made of steel and black vinyl was secured solidly to the gray linoleum floor. A work light sat on a rolling table with a glass surface. On another table sat a tattoo machine, foot pedal and power supply, tattoo tubes, bottles of ink, a box of disposable gloves, paper towels and a pair of scissors. The bench below held more supplies: a large bottle of distilled water, a pack of disposable razors, lap cloths and antibacterial soap.

"He seems to know what he's doing," Pelayo said.

"Indeed," Gabriel replied. His attention was drawn to a filing cabinet. He opened the top drawer and flipped through numerous files of designs until he found what he was looking for: The image the artist had tattooed on Arianna, along with a list of clients who had requested the same image. He took out his phone and took pictures of the information, and then forwarded everything to Christopher. He was careful to place everything back as it had been.

Before they departed, Gabriel tossed a rune into the air and waved an arm; his movements resembled those of an orchestral conductor. He snatched the rune from the air and left with Pelayo the way they had arrived.

"Was that to lift our scent?" Pelayo asked.

Gabriel nodded. "Yes, something else I need to teach you."

"Do you think Kenan knows about this place yet?" Pelayo asked.

"My guess is yes," Gabriel said, "although I didn't sense vampires in the studio, but I'm fairly sure a few of the names of his clients matched the names of missing girls."

Pelayo glanced up and down the street as they crossed to the other side. "Why's Kenan preying on young female atheists?"

"His hatred is inherent and runs in his blood," Gabriel said. "Kenan is blind to any form of worship other than the archaic, one-dimensional branch of Catholicism he was fed from his mother, and later his maker. Their fear of the strength of the feminine brewed for centuries until it reached borderline hysteria at the beginning of the darkest ages. This then set the horrors of heresy in motion. By taking women out of their stature in society and claiming they were witches, the Church gained control, but in doing so, cities collapsed and sent society spiraling back hundreds of years. The small section of the Catholic Church that Kenan supports does not want equality for all, or an educated society. They prefer the opposite. A society led by a puppet whose strings they pull."

"A male-dominated society," Pelayo said.

"Yes," Gabriel agreed. "Specifically, a sect of religious sociopaths, who in reality have no interest in conforming to the rules of Christianity."

The two men walked down the alley, and disappeared into a shadow of darkness.

# 19

*ARIANNA SAT ON the front steps at Jeremy's home in New York. She looked up as a tall, slender man with white hair opened the front gate. His gaze met hers, and she was instantly drawn to his cerulean blue eyes. "Hello, Arianna," he said. "There's a reason why Prudence seems familiar to you."*

*Arianna stood and walked toward him. "What is it?"*

*"You already know…"*

*Arianna reached toward the man, but he began to fade. "Please, tell me…" she said.*

*He smiled and sang; "Lulla, lulla, lullaby, lulla, lulla, lullaby."*

*His words caught in a wisp of a breeze before his image disappeared.*

Arianna woke with a start and stared up at the ceiling. She replayed the dream in her mind. "Lulla, lulla, lullaby, lulla, lulla, lullaby…" she sang the song over again to herself, and then froze. Her eyes widened, and then the corners of her mouth broke into a wide smile. She grabbed her laptop and phone and went to find Jeremy. She found him sipping coffee in his suite next to hers.

He looked up from his computer. "Hey," he said.

Arianna stood in the doorway. "I think I know where I've seen Prudence before…I mean, her face."

"Where?"

"It'll be easier if I just go over this once," she said. "Have you seen Isabel?"

"Yeah, she went in search of the library," Jeremy said.

Arianna dropped into a chair opposite Jeremy, and opened her laptop. "I need to upload some photos, won't take a minute."

"You don't want to tell me what this is about?" he asked.

She shook her head. "Not yet. Just want to check I'm not going insane."

Jeremy clasped his hands together and stretched his arms above his head. "I'm thinking we might be the only sane ones around here."

"I don't," Arianna said, "in fact, I'm really comfortable here. I just hope Mom's okay."

"She looked fine the last time I saw her," Jeremy said. " She was armed with a cauldron and a wand."

Arianna giggled. "No black cat?"

"Just a couple of rats," Jeremy replied. "Haven't you heard? Rats are the new cats."

Arianna shook her head. She scrolled through the mass of photos on her phone and checked when they were available on her laptop. When she was done, she closed her computer and stared at Jeremy. "Okay, let's go find Coco and the others."

"Oh great," Jeremy said. "Another intimate get-together of The Walking Dead."

○

Caprecia entered the suite and closed the door. Eduardo stood before a window, looking out at the snow-covered mountains tipped with sunlight. His dignified pose was exactly how she remembered him. "There are too many words unsaid between us," she said. "I'm so sorry for what I did."

Eduardo turned to her, and when he spoke, his somber tone reflected that of a broken man. "I forgave you long ago, Caprecia, and strangely, even after all of the heartache your initial betrayal gave me, I find I still love you."

Caprecia held up a hand. "Eduardo, I'm not here to ask you to take me back."

"We were young, and when our love was tested, we failed," Eduardo said. His tenderness touched her core. "I shall always hold a space for you in my heart, but not as my wife. Do you understand?"

Her eyes brimmed with tears. "That's more than I deserve."

Eduardo shook his head. "We both made mistakes and have paid dearly. I failed to give you the attention you needed and deserved. Instead, I threw my passion into my art, not realizing until after you were gone that you were my inspiration."

"Your kind heart helped me get through Kenan's degradation and abuse," Caprecia said. The silence that lingered between them broke her heart.

"What will you do now?" he asked.

"Help Prudence bring our daughter home." Caprecia slid the wedding ring off her finger and placed it in Eduardo's palm. "If by chance something happens to me, please give this to Louisa." She handed him a small package tied with a ribbon. "I wrote letters...maybe they'll help her understand me. I don't want her to make the mistakes I did, but to keep talking to Ignacio when times are difficult rather than look for an escape."

Eduardo wiped the moisture from his own eyes. "My life is empty without her."

"I'll do what it takes to bring her home, Eduardo, you have my word." Eduardo set the package on a nearby table, and embraced Caprecia. She heard him breathe in her scent of lilacs.

He let her go, and stared at the floor. "I warned her about Ignacio... did my best to stop her from seeing him, but then one day when she left the studio I observed him while he waited for her. When I saw them together, I realized they were deeply in love. Of course I feared for both of them...they shared a deadly addiction."

Caprecia walked over to the fireplace. "I would have been dead in a gutter like my mother if you hadn't found me, Eduardo. Sobriety gave me Louisa and you, but I didn't have the strength nor the courage to keep doing the work."

"You've shown more courage than I'll ever have," Eduardo said. "I hated myself for refusing to let you go when you pleaded for a divorce. In truth, I wanted to protect you."

"I know, but I didn't understand and I felt trapped. I gave up one addiction for another." Caprecia stared into the embers. "You and Louisa are the greatest gifts this life has given me...I'm so sorry for deserting you both and destroying what we had. I was caught in a moment of weakness, and not a second goes by when I don't hate myself for my betrayal. But now I have a chance to help bring Louisa and Ignacio together again. Perhaps in time, Louisa will find it in her heart to forgive me." She turned to him. "Did you ever tell her how we met?"

"Not the whole story," Eduardo said, "only that we were introduced while I was in Spain for an art gallery opening. I told her nothing more, although she begged to hear the story over and over again, as if searching for the missing pieces of a puzzle. She would listen intently in case I added or changed a word, but I never did.

"She went to Spain once, and although she told me the trip was purely a vacation, I found out later that she'd also traveled to Portugal. I don't know what she found, if anything, but she seemed aloof for months after she returned. Then I saw the marks on her arm...I thought I would lose her too. Gabriel helped me get her professional support, and for a while she seemed stronger, but in retrospect Louisa had just become clever at hiding her addiction. She was on a path to self-destruction."

"How long had she been using before Ignacio entered her life?" Caprecia asked.

"She'd been clean for two years, but something triggered her to use again, and it was just before Ignacio arrived in San Gimignano."

"Kenan knew my heart ached for my daughter, although I did my best to hide my sadness. I wouldn't put it past him to have discovered her illness and found a way to tempt her. The thought makes my intent to kill him even stronger."

"Louisa's demeanor changed about two months before Ignacio arrived...before Coco landed in Tuscany," Eduardo said. "She moved out of our guesthouse where she'd lived for years and into her own apartment on the outskirts of town. The only reason I had a key to her apartment was because once when she was ill, Maria insisted on delivering food to her."

Caprecia shook her head. "The time frame fits. I think Kenan planned to destroy Ignacio all along. I'd heard him speak of 'the English vampire's addiction,' and there was something else too, about Ignacio's family, but I didn't catch the whole story."

"Stefan may know something about Ignacio's history...something that would cause Kenan to execute such vengeance," Eduardo said.

"Kenan is a cold-hearted psychopath," Caprecia said. "Extreme violence seems to calm him like a lullaby, and he methodically plans revenge." She leaned into the back of a chair and looked at Eduardo. "Tell me about Louisa's personality, her likes and dislikes. Does she sing and dance, or paint?"

A proud smile caught Eduardo's lips. "Louisa's creativity flows through words and photographs. She combines the two mediums. Her images are stark and often surreal, but her words are delicate and emotional." He paused for a moment, lost in his thoughts. "Christopher encouraged her to further her career in the arts and journalism, and apply to universities in the United States...but Louisa's reply was always the same. 'I'll think about it,' she'd say. I think she believed you'd come back one day, and wanted to be here when you returned."

"I'd love to see her work," Caprecia said.

"Ask Christopher, he has quite a few of her pieces on the walls of his rooms upstairs. She has your sensitivity, Caprecia, and your grace and beauty."

"How was she in school?" Caprecia asked.

"Determined, stubborn, kind." He caught a breath and his words wavered. Caprecia reached out to him. "One of her high school teachers used the word 'altruistic' to describe her. Even as an adult she carried an innate sense to protect others...she just wanted everyone to be happy."

"She sounds like you, always concerned for others before yourself," she smiled. "There were times when this facet of your personality drove me crazy. I witnessed your health suffer when you'd stay out late encouraging your friends to finish paintings, or making sure they had food and art supplies. Nurturing others is inherent in you, and one of the many things I love about your personality."

The corners of Eduardo's lips curved into a sad smile. "It can be both a curse and an asset," he said. "When does Prudence plan on departing?"

"In a day or two." Caprecia walked toward the door.

Isabel made her way down the staircase to the main floor, stopping every now and again to marvel at the portraits lining the walls. She thought about the events that had transpired over the past twenty-four hours, and smiled when she realized she had woken this morning eager to get on with the day.

According to Gabriel's directions, the next door on her left should be the library. She reached for the brass handle just as the door opened. An exquisite woman with alabaster-toned skin, and waist-length, dark-chocolate brown hair, and matching eyes, stood before her. But Isabel's gaze was drawn past the woman's shoulders to an elegantly dressed gentleman who stood about ten feet behind her. When he looked up at Isabel, it was as if a veil lifted from her eyes, and for a moment, life seemed to take a breath and then pause.

Something icy cold touched Isabel's arm. She gasped and returned her gaze to the woman. The temperature of the woman's fingers through Isabel's silk shirt told her the woman was more than an ordinary human. And although her smile was warm and genuine, Isabel saw great sadness in her eyes.

"My apologies," Isabel said, "I'll come back later."

The woman looked back at the gentleman, and then to Isabel. "Please, stay, I believe you are exactly where you need to be."

Isabel's eyes darted around the room. "Actually, I thought this door led to the library, but now I see my mistake."

"I'm sure Eduardo would be happy to guide you," the woman said. As she walked by Isabel, she breathed in deeply. "Are you a dancer?" she asked.

"Yes," Isabel said, "but it's been a while."

The woman closed her eyes for a moment. "Do you sing?"

Isabel nodded. "Yes, I sing the songs from the country of my mother's birth."

"And where was your mother born?" the woman asked.

"Veracruz, Mexico," Isabel said. "She taught me songs from her heart."

The woman smiled. "I also sing the songs from the birthplace of my mother," she said. "It's important to remember where we are from."

Isabel held a hand toward the woman. "My name is Isabel."

"I'm Caprecia," the woman said, and nodded to the man, "and this is Eduardo." Caprecia placed her hands on Isabel's shoulders and kissed both her cheeks. "Prudence is asking for us all to meet in the main living room. Eduardo will guide you, I will see you both there shortly."

It seemed to Isabel that Caprecia just suddenly disappeared. She turned to Eduardo. "I'm not sure I'll ever get used to how fast they are."

"It takes time," Eduardo said. "The library is next door, and is quite an extraordinary room. Perhaps you would allow me to show it to you after our meeting with Prudence."

Isabel felt a warmth flood her cheeks. "I'd like that," she said. "Thank you."

# 20

ARIANNA AND JEREMY found Coco and Gabriel in the main living room. They were standing arm in arm, staring at a portrait of Prudence that hung over the mantle. The painting appeared old and slightly damaged, as if flames had licked up one side. Arianna glanced around the crowded room; most of the household was there, including Prudence. She took a seat next to Isabel.

Jeremy stared at Thalia. "So, is that just a cat?" he asked, "or is it something else disguised as a cat?"

"Thalia is related to Algiz," Gabriel said, "and yes, she has the ability to change into other forms, but only in the feline family."

Jeremy fell into an armchair near Christopher. "You mean like a lion, a cheetah, a—"

"Mountain lion is her favorite form," Coco cut in. "Maybe later she'll give you a demonstration."

"Can't wait," Jeremy said. "How about this chair I'm sitting on, does it morph into something else or is it just a chair?"

Gabriel raised an eyebrow. "I can say without a doubt that the chair you are sitting on is an inanimate object," he said. "It has no hidden agenda."

Prudence turned to Arianna. "You need to speak with me, dear?"

Arianna wondered how Prudence knew she had something to say, but threw the thought aside and nodded. "Yes, I think it's important."

The room went quiet, and Arianna decided to jump straight into her story. "When I first saw Prudence, it seemed to me like we'd met before, but it wasn't until about thirty minutes ago that I realized why. I dozed off for a while and dreamed." She took in a breath. "I dreamed I was sitting on the front steps at Jeremy's home in New York. I looked up and saw a tall man with snow-white hair standing at the gate. We stared at each other, and I remember being instantly drawn to his eyes. They were an unusual tone of blue. Cerulean blue. He smiled and said hello, and then told me there's a reason why Prudence seemed familiar. I asked what the reason was, and he said: *'You already know…'*

"I reached out to him but his image began to fade. I asked him to please tell me, and instead of talking, he sang to me: *'Lulla, lulla, lullaby, lulla, lulla, lullaby.'* When I woke up, I knew where I'd seen Prudence." She opened her laptop and turned it around so the others could see the screen. It showed a photo of the gnomes and fairies clustered into a corner of Katya's garden. Arianna clicked the screen and another photo appeared, a close-up of one particular fairy's face. Arianna looked to Prudence, who seemed transfixed on the image.

"The lines the man quoted are from *A Midsummer Night's Dream*," Arianna said. "It's the song the fairies sing to Queen Titania. This story is my favorite of Shakespeare's plays."

The room fell quiet. Stefan rested his hands on Prudence's shoulders. To Arianna, this moment seemed so private, as if it was not common for Prudence to show her feelings in front of others.

"What is it?" Arianna asked. "What have I said?"

"My mother's response is partly from joy," Gabriel said. His gaze met Prudence's. "May I explain?"

Prudence nodded, and Gabriel continued.

"The statue you speak of was crafted by the artist Jacques Callot. He lived in Florence for a while in the early 1600s and it was there that Prudence met him. She became captivated by the intricacy of his work, particularly the attention to detail in the characters he replicated from the Italian festivals…*commedia dell'arte*. She would visit his studio and encourage him to continue his work. He used to call Prudence *'la dame de fees.'*"

Arianna smiled. "The Fairy Lady."

"Yes," Gabriel said. "Before he left Florence, Callot presented Prudence with a gift, a statue of a fairy whose face mirrored hers. In later years, she gave this statue to a dear friend in return for a kindness he had shown."

Prudence looked at Jeremy. "You look so much like him," she said. Her words seemed to float across the room. "The statue of the fairy in your mother's garden is invaluable, and the man I gave her to… was your father, and my dear friend, Elion."

Arianna glanced around at everyone in the room, and decided this was as good a time as any to lay her cards on the table. She closed the laptop. "I want to get Katja's diaries and the letter from Elion. They're in a safe deposit box at a New York bank. I'm the only one who can go," she said. "It has to be me. This Kenan person knows what Jeremy looks like, but is clueless about me. About us being twins."

Prudence nodded. "You may be correct, but I'm not sure I want to take the risk."

"With due respect, Prudence," Arianna said, "I need to do this, and it makes sense."

Prudence thought for a moment, and then looked up at Gabriel. "Take Pelayo with you."

"May I go too?" Isabel cut in, "I don't want my daughter to be alone."

Arianna placed a hand over her mother's. "Mom, I need to do this alone," she smiled. "I feel like it's my destiny, for want of a better word. Maybe this is the part I play in this strange world. No one knows me, I'm just another human."

Isabel nodded and lowered her head. The tears that welled in her eyes rolled down her cheeks, but were caught in a bright white handkerchief. When she looked up, she saw Eduardo's kind face and his outstretched hand.

"You have raised a courageous daughter," Eduardo said, "I know what that's like. And at some time, we must let them go."

Isabel took the handkerchief and wiped away her tears. "I know," she said, "but it's so hard."

"Isabel," Prudence said, "perhaps you can assist Layla and Coco in preparing Arianna for her quest. I suggest she look…a little upscale New York, perhaps."

"Let's go upstairs," Layla said, "I have the perfect outfit in my wardrobe."

"You have an hour, ladies," Gabriel said.

"An hour?" Arianna asked. "They'll need way more time to transform me into a trendy New Yorker."

Gabriel held up a finger. "One hour," he said. He looked at Alessandro, Christopher, and Pelayo. "I need to meet with you all in my study."

# 21

*Midtown Manhattan, New York*

GABRIEL, ARIANNA, AND Pelayo materialized in a room painted a light shade of coffee. The late afternoon sun cut a shadow across a black ink drawing of a gothic church that hung on a wall opposite. Car horns and the dull drone of traffic seeped through the windows. A cat meowed. This was not a sound Arianna expected to hear. However, since being thrust into Coco's world, she was surprised at how quickly the extraordinary often teetered on the brink of being mundane.

Gabriel knelt down on one knee. "Hello to you too, Matilda," he said, scratching the vocal feline under the chin.

Arianna noticed that the cat resembled Coco's cat, Thalia. "Is that just a cat?" she asked.

Gabriel picked up Matilda and walked over to the window that looked onto 44th Street. "She's related to Thalia, but prefers her ragdoll persona. Anything else and the hotel guests might complain." He placed Matilda onto the window ledge where she rolled her plush body across Gabriel in search of more attention. Her persistence was rewarded with a small treat he retrieved from a pocket. He turned around. "I'll watch you from the roof opposite the bank," he said. "When you enter the building you'll be out of my range, but Pelayo will keep an eye on you via the hidden camera."

Arianna nodded, while her fingers touched the thick silver chain around her neck and trailed the outline of the locket that hid the tiny camera. Pelayo set up the laptop and checked that the links were live and ready. "All good here." He stood face-to-face with Arianna. "Are you sure you still want to do this?"

"Of course," Arianna said.

Gabriel smiled at her. "Elion would be proud of his daughter."

"Thanks." Arianna turned to Pelayo. "Wish me luck."

"Good luck, *mi amiga*," Pelayo said.

Matilda sprang down from the window ledge and sauntered beside Arianna. "Matilda will escort you downstairs to the foyer," Gabriel said, "but once you're on the street you'll be on your own."

Arianna stroked Matilda's soft fur. "Don't you think guests might think it's a little strange seeing a cat guiding me through the hotel?"

Gabriel grinned. "There's been a feline connected to the Allegiance living at the Algonquin since 1902."

"Why the Algonquin?" Arianna asked.

"Prudence envisioned this building as a haven for writers," Gabriel said. "Although I think Stefan encouraged her a little."

"Your parents live here?" Arianna asked.

Gabriel shook his head. "No, when they're in New York they stay in their apartment opposite the Metropolitan Museum of Art. But they've had this room since the building was first built. It gave Stefan the opportunity to mingle with writers of times past, such as Harold W. Ross. I think Stefan may have planted the idea for Ross to create The New Yorker magazine over a few brandies late one evening," Gabriel said. "Stefan reads the magazine habitually."

"I love these tidbits of historical information," Arianna said. Matilda rubbed her head against Arianna's ankles and nudged her forward. Gabriel opened the door and Arianna followed the cat into the hallway. "Can I hear more when I return?"

"Of course," Gabriel said, "but let's take care of the issue at hand first."

Pelayo gave her a wave before the two immortals disappeared behind the door. The clicking of the lock made Arianna more alert. She walked along the carpeted hallway and past two other hotel room doors. She noticed that at the center of each door hung a framed picture of Matilda, with a quote from different literary figures. One of the quotes by Dorothy Parker made her smile:

*This is not a novel that should be tossed aside lightly.*
*It should be thrown with great force.*

Arianna paused for a moment on the first set of stairs. With ten sets of stairs before her, she was grateful for the extra cardio routines she'd recently applied to her daily exercise schedule. She rested a hand on the wooden rail and began her descent, taking each gray marble step one at a time, Matilda keeping pace by her side.

When she reached the last step, she pushed open a door and entered the lobby. A gentle prod from Matilda urged her forward. She stepped onto a white tiled floor and glanced around. Two women were busy at the front desk, and a few guests were reading in the lounge area to her right. A bellman pushed open the front doors for her. She stopped for a moment to stroke Matilda before she stepped outside to the noise of Manhattan.

A bitter wind hit her face, and she pulled up the collar of her coat. She was grateful for the clothing Layla had given her to wear, and although the medium-heeled black ankle boots and stylishly cut two-piece black pantsuit were a far cry from her familiar faded jeans and baseball undershirts, she found it easy to rise to the character of a trendy New Yorker. The short chestnut-colored wig she wore gave her an added sense of anonymity, a trait she could get used to.

She immediately noticed the landmarks Gabriel had suggested she look out for, the most significant being the weathered gray cement façade of the New York Yacht Club building. The curved windows looked as if they belonged on a pirate ship, with their intricately carved goat heads staring out at her as she walked by. Yellow cabs were lined up outside hotels, and people rushed by her on the sidewalk wearing business suits and sneakers. A few minutes later, Arianna saw the bank to her left and entered. She walked toward the first available teller, a young man, who smiled as she approached.

"I'd like to open my safe-deposit box, please," Arianna said.

"Of course," the teller replied. "Just swipe your bank card, punch in your PIN number, and I'll be happy to get you started. I'll also need to see a picture I.D."

Arianna ran the bank card through the machine and punched in the PIN Katja had assigned to her before she died. She handed the teller a small card with the number of the box, along with her driver's license. The teller checked that the photo on the license matched the young woman standing in front of him.

"Fabulous photo," he said. "How'd you manage that?"

Arianna ran a hand over her hair, wondering how the hell Pelayo managed to get her a new license in under an hour. "Luck, I guess," she said with a grin.

The teller pointed toward a small gate at the end of the row of cubicles. "Come right through," he said.

Arianna fiddled with the key that would unlock the secrets of her past. She used it as a touchstone to calm her fluttering stomach. The teller opened the gate and ushered her forward. She followed him to a room where the walls were lined with numbered boxes and accessed through a steel grate. It was all she could do not to push past the teller. She thought of the words Gabriel had said to her before she left. *Elion would be proud of his daughter.*

The teller's voice brought her out of her thoughts. "It sure is cold out there today, isn't it?" he said.

Arianna nodded. "Yes, it is, but I kind of like it."

"I'm kind of done with it," the teller said. He motioned her into the room and slid the grate closed. The click of the lock brought a tickle of excitement over Arianna. She handed him the key and he walked over to the corresponding box. With ease, the key slid into the lock, and he pulled it out from the wall.

She followed him into an adjoining smaller room where he set the box onto a table. "Take your time," he said, "I'll be right outside." He left and closed the door.

Arianna lifted the lid of the box. A sense of calm swept across her mind. She put her purse on top of the table and reached into the box. Her fingers wrapped around the journals, and she allowed herself a few seconds to fixate on the history she held in her hands. She placed the journals inside her purse, and then peered into the box. It looked empty, and yet for some reason she made a sweep with a hand and gasped when she felt something else. The moment she lifted her hand out of the metal box a package wrapped in purple velvet and tied with a delicate lavender ribbon appeared in it. "My father's letters," she whispered, holding back tears.

She placed the package on top of the journals and then checked the box one more time. Confident there were no other surprises, she closed the lid, zipped up her purse, and opened the door. She watched as the teller replaced the box, locked it, and handed the key and card back to her.

"All done," he said.

"Thanks," Arianna said, "see you next time."

She walked through the lobby eager to be outside, back in the chill of Manhattan.

O

Gabriel crouched on a rooftop at the corner of East 44th and Fifth Avenue. This gave him a perfect view of the bank. He had not been keen on the idea of Arianna going into the building alone, but he could not argue with her rationale for doing so. Kenan was not aware of her existence, only Jeremy's. Gabriel had personally checked the birth certificates and hospital records for the twins, and noted that someone had taken great care to see that Elion's heirs could not be traced to each other. Jeremy's birth certificate said nothing about him being a twin, and Pelayo had lifted all evidence of Arianna's adoption from any files in New York and California.

The muscles in Gabriel's neck suddenly tensed. Across the street from the bank stood a vampire. Gabriel sent a text to Pelayo:

*Immortal on street opposite bank, do you see him?*

Pelayo replied immediately.

*Got him.*

Gabriel contemplated the situation. For now, the vampire seemed unaware of Arianna as she exited through the double doors and headed down 44th Street toward the hotel. He pulled his runes from a pocket, ready to go into action if needed. The vampire began walking parallel to Arianna on the opposite side of the street.

It was clear to Gabriel the vampire had spotted her. A crowd had gathered outside a hotel and rain began to fall. Numerous umbrellas popped up around Arianna. The crowd crossed the street in unison. The vampire waited, watching to see if Arianna crossed the street.

A woman tripped on the sidewalk and fell to the ground. The vampire seemed momentarily distracted. Gabriel knew why. The vampire feasted his eyes on the blood seeping from the unfortunate woman's knee. In a flash, the vampire was beside her, helping her to her feet and leading her in the opposite direction to Arianna.

Gabriel dropped the runes into his pocket. Although it seemed that the vampire had not been waiting for Arianna, there was definitely something about her that caught his interest. Yes, she was young and beautiful, but Gabriel couldn't help wonder if it was something more. He made sure Arianna was safely inside the hotel and then disappeared.

○

Arianna didn't stop until she made it back to the foyer of the hotel. As promised, Matilda was sitting, waiting for her, and escorted her back up multiple flights of stairs to the room where she had left Gabriel and Pelayo thirty minutes earlier. The door opened and she fell into Pelayo's arms.

"I have questions," she said.

"*Estás bien?*" Pelayo asked.

Arianna nodded. "*Si gracias*...I'm fine."

Gabriel appeared in the doorway, and Pelayo grinned when he saw what he held in his hands. "I had to dig it out of the ground," Gabriel said. "Elion secured it rather well."

Arianna stared at the fairy statue in his muddied hands. "Thank you," she said, "you're an absolute gem!"

Gabriel knelt down, patted Matilda, and gave her another treat. She trotted off down the hall, jumped onto a luggage cart and began eating. He closed the door. "You did well, Arianna. Let's go home." He patted the fairy on the head. "This little lady has been away from Italy for too many years."

# 22

## *Casa della Pietra*

WITH THE ARRIVAL of Jason and the need for more workspace, Christopher moved his office into the main library. While Jeremy pinned names and photos of each missing girl onto display boards, Jason created a portfolio of charter schools set up around the U.S. that had either closed shortly after opening, or had ties with the Catholic Church. Layla sat at a computer, scrolling through social media pages that related to each of the missing girls, hoping to find pertinent information or photos that revealed tattoos.

Gabriel leaned against a bookcase and scanned over a list of properties owned by the same European investment group as the D.C. mansion they had raided. Jason had also discovered other properties, where one or more of the names attached to the group were linked to real estate transactions in various countries around the world. Alessandro, Pelayo, Stefan and Dr. Fiore entered the library. Christopher picked up a bunch of folders and gave one to all present.

Jeremy dimmed the lights, and Jason projected a power-point presentation onto a screen at one end of the room. While Christopher narrated, Jason flicked through images, beginning with the stories behind each girl they had found in the D.C. mansion, and the vampires involved.

"Here's what we know so far," Christopher said. "Two of the girls you rescued attended Todos los Santos Community School. One was reported missing a week ago, the other had been missing for two years.

Girl number three resided in Virginia, reported missing three months ago, and the fourth girl was from Florida, missing for a month." He looked up at Jeremy. "What can you tell us about the tattoos?"

"All four girls had the same tattoo," Jeremy said, "however, Sarah, from Virginia, still attended mass with her family. She might have just had the tat done as a statement, and I'm guessing she's not the only one who did this."

Gabriel stared at the image that showed photos of the four girls. "Have you been able to trace the tattoo artists who worked with each girl?"

Jeremy nodded. "The two girls from D.C. went to the same tattoo studio, but I'm still working on the locations of the others. I'm guessing they both paid cash, so that's why it's a little more difficult, and the tattoo artists I've spoken with aren't willing to give out private information."

Dr. Fiore cut in. "One of our kind needs to question them."

"Agreed," Gabriel said. "Jeremy, give the information to Dr. Fiore."

"Sure," Jeremy said, "but there's something else I noticed. On their social media pages, all the girls talked about prepping for the SATs early, so that tells me they were studious and intended to apply to colleges."

"I noticed similarities too," Layla said. "These girls are smart. They share information regarding important topics: climate change, social justice, equality, etcetera, not just girly-teen stuff."

"And at one time or another, they've all liked the same page," Jeremy said. "It's a tribute page to the girl found in the dumpster in L.A. who just happened to be a star pupil herself."

Gabriel frowned. "Have you cross-checked the names of people who have liked the page, against the list of missing girls?"

"We're working on that," Jeremy said. "Should be through within the hour."

Jason clicked to the next image. "This is a list of the other properties owned by the European investment group listed as the current owners of the D.C. mansion," he said. "There are a few properties that have been grandfathered to the same group for a hundred and fifty years. One's in Virginia, another in New Orleans, and the other in New York City. I'm currently looking into properties owned by the same group in other countries, but we need to remember that this group probably has listings under multiple names."

Dr. Fiore looked up from her folder. "Do you know if they own real estate in Italy?"

Jason nodded. "Yes," he said, "multiple properties, but the largest is in Rome, and they have one nearby on the coast. The villa in Rome was difficult to find, because it's not listed under the investment group's name. The only reason I found it is because I ran a search on properties that have been owned by the same family or group for a period longer than one hundred years. The interesting fact about the property in Rome is that only a small piece of the land was used to build on. I'm guessing it's a modest villa by Italian standards."

"What year was the villa built?" Alessandro cut in.

Jason referred to his papers. "Late seventeenth century."

"Anything else unusual about the property?" Stefan asked.

"No," Jason said. "But that's what made me delve further. You see, almost every other building in Rome is built above two or three previous buildings, correct?"

"Correct," Stefan said.

"Not so with this one," Jason said, "well, that's according to the department of records, but I'm not buying that."

"Rightly so," Stefan said. "There are ways of hiding such things as underground tunnels and ancient buildings from modern technology, or at least to wipe the fact that they exist from human memory."

"Chantal has repeated over and over that when Kenan changed her, she could smell earth," Alessandro said. "She thought she was in a cave of sorts."

Christopher nodded. "Or perhaps in a hidden dwelling under the present building. By the way, where's Prudence?"

"She's with Arianna," Jeremy said. "There's a lot of information in one of the letters that we thought she'd want to read, and we found a letter addressed to Prudence written by my father."

Stefan flicked up the lights. "I shall pass this information on to Prudence." He exited the room.

Gabriel took out his phone and sent off a text. "Frederico's on standby to take a look at the addresses. He's worked with a group of spelunkers who're mapping out the subterranean tunnels beneath Rome, and he's familiar with anything built after the late 1400s in that part of the country."

Jason scribbled the addresses onto a piece of paper and handed it to Gabriel. "Thanks, and well done," Gabriel said. "Let us know if anything else comes to light."

# 23

THE MAIN ART studio at *Casa della Pietra* was situated in a loft space with views that encompassed the mountains beyond. Multiple dormer windows jutted out; their recessed ledges decorated with pillows and blankets. At the back of the studio, the walls echoed the original stone, and pieces of weathered wooden framing still remained. In front of this area stood an aged easel, and various brushes and palette knives were arranged on a table close by, as if waiting for the tender hands of the artist who once painted there. Every ten feet or so, easels were set up, and the surrounding wall space seemed to update in age, as did the attending brushes and art supplies.

Prudence stood with Chantal and watched her while she painted. She glanced toward the door as Coco entered with Arianna. The young girl seemed visibly upset, and Coco held an arm around her shoulders. "What is the matter, Arianna?" she asked.

"Jeremy and I read the letter Elion wrote to us," Arianna said. "We're hoping you can help us understand more about the content."

Prudence gestured toward the sofas by the fireplace. She nodded to Chantal, who put down her paintbrush and joined the others. When they were settled, Prudence spoke to Arianna. "Would you like to read us the letter?"

Arianna nodded, cleared her throat and then began to read.

*My dearest Jeremy and Arianna,*

*If you're reading this letter it will mean that Katja and I are no longer in* this world. And it will also mean you've found each other and are safe with my friend Prudence, and members of the Allegiance.

In an effort to bring you solace, I shall explain a few of the relevant circumstances in my personal history. Please know that I'd hoped to share this information with you both in person, but fate has seen differently. When I fell in love with Katja I made the choice to give up my life in the world of fae. But I should have seen that dark forces would never allow such peace for us.

Centuries ago, a vampire named Domenico was single-handedly responsible for the deaths of many seers, including my mother and sister. The year was 1326, and the people of Europe lived under the shadows of dark times. I was five years old when my sister, herself barely a young woman, hid me in a secret place. She cast a spell of silence around me so my cries would not be heard by anyone other than my father, when he returned from the fields.

To this day, when Midsummer arrives, I hear the cries of my mother and sister being stolen from us. Cries matched only by the howls from my father when he realized what had happened. He gathered me into his arms and together we rode into the night, determined to find our loved ones.

For twenty years we searched, until we heard of a cave in Northern Italy where heretics had once been tried. When we arrived at this place, branches, weeds, and layers of rock covered the entrance. Father and I worked until we could access the portal, and together we entered the cave.

Walls painted with frescoes depicting scenes of barbaric torture greeted the glow of our torch flames. A long passage ran deep into the mountain and opened up into a circular room. Here, a series of small cells lined the walls, their heavy wooden doors stood half open, as if waiting for a victim. Father and I searched every room until I found a corner where Mother's scent lingered.

We knew, then, that she had died in this cave. Father fell to his knees and wept. I lifted my torch to the walls and saw where figures and words had been carved into the stone. One carving stood out: a figure with two faces, one male and one female. I traced a finger over the grooves cut into the stone and heard Mother's voice whisper the words, sine virtute omnia sunt perdita. Father heard her too.

It would be centuries later that I'd finally understand the importance of Mother's etchings. It happened when I realized Katja was pregnant with *twins. I knew then that in order to protect you both, we'd have to separate you. We couldn't risk anyone discovering the allure of magic in your blood. I apologize for not being honest with you both, but your safety is of great concern to your mother and I. If my intuition is correct, then you are now together and protected by the Allegiance.*

*Domenico is dead, but is survived by his vampire son, Kenan, and he is a tyrant like no other. He watched, as thousands of women like your grandmother and aunt suffered under Domenico's thirst for their blood.*

*My mother's essence was not all we found that day. She left a coded message, a diary of sorts, embedded into the walls of the cell. Knowing that she would not survive the torture of Domenico, she passed along her knowledge of our ancestry and of seers she knew, so we could search for them and offer our protection.*

*My father was human, a gentle soul with a stronger connection to the other world than most. He waited patiently in the cell while I gathered Mother's diary that she had left drifting in a sphere of unseen words. When I was done, my father and I left that place of pain and death.*

*When we exited the mouth of the cave, we were greeted by a woman. Her eyes sparkled with gold and her white hair flowed down her back. Tears shone in her eyes and sent fractured rays of light into the lulling twilight. And when she spoke, her voice seemed to ease my pain. I knew then that she was a powerful seer, and that somehow we were connected.*

Arianna paused and cast her gaze at Prudence, whose eyes had a faraway look. She continued reading.

*She explained that she was a friend of Mother's, and that she had not arrived in time to save her, only to numb her pain. She said her name was Prudence, of the Allegiance, and that they offered protection for fae, seers, creatures, and Creatives. She wanted to help us.*

*Father and I traveled the Italian peninsula alongside Prudence, searching out the seers who were hiding. We told them of my mother's death, and asked after my sister, but to no avail. But the Allegiance was true to their word. They escorted hundreds of gentle creatures to a safe fortress hidden in the mountains. It is protected with magic, and when one chooses to leave all knowledge of its existence vanishes.*

*Prudence and the Allegiance protected us all, until gradually the world saw creatures in a different light. Many forgot about our existence, and this made it easier for us to emerge from hiding and re-enter the world of humanity. I stayed for a while in Italy and searched for my sister, but not a hint of her essence existed. Father had long since passed, and I left Europe, taking with me only one treasure: a sculpture by the artist Jacques Callot. Prudence gave this to me, and for years it has rested in Katja's garden. The statue is embedded with the information I gathered on the wall in Mother's cell.*

*Lately, I have sensed three young vampires in New York. Normally this would not be cause for alarm, but they share Kenan's scent, and therefore he is their maker. Because of this, I arranged my own fake death. By the time you enter this world, I will be gone from New York. I plan to return to Katja in a few years, once I have found a way to end Kenan's life. For only then will you both be safe. If I do not return, know that I shall love you both always. The strands of magic within your blood are the touchstone to our heritage, and because of this you must stay with the Allegiance and accept their protection.*

Arianna folded the pages, clutched them to her body, and stared at Prudence. "You knew my father and grandmother?"

Prudence gazed at Arianna, and her mouth curved into a somber smile as a memory brushed by. "Yes," she said. "Would you like to hear more about your family?"

Arianna nodded. "I'd like that."

Prudence clasped her hands together in her lap. "Your grandmother's name was Birgit," she said. "We were brought together in the latter part of the ninth century, when the *Scuola Medica Salernitana* was founded in Salerno. This became the world's first school of medicine, and as such, attracted students, teachers, and those seeking to be healed. Women were welcomed at *Salernitana*, not only as students, but as teachers too.

"This place of learning was a beacon of hope, guiding us out of the harsh oppressive years of darkness, and into a world where education in the field of medicine was openly associated with the Church. For those of us who witnessed the growth of *Salernitana*, it seemed, for a while, that the world of learning had endless possibilities. The school graced herself within a valley above Salerno, caressed by the healing waters of the Tyrrhenian Sea."

Prudence closed her eyes, and a nostalgic smile caressed her lips before she continued. "During the late eleventh century, in the city of Bologna, students and masters gathered together and dedicated themselves to the study of law. The *Universita Di Bologna* became the first university in Italy, although it would take centuries for a female to hold a teaching position, and even longer for women to be accepted as students. Unfortunately, society tends to swing like a pendulum in regards to accepting the attributes of women.

"The Italian *Universitus* were established as *societeas di socii*, meaning 'group of students.' It was a place where the students decided on the courses offered, and here is where they differed from the universities of the northern countries. Birgit was so happy at Bologna. Of course, people recognized the air of mystique around her, but because of her gentle way and ability to heal, they accepted her and encouraged her to stay."

"So you were both safe there?" Coco asked.

"Yes," Prudence said, "but when the Crusades began, I left Bologna. I had foreseen the tragedies that lay ahead. I returned here, to *Casa della Pietra*, where I could work with members of the Allegiance. The Creatives helped us save thousands of historical relics, books, and works of art, and we set up secret areas beneath the cities, and hid the treasures. The Allegiance cannot interfere with the template of this world, but we helped the wounded, no matter on which side they fought.

"War equals death. To kill a human, whether it be man, woman, or child, sows the seeds of destruction. This is the worst kind of virus, for once the seed of hatred is planted, it is difficult to stop the frenzy of war. Once human life is gone, books and artifacts follow, but often they are destroyed as the precursor to war. It is strange to think that men whose eyes mirror the madness of war destroy statues created in the essence of devotion and passion.

"Shortly after the Summer solstice in the year 1304, Francesco Petrarca entered this world. I remember, because this was also the year Birgit met her beloved. Their daughter was born in 1309, and your father, Elion, in 1321. As his letter states, we first met at the cave where your grandmother's life was taken in the year 1346. Your father worked alongside the Allegiance, helping other creatures. I traveled throughout Europe, stopping for a while in Serbia."

"Were you aware of what would happen to him, even back then?" Arianna asked.

Prudence closed her eyes and shook her head. When her eyes opened they swam with tears. "I cannot change outcomes, Arianna," she said. "To interfere in matters of death—"

"But you saved your own husband," Arianna cut in. "So why didn't you save my father?"

Prudence stood and walked over to the window. "Because I had also seen his alternative fate. He did not deserve to die like his mother. Elion also had the sight, Arianna. He chose to protect you and Jeremy, and Katja. Not himself. This was his choice."

Arianna pulled a small and aged envelope from the pages in her lap. She walked over to Prudence and handed it to her. "This is addressed to you," she said.

Prudence accepted the envelope.

"Thank you for telling me about my family," Arianna said. "I understand everything, but I just need some time alone." She turned and hurried out of the room.

Chantal stood at Prudence's side. "Alessandro shared with me stories of that time, they were violent years," Chantal said. "Give her time, Prudence, she has a lot to take in."

Coco walked over to the two women. "Are other Creatives, apart from our own bloodline, still living?"

Prudence looked over to Chantal. "Do you remember asking me that very question?"

Chantal nodded. "Yes, when I first arrived in Tuscany."

"It seems that you are both the only surviving line of Creatives," Prudence said. "Kenan's maker hunted the others like wild animals, accused them of heresy and handed them over to the Inquisition. They were subjected to torture and, later, death by fire."

Coco frowned and shook her head. "But what of the Allegiance, couldn't you have stepped in and saved them?"

"We were able to save a few, Colombina," Prudence said. "They were turbulent times of war, death, and famine. Fear spread across the whole of Europe quicker than the plague, and so often Creatives died trying to save their families. The Allegiance does not wish to control anyone's life. We are here to protect as best we can. We saved many, but sadly not all, and the ones we saved chose to stay with their families." She took in the room and smiled. "It has been many years since this space has been used, and centuries since more than one Creative has stood within this fortress."

Chantal placed an arm around Coco's shoulder. "You're tired, little one."

"I'm fine, Mom," Coco said. "But I've been fighting to keep awake since I arrived. I don't know what's up with me."

"I remember feeling the same way," Chantal said.

"Best to not fight it, Colombina," Prudence said. "In essence you are tired because you are waking up."

Coco yawned, and nodded. "Believe it or not, I kind of get what you're saying. But for now, I'm going to go and take a nap. She gave Chantal a hug and left the studio.

O

Prudence ran the envelope written in Elion's hand under her nose before she broke the seal, unfolded the paper, and read the letter silently. As if she had called to him, Stefan entered the room, and strode over to where she stood and embraced her.

"What is it, *tesoro?*" Stefan asked.

Prudence gave him the letter to read, and then turned to Chantal. "During your time as prisoner, did you ever hear any talk of Kenan having a biological daughter?"

Prudence sensed Chantal's anxiety rise. "No," Chantal said, "and I think if he knew of this, he would have hunted her down."

"This letter is from Elion," Prudence said. "He writes that in his long search for Kenan, he spent time in Florence where he made contact with an elderly seer. She shared stories of the past with him, and one in particular resonated with Elion. There is a story, from the year 1517. It was thought that a young woman who worked and lived in the Medici household was a seer. She went missing one night. That same night, a prostitute found a young woman lying in bloodstained snow in the foothills of Florence. When the woman opened her eyes, the prostitute saw she had eyes the color of amethyst. She asked the young woman who had hurt her, and she answered, 'The man from my nightmares: *il diavolo che beve*—the devil who drinks blood.' The prostitute went in search of help, but when she returned, all that was left were spots of blood on the ground.

"The winter of 1517 was the year Stefan and I caught Kenan stealing from peasants. We believe that Domenico turned him around that time." She turned to Stefan. One look at him and she knew his thoughts were of a tragic night centuries ago; a night when a little girl had been born with amethyst eyes, in the city of Florence.

In a show of understanding, Stefan nodded. "If Kenan knew he had a child, I have no doubt he would not have rested until she was found," he said. "He was an angry and cruel human when we first met him, he believed God had sent you to him. Let us not forget, he thought you were his angel. Jealousy and anger could have driven him to self-destruction that night, but I had to get you away from him, *tesoro*, and I would do the same again."

Prudence touched a hand to Stefan's cheek. "We need to find her and the child she bore."

# 24

## *Svalbard Islands, Arctic Ocean*

KENAN STARED AT a tear of wax as it slid slowly down the stem of an ivory-colored candle. The flame flared, as if in response to the sudden jolt of agony pulling at his muscles. His jaw clenched as the poison worked its way through his veins. The tarnished blade Alessandro had thrust into his heart had seared quickly through the nerves in his body. Freyja had been quick to hear his call, but the poison acted instantaneously. After all, he'd planned it that way, although he had not expected to have the weapon he'd used against Prudence used against himself. The careless mistake had cost him time, and caused excruciating pain. His face twisted into a grimace, as his thoughts drifted to the past.

## *Florence 1517*

Kenan stared at the bodies of the two dead boys splayed out beside him in a Florentine alley. He turned away and vomited, ridding himself of the sins he had committed in his drunken stupor mere hours ago. Whispers of a second memory tugged at his mind. A young woman…she had witnessed his atrocities. He surrendered to another wave of nausea, and then looked around, hoping to see the woman; perhaps she'd be alive. When Kenan saw he was alone, he went through what was left of the boys' clothes, and grabbed any coins he could find. He staggered to his feet, took one last look at the battered bodies, and then made his way through deserted alleys in search of redemption.

At the edge of the city, he ascended a set of wide stone steps that led up a hill. The organized formation of stones gradually withered into the dirt road that he remembered from his youth. He crested the hill, and saw the derelict stone chapel and cottage. The first light of dawn crept across the sky, pushing through threatening thunderclouds. He dragged the overgrowth of weeds away from the side door of the chapel, entered, and pulled the door closed behind him.

His gaze swept across the dim room. A thread of sunlight burst through a crack in the roof, spilling a misted arc of dust-motes across to the opposite wall, and falling onto a man's boot. The hairs lifted on the nape of Kenan's neck at the realization that he was not alone. His heart raced. He tried to escape, but found he could not move. He fought against the pull to face his captor.

"I have tasted your blood. There is no escaping me." The man spoke in the Latin of ancient times.

Although he had no recollection of moving, Kenan abruptly stood face-to-face with his past. "What do you want from me?" Kenan asked through clenched teeth, trapped in the gaze of the hooded man he'd hoped never to see again.

"How quickly you forget. I wish to make you one of my kind, to offer you eternal life."

"I only wish to die."

"Oh, and you shall…only to rise again."

The hooded man beckoned to him with a long, bony finger, stained with blood. And as much as he wanted to bolt out the door, Kenan knelt on the frigid stone floor in front of the darkly-dressed figure. The man leaned down, his breath thick with the stench of carrion. He grazed his lips along Kenan's forehead, and then trailed his ice-cold tongue down the side of Kenan's face, finally resting at a vein in his neck. The man breathed in deeply through his nose, and Kenan felt a surge of warmth as blood rushed to the place on his neck where the man now stroked at the throbbing vein with a thumb.

The allure to this man was balanced somewhere between revulsion and seduction. Kenan's mouth grew moist, as thoughts of lust for this man grew stronger. While the man stroked Kenan's neck, he pushed away the cloak and eased Kenan's head between his legs. Kenan trembled with ecstasy as he took him into his mouth. He moved back and forth until both men climaxed. But his pleasure was short-lived as a burning pain erupted in his neck. He screamed with a newfound tormented euphoria, as agony shot throughout his convulsing body.

"Sweet bliss!" Kenan cried.

They were the last words to escape Kenan's mortal lips.

Liquid fire burned along Kenan's veins, while an insatiable thirst ripped at his throat. He caught a trace of sweetness in the air, and in that instant, his mouth filled with nectar. The scorching flames that lapped at his body began to recede, replaced by a glorious sated elation. But with a tug, the rapture disappeared.

A surge of exhaustion broke over Kenan's mind, bringing darkness and sleep. This pattern was repeated three times before Kenan was fully awakened. A deluge of sounds thundered around him, and in an effort to cease the deafening noise he pushed his palms against his ears. This seemed to awaken other senses: the stench of decay, the taste of metal. He opened his eyes to a clouded darkness.

He was in a room that resembled a cave. He removed his hands from his ears and listened to the layers of sound around him: water dripping, a rodent's feet scurrying across the rock floor, the solid thumping of a human heart. The familiar thirst began to burn in his throat. He leapt to his feet and froze.

Kenan's lips parted. His tongue caught on two sharp fangs as they descended into his mouth, bringing with them the need for blood. Caught in the throes of bloodlust, he did not hesitate to lunge at the neck of the human thrown at him. He plunged his new fangs into the throbbing jugular vein, dropped to the floor, and gorged on the blood until the pulse of life fell away with the screams of his victim. He dropped the dead body, lifted his head, and stared into the face of the hooded man.

"I asked for death," Kenan said.

The hooded man's lips lifted into a sardonic smile. "Some call us the living dead."

"What have I become?"

"Immortal. Powerful. A Vam*pir*," the hooded man said. "You have been granted eternal life. In exchange for this greatness, your piety will be strengthened."

Kenan's body shook with intensity, and he cried out as pain twisted his insides. "Help me!"

"The pain will pass, my son. Welcome the changes in the name of God."

"Who are you?" Kenan spat through chattering teeth.

"Domenico," he said. "The light of dawn approaches. We shall speak again at dusk."

He waved a hand, and the chill lifted from Kenan's body. "Sleep, my son."

"Sleep..." Kenan whispered, as a wave of darkness fell over him.

# 25

## Casa della Pietra

PRUDENCE DESCENDED INTO the deepest part of the fortress. As she hurried down the steep staircase, the smell of earth began to mingle with the scent of fresh water. When she reached the final step, she was standing at the edge of an underground lake. She gazed across an expanse of still water, crystal clear and aqua, and then upward to the cavernous domed ceiling. Parts of the walls that surrounded the interior lake showed they had once been adorned with bright frescoes. The faded paintings displayed various scenes from ancient mythology, and Prudence stared at one particular painting that depicted a raging storm at sea, and a man holding a woman in his arms on a battered raft.

With tempered grace, Prudence stepped down into a small wooden boat that drifted across the water. The boat stopped at an outcrop of stone. Prudence stepped up onto the ledge. She raised a palm, and a small crystalline sphere materialized. She blew a gentle breath and the ball rolled to the end of her fingers, where it stopped and became cloudy. Once more she blew onto the ball and a door became visible amongst the clouds while simultaneously appearing in the solid rock wall before her. She wrapped her hand around the sphere and walked through the door, which slid closed behind her. Prudence walked across a foyer and ascended a spiral staircase. When she reached the top, she stood in a vast gallery. She stepped onto the thick wooden floor, and looked around.

She made her way to the opposite end of the gallery, past works of art long thought destroyed, both in fires created by religious zealots, and the greed of Holy Wars. Prudence sat on a bench and gazed with adoration at the collection of Botticelli paintings in front of her. She studied one particular piece in the collection, and allowed her mind to drift back to the day Sandro had first seen the young dancer, Colombina.

## Florence, 1476

*Prudence stood on a balcony, and watched the artist stroll through the garden. His lips curved upward, as he drew in the sweet scent of citrus blossoms that waited in earnest to open their white wings and give birth to fruit. The humming of bees and twitter of birds made him pause. He closed his eyes, and Prudence sensed him picturing the colors of the noises around him.*

*The sound of a woman singing a sweet melody forced him to open his eyes. Drawn to the joy in her voice, he followed her song, and stopped when he saw a young woman dancing amongst the plane trees. He leaned against one of the mottled and sturdy tree trunks, took a piece of tinted paper and small nub of charcoal from a pocket, and brought her body to life on the page.*

*Delicate, diaphanous fabric teased her breasts as she moved her body in a series of heartfelt emotions. Strands of her golden hair bathed with strawberry tones swayed in rhythm with her. The artist's hand guided the charcoal over the paper, moving with her, capturing her joy and innocence. She looked up at the sky, and it was at that moment, that Prudence knew the artist had fallen in love with the dancer.*

*His hand never ceased to move, smudging lines that caught the rise and fall of the delicate creature before him. Prudence caught flashes of the artist's thoughts. He saw her suspended in time: the curves of her body, the pink of her lips, and the mound of her sex. The wind had picked up again, swooping up blossoms from the nearby rose garden, and showering the dancing beauty with petals, like snowflakes. He thought of birth, and Spring, and of the goddess Venus.*

*Girlish giggles broke through his vision, as five young women ran toward the goddess he was drawing. One held a babe in her arms, and she cradled the infant against her body as if to be apart from him would break her heart. The women joined his goddess in song, twirling and skipping with such joy that tears brimmed in the artist's eyes. Still he sketched, and as he did, a story of springtime emerged from his heart and onto the page.*

*The dancers moved further along the garden until they had become specks in the distance, and their voices were lost in the heat of the day. The sound of footsteps on fallen leaves brought him back to the moment.*

*A hand rested on his shoulder.*

*"From what you have drawn, it seems you are besotted with the daughter of our cook," the man said. "And unless I'm mistaken, there are five others who share her image."*

*The artist's mouth broke into a grin when he realized that each of the dancer's faces mirrored the image of his goddess.*

*"Do not be concerned, my friend," the man said. "I shall carry your ode of love to my grave."*

*"Is that a promise?" the artist asked.*

*"Consider it so, but on one condition."*

*"Your conditions always amount to a painting, Lorenzo," the artist said.*

*"Only when I see beauty, my friend," Lorenzo said, "and how can I not when I look upon the lines you draw."*

*"Will you arrange for me to meet with her?"*

*Lorenzo nodded.*

*"Today?"*

*Lorenzo grinned. "When was the last time you visited the kitchen with me, Sandro?"*

*"When we were children."*

*"Come and join the others in the salon," Lorenzo said. "We shall visit the kitchen later, and you will meet your Colombina."*

The vision passed, and Prudence slipped back to reality. She stared at the collection and mourned for the life of happiness that the artist once had, which had been stolen from him. His beloved had been poisoned, causing her to go into labor. She died moments after she had given birth to their daughter.

Prudence stared at the original paintings Sandro had sketched of *Primavera* and *The Birth of Venus*. She smiled at the faces of all the women he had portrayed. They all shared the same face: the face of his Colombina. A smile rested upon Prudence's lips. "Of course, Sandro," she said, "how could I have missed your clue? When Chantal chose to name her daughter Colombina, I knew then that the two women would somehow be connected." She opened her hand, blew once again on the crystal sphere, and disappeared.

Prudence entered the bedroom silently, and noticed Algiz lying by the fireplace. The jaguar raised her head in recognition of her, but with a wave from her mistress the large feline lowered her head, and went back to sleep. Prudence saw Stefan sitting outside on the balcony, his booted feet resting on a ledge as he wrote in his journal. The room filled with the impassioned orchestration of Fauré's Cantique de Jean Racine Op. 11, causing Prudence to linger for a moment in the presence of such divine inspiration.

She breathed in her beloved's scent, and brought a hand to her heart. She marveled that even after centuries the very sight of him still made her lightheaded. On tiptoe, she made her way across the floor, under the domed roof painted with goddesses and angels. At the steps leading out to the *terrazzo*, she lifted her dress so as not to trip.

Prudence instantly felt the blade of Stefan's dagger flat against her heart. His warm breath lingered over the side of her neck before he whispered in her ear. "I believe I won this game," he said.

Prudence shook her head. "What gave me away?'

"That is my secret, *tesoro*, just as you shall keep your reasons secret for visiting the gallery." He lowered the blade and slid it back into its sheath. "Have you forgotten that Sandro chose his path, albeit a path decided while wracked with sorrow?"

"I miss those days, *mi amore*."

"You miss his presence," Stefan said.

Prudence placed her hands on either side of his face and kissed his lips. Their kiss deepened, and Stefan's strong arms embraced her. She pulled him to her, but she felt him resist.

"These are dangerous times, *tesoro*," he said. "I need to know what you are planning."

Prudence ran a hand through his dark hair. "I must see Sandro's *Madonna and Child with Adoring Angel.*"

"I do not believe that painting hangs in our gallery," Stefan said.

"No," Prudence said, "but I am sure there are secrets hiding beneath the paint, something I have missed before."

"Or perhaps you were not meant to see the image until now," Stefan said. "But the painting you speak of was painted before Sandro and his beloved Colombina had even met."

"It would not be the first time this has happened," Prudence said, "and Sandro himself said that particular painting was one of his most cherished. He broke conventional rules when he created the piece. He showed the deep love between the virgin mother and the holy child, they have a relationship, a bond not seen prior. He painted the image from deep within his sub-conscious, I am sure of this."

"Then we had best leave," Stefan said.

Prudence shook her head and gazed into his eyes. "Coco needs to be there, too," she said. "I cannot say why, but I feel she is the only one who can unlock the painting's secrets."

"Gabriel will be hesitant for her to go with us," Stefan said. "She may be in danger the minute she leaves the fortress."

"I understand," she said, "and I have spoken to Dr. Fiore about this. She has come up with somewhat of a solution."

# 26

DR. FIORE WATCHED blood run down the tube and into the first of seven vials. When the last vial was filled, she removed the needle from Stefan's vein, covered the tiny hole with a piece of gauze, and applied pressure to the point of entry. She removed the gauze knowing that the pin-sized hole in her patient's arm had already healed.

"*Grazie*, doctor, your aim is perfect," Stefan said. He unrolled the sleeve of his shirt and looked across at Prudence. "You are next, *tesoro*."

Prudence waved a hand and the tiny buttons that ran along the long sleeve of her satin dress popped open to reveal her flawless skin. Dr. Fiore drew Prudence's blood, followed by Gabriel's.

"And now the Creative's blood," Dr. Fiore said. "You must be careful, my dear. We cannot be certain how blades cast from coins used to cross the River Styx will affect you."

"I understand," Coco said. She held out her arm, and Dr. Fiore sighed as Gabriel's protective ambiance flooded over Coco. "I'm drawing her blood, Gabriel, not attacking her," she said, her eyebrows raised questioningly. "You can ease up on your protective issues. I prefer my patients relaxed when I draw their blood. I am a vampire after all."

With practiced finesse, Dr. Fiore tightened the rubber tourniquet around Coco's arm, waited while her vein filled with blood, and then stuck the skin with the fine needle. Once her task was completed, Dr. Fiore set the labeled vials of blood on separate trays. She took six of the seven vials from each of her patients, and put them in a centrifuge to separate the platelets from the other blood cells. While she waited for the centrifugation process to be completed, she passed the remaining single vials of blood to Prudence.

Prudence placed her hands above the first vial that contained her own blood. The vial floated onto her open palms. She closed her eyes and breathed in deeply. On her exhale, the vial shifted and molded together, until all that remained was a small ampule approximately half an inch in length and a quarter of an inch in width. Prudence closed her fingers around the ampule and held it against her heart. When she opened her hands, the ampule was gone.

Prudence looked up at Stefan. He opened the first two buttons of his shirt to reveal the small, teardrop-shaped ampule attached to a piece of rolled leather hanging against his pale skin. "These ampules are enchanted," Prudence said. "They can only be seen by us and Dr. Fiore. We will each wear our beloved's blood, and one vial alone will save us from Kenan's knives. Let us hope we never need it."

Prudence cast her spell over the remaining vials. When the centrifuge had finished spinning, Dr. Fiore removed the vials and arranged each of the five respectively on trays and watched while Prudence repeated the same procedure she used with the blood, on the vials containing platelets.

"Using the platelets, along with the blood of your partners, will protect you for a limited amount of time," Dr. Fiore said. "If you're injured, break the vial. Within seconds you should feel the benefit." She turned to Coco. "I cannot stress enough that we do not know how tainted blades will affect you, Coco. Time is of the essence."

Coco nodded and turned to Prudence. "Do you think Kenan is still alive?"

"I know it," Prudence said.

"So where are we headed, Mother?" Gabriel asked.

"Los Angeles."

# 27

## Norton Simon Museum of Art, Pasadena, California

"ARE YOU ABSOLUTELY positive no one can see us?" Coco asked. She gave her eyes time to adjust to the darkness, and then brought a hand to her mouth when she realized she was standing next to a Picasso. Not just any Picasso, but one of her favorite pieces, *Bust of a Woman*: oil with fixed black chalk on canvas. "I have the urge to see if there are secrets behind all of the paintings here."

"Another time, *il mio amore*, I promise," Gabriel said. He squeezed her hand. "Consider my words assurance of our first real date."

"I'll hold you to that," Coco said.

"Now, lead the way," Gabriel gestured to the rest of the gallery, "the sooner I have you back at the fortress, the happier I'll be."

Coco guided Gabriel, Prudence, and Stefan through the twentieth century gallery, past the main door, and into the gallery of fourteenth and sixteenth century art. She turned left at the entryway, and stopped directly in front of Botticelli's *Madonna and Child with Adoring Angel*. "I'm ready," she said. "But I still can't believe I'm going to do this to one of Botticelli's paintings."

"I believe this painting has been waiting for you," Prudence said. "Please, go ahead."

Coco stretched a hand toward the painting. The pull of the pigments was strong, and seconds later scenes appeared from the artist's life.

*Prudence ran along a stone floor toward a heavy wooden door. She waved a hand, and the door opened. A man cradled the body of a woman in his arms. The sheets around her were drenched in blood. Stefan stood at the end of the bed. In his arms, he held a baby wrapped in blankets. He handed the child to Prudence. "Tend to the babe," he said. "I will stay with Sandro until you return."*

*With the newborn baby clutched to her body, Prudence crossed a courtyard, framed with Corinthian columns, to a set of double wooden doors, adorned with a bust that sat above a keystone. She tapped on the door in a particular rhythm. The door opened, and a man with ink-stained fingers ushered her inside.*

*The room was lit with candles that lay shadows across the man's face. His dark eyes and prominent nose were framed with straight dark hair. "What has happened?" the man asked.*

*"Colombina died during childbirth," Prudence said. "Sandro is buried in grief and their child is in need of milk and love. I need your help, I cannot interfere more than I already have. Look at her eyes, Lorenzo."*

*Lorenzo pulled back the blanket, and sighed. "I promise to keep her safe," he said. "There are new mothers in the household, I shall see to it they look after this child as if she were one of my own."*

*"Eventually she will draw attention, Lorenzo," Prudence said. "It would be best if she lives as her mother did, with the people who were her family."*

*"But her parents both died within months of each other. Sandro was all Colombina had," Lorenzo said.*

*Prudence shook her head sadly. "I am not sure he will ever recover from this loss, and he showed no interest in this little one. His whole world, his creative muse, was Colombina. His heart is shattered."*

*Lorenzo reached for the baby and kissed her forehead. "For as long as I live, I promise she will be protected."*

*"Her heritage must be kept secret, Lorenzo," Prudence said. She placed a hand over the baby's forehead, and when she lifted her hand, the baby's eyes were blue. "Her secret is safe for now, however, this magic is bound to her own fate. She is our light, Lorenzo, and as such her name will be Luciana."*

*A woman with long, dark brown hair and full lips wakes up and stares into the semi-darkness. Her eyes are almond-shaped and blue. She throws a robe over her chemise and opens a door to a hallway. As she stumbles through a darkened villa, the hem of her robe catches the edge of a paneled wall. She runs through a courtyard, past columns and ancient statuary, to a gate that empties onto a cobblestone street. She takes off running, peering into side streets as if she's searching for something. She stops suddenly and stares down a narrow alley. Her breath comes in short gasps. She walks toward a man who is crouched over the bodies of two lifeless boys. She falls to her knees and cries.*

*The man lifts his head. It's Kenan. He pushes the young woman to the ground and rapes her. When he is done, he rolls away and passes out. The woman struggles to get up, her chemise ripped and stained. She makes her way back to the villa and throws her travel clothes and cloak over her bruised body, and leaves the villa the same way she entered.*

*By the time she reaches the outskirts of Florence, snow is sticking to the ground. She pushes onward to the hills, but trips and falls. Her eyes flutter open as a woman approaches. She kneels beside Colombina, and gasps when she sees the color of her eyes. She runs to get help.*

*A couple approaches Colombina and sits beside her. The woman leans in and kisses her forehead, while the man holds her hands in his.*

"Sine virtute omnia sunt perdita," *the man says.* "Be the light, not the shadow, our dearest Luciana."

Coco collapses into Gabriel's arms.

"Get us home, Mother. Now!"

A couple stepped out of the shadows by the altar in the room dedicated to fourteenth and sixteenth century art at the Norton Simon Museum. They were not of this present time, but from a time of enlightenment. The man gazed at Prudence as she disappeared with Stefan, Gabriel, and a young woman he did not know. For a fleeting moment, their gaze met, and he saw a tear fall down her cheek.

A halo of light shimmered around the couple as they walked up to the small but significant painting, *Madonna and Child with Adoring Angel*. The man held a hand toward the image, and his fingers lingered over the face of the mother.

"My soul was guided by something much greater than my own hand when I painted this," he said. "We had not yet met, though I saw a vision of you as I made the first sketch for this piece." He ran his hands over her hair, and then kissed her. "Perhaps it is time that Prudence shared your beauty with the world."

The woman smiled and leaned into him, her face similar to the Madonna before her. "Not yet, my beloved Sandro, not yet," she said. "Luciana's story is still to be told."

The man reached into his cloak and handed the woman a small sketch of a couple entwined on a bed. "Do you remember this day, Colombina?"

"Of course, you woke me in your special way," she said. A smile broke onto her face. "Take me there again, my love."

Their lips met.

The drawing fell from Sandro's hand and came to life…

## Florence, 1477

*Sandro reached for Colombina's hand, and trailed kisses along the inside of her arm, lingering for a moment at her breasts. Her sudden intake of breath made him smile, and he knew he had been successful in waking her from a deep slumber. In anticipation of where his lips were headed, her body writhed beneath the linen sheet. He outlined her salmon pink nipples with kisses, and gazed upon them as they sprang to life. An image of rosebuds greeting the warmth of the sun flickered in his mind.*

*Colombina arched her body toward him, but he swung his body over hers. "Be still, little dove," he said.*

*The corners of her mouth lifted upward. "You ask the impossible, Sandro," she said, her waking voice breathless with pleasure.*

*Sandro wove a trail of kisses over the rise of her belly. "Our child made with pure love," he whispered.*

*Colombina wove her fingers around his hair.*

*"Ti amo," Sandro whispered.*

*He moved a hand lower, until his fingers slipped between her thighs. Colombina moaned. His lips and tongue replaced his fingers. She pulled on his hair, and brought his lips to hers and kissed him. Her body trembled as he entered her, then moved with him in waves of ecstasy. Colombina cried out his name as they found release together.* "Tranquillità," *Sandro whispered. A vision entered his thoughts...*

*Three women dancing together in a garden—Colombina dances to their right with her head held upward. Rose petals, dappled with dew, are picked up by the wind as they fall from full blooms. They land on her rounded belly filled with life, and on the grass beneath her feet.*

*"My muse, my beloved," he whispers. "Your beauty has cast me out of the shadows and into the light." Colombina goes to speak, but Sandro brushes a finger across her lips. "Your face will always be our secret,* mi amore. *I shall ask Prudence to protect the images I paint of you."*

# 28

KENAN STOOD AT the crest of a hill, and stared at the village below. From this vantage point, he could hear the whispered conversation between two women as they walked along a narrow alley. They spoke of a child born with eyes the color of violets.

"The Holy Trinity of flowers," one of the women said.

"A Creative," said the other. She tucked a hand around her friend's elbow, and whispered. "It is said she grows more beautiful with each full moon." She patted her friend's hand, and kissed her cheek. "We are blessed." The two women smiled, and parted ways.

The air chilled, but Kenan's immortal body did not feel the cold. He waited until light from candles illuminated windows, and then made his way to where one of the women lived. He watched through a window as the fire she had built struggled to catch. She threw a shawl over her shoulders, and headed outside toward a pile of wood.

He knew the second the woman realized she was not alone; her breath quickened, her heart raced, and the throb of fear pulsed in her veins. Kenan placed the tip of a finger behind her right ear, and ran it slowly around to the base of her neck. His icy touch made her shudder. Her shawl fell to the ground in a continuous stream.

"What is it you want?" she asked.

"Tell me of the Creative," Kenan said.

Her body froze.

"The Holy Trinity of Flowers," Kenan said. "I believe that is how you described her."

"I do not know of whom you speak," the woman said.

Kenan edged closer, his mouth grazed her ear. "Lies, like a rotting corpse, emanate the stench of death." He noticed the hairs lift on the nape of her neck. "Where is she?"

The woman shook her head. "I do not know."

Kenan pulled her back to his chest, and licked the salty tears from her cheek. Her body trembled. "Another lie," Kenan said, his voice barely a whisper. "Tell me what you know of the Creative."

"I know what you are," the woman said.

"And what is that?"

She drew in a quick breath. "You take away our freedom. Our joy. Our souls."

"Tell me about the Creative!"

"I would rather die."

Kenan kneed her in the back, and she fell to the ground. "Where is she?"

With staggered effort, the woman lifted her head and glared at him. "I will never tell you."

Kenan's hand caught her face hard. She fell back, gasping for breath. "Then you will lie here and listen while I feast on every woman in this village." He turned to leave.

"Wait…" she said.

Kenan stood perfectly still, a sinister grin claimed his face.

"You take me for a fool," the woman said. "You would feast on every woman in this town whether I tell you or not. A long time from now, you will remember this night and pray for my forgiveness. It is a weak man who threatens women, but then again, you are not a man."

Kenan spun around and lunged at the woman, hoisted her up by her throat, and plunged his fangs into her neck. Her honeyed blood gushed into his mouth. Domenico had told him the taste of a seer was bitter, but now he knew that was a lie. He had intended to make the woman suffer for eternity, to make her a vam*pir*, but instead he sucked on her vein until her body caved in to death.

He fell to the ground, drunk with the ecstasy of her blood pulsing through his body. An image flashed before him...*a darkened night, a young woman.* Kenan pulled at the wisps of a memory belonging to his mortal life, but like always, the image dissolved. He pushed himself up and gazed at the corpse. He considered hiding her body, but instead, he hoisted her over his shoulder and dumped her at the front door of the cottage of her friend. He thumped on the door, waited for the sound of footsteps, and then fled into the dark of night. A woman's high-pitched scream faded behind him.

O

On his return to Domenico, Kenan had one thought on his mind. *Why would his maker lie about the taste of a seer's blood?* The thought of returning to Domenico without a morsel of information did not sit well with him. When he entered the underground refuge on the outskirts of Rome, he made his way to his maker's sanctuary. Candles lit the narrow passageways, throwing flickering shadows onto the rock walls as he passed by. Trepidation deepened with each step, and he wondered if it were possible his maker already sensed his failed task. At his approach, the door creaked open and a familiar voice greeted him.

"My son," Domenico said. "I have been waiting for you."

Kenan entered Domenico's quarters and knew immediately he would be punished for his reckless behavior. He stood before his maker and awaited judgment. Domenico's nostrils flared, and his head fell back. The yellowish tinge to his eyes flushed with blood, and in a blink he had Kenan's head caught in the crook of his elbow.

"What news do you bring of the violet-eyed Creative?" he asked.

"I have none, Father," Kenan said. "The threat of death did not loosen the lips of those who spoke of the child."

The whiff of decay alerted him to the fury brooding below the surface of Domenico's persona. Kenan knew what would follow. He sensed the labor of Domenico's transition, and from the corner of his eyes he saw his maker's fingernails extend to filthy claws. Domenico forced Kenan to face him and watch his face shift into a decrepit form. His teeth yellowed and the foul stench of sulfur seeped into Kenan's nose.

As Domenico's sharp fangs tore into his neck, intense heat spread over Kenan's skin. Pain shot like arrows through his veins. He wanted to fight, but Domenico's power cloaked his mind with paralysis. His life force faded, and for a moment, he contemplated death. Perhaps this time, Domenico would show mercy. But as if to remind him of his entrapment, Domenico threw him across the room, and then landed a swift hard kick to his chest.

"You drank the filthy blood of a seer," Domenico said. "Your weakness sickens me. Have the horses ready upon the hour, and wash the scent of that whore from your body."

Domenico stormed out, leaving Kenan in the throes of death. But the popping of bones and the prickling sensation pulsing over his body reminded him that he was immortal. His body healed. There would be no telltale scars of abuse. Until he found an escape, Kenan was bound by blood to the trials of eternal life with Domenico.

○

The horses thundered to the top of the hill, their necks lathered in white foam, nostrils wide and eyes alert. The scent of seaweed and the sting of salt urged them forward. They pushed through the angry wind and began the descent across the steep hillside. The immortal riders gave them full rein.

At the foot of the hill, the terrain changed. Velvety grasslands and scrub fell away, replaced by weathered rocks and pebbles. Kenan and Domenico rode toward the wet sand. Spray from crashing waves splashed onto the horses' muscular bodies, and they neighed in response, sensing they were close to home.

In the distance, masked by a creeping fog, light from a lantern marked the end of their journey. Huge gates opened upon their approach and closed quickly once the horses were inside. Kenan and Domenico dismounted, and strode across the loggia, and up the stairs to the main living area of the villa. Kenan followed Domenico into the entrance hall, the walls of which were covered in tapestries and paintings depicting religious images. When they reached the main room, Domenico waved a hand, and the thick door slammed shut behind Kenan.

"Tomorrow we leave for Valcamonica," Domenico said.

He downed a goblet of liquid, his tongue catching a garnet-tinged droplet from the corner of his mouth. The smell of blood caused Kenan's fangs to elongate. He needed to feed.

"Leave me now," Domenico said. "You will find sustenance in your quarters."

Kenan hurried to his room. Tied to the bed was the naked and bruised body of a seer. She was the friend of the woman he had killed in the village. He wondered if Domenico had forced information regarding the child with the amethyst eyes from her. Or perhaps her torture would be dying from his mounting hunger.

A rag had been stuffed into her mouth, and a stream of tears ran from her wide eyes. She pulled at the ropes securing her hands and feet. In an instant, Kenan fell upon her. He savored her fear-filled scent, and traced the dips and curves of her body with his tongue. When he reached the crease of her womanhood, he inhaled, and then plunged his fangs into her femoral artery.

The taste of her fear excited him, and he pulled back, lowered his britches, and thrust into her hard and deep. She gagged, and he ripped the rag from her mouth and latched onto her neck. Her screams dissipated along with the pulse of her heart. Kenan collapsed on top of her.

He heard the door open, and shuddered at what he knew would happen next. Domenico's hands caressed Kenan's body, always the precursor to his rape.

Kenan awoke with the cold and stiff body of the dead woman beside him. He jumped up, ran from the villa, and dove into the frigid waters of the Tyrrhenian Sea. He thought of his past: his uncle's violent death at the hands of Domenico, the stench that clung to his mother's death, and a woman in a Florentine alley.

While he floated atop the water, an image from a happier time brushed his consciousness; kneeling beside his mother on the hard and chilled stone floor of the chapel, and listening to an angelic chorus singing the *Agnus Dei*. He thought of how Savonarola's men had saved him from starvation. But mostly he thought of a woman with golden eyes. His angel.

He rolled over and enjoyed the feel of the water as it lapped over his scarred back. He stared at the ocean floor. As if by fate, the moon peeked out from dark clouds, and a streak of light filtered through the water, exposing a mountain of human skeletons rising up from the sand below. A curtain of darkness crossed over the moon, and the gruesome mass grave became a memory.

○

While Domenico savored the blood of imprisoned seers at Valcomonica, Kenan took stock of the hundreds of local inhabitants dragged in for questioning by Inquisitors. Cells were crammed with peasants, and like the Inquisitors, Kenan had no tolerance for their Pagan beliefs. He saw the need to rid the entire republic of Venice of heresy.

Kenan recognized the importance of the work of the Inquisitors, especially with Pope Leo X choosing to ignore the threat of the German Augustinian monk, Martin Luther, whose cause continued to gather momentum. Whispers had spread of Leo's lavish lifestyle and over-spending, and this angered the more conservative members within the Church.

From Valcomonica, Domenico and Kenan traveled across the Holy Roman Empire and France to Spain, where the dark cloud of Juan de Torquemada's Inquisition still threatened anyone thought to have committed crimes of heresy, including acts of blasphemy, sodomy, and polygamy. The wave of the Reformation beckoned with the strong force of a constant undertow. This threat caused the Catholic Church to continue their torture amongst Jewish and Islamic communities, often coercing them into conversion.

For ten years, Domenico hunted seers, and Kenan's distaste for him deepened. However, he used this time to his advantage, paying attention to his maker's every move. He learned how to live as a vampire, but more importantly he learned one of his maker's secrets. The trigger to Domenico's distorted change resided in his inability to control his anger.

When this metamorphosis took place, the stench of sulfur seeped from Domenico's pale skin, causing the unlucky benefactor of his wrath to gag involuntarily. Often his prey did not bear witness to the blood flooding the whites of the vampire's eyes, or the yellowed fingernails that morphed into claw-like weapons. And if by chance they had not fallen to their knees gasping for breath, one brief glance at the grotesque creature that stood before them forced their bowels to empty and a river of vomit to erupt from their mouths. Domenico would laugh and wait for the gleam of terror to glisten in his prey's eyes, before plunging his fangs into their jugular vein, and feasting on their blood until the last spasm of their mortal life perished.

In the year 1527, news reached Domenico that Rome had been assaulted. Kenan knew that Domenico hated the humanist ideals of the Medici cardinal, who he saw as a weak choice for the papacy. But worse than this, Pope Clement VII had chosen to be ignorant to the seriousness of the reformists. Knowing his maker would want to leave for Rome immediately, Kenan prepared for their departure.

"Leave everything!" Domenico said. He grabbed Kenan, and launched into the night sky. Kenan had heard that flying was an ability vampires gained with age, and from the ease at which he had witnessed Domenico leap across rooftops, he knew it would only be a matter of time before he would display this talent. Kenan learned many of Domenico's secrets during the ten years he spent at his maker's beck and call.

As they neared the coastline of an island, dark shadows jutted up from the land below. Domenico touched down in a valley shrouded by dark clouds. He threw Kenan to the ground, leaned back his head, and inhaled deeply. "There is a seer nearby, she is mine, but you may feast on her lover." His mouth grew into a cruel smile, and he took off on foot toward a group of houses crouched at the end of the valley.

From a ridge close by, Kenan watched Domenico stalk his prey. He knew the second the woman caught her stalker's odor. She dropped the bundle of wood she carried in her arms, pulled something out from around her neck, and clutched it in her hand. Kenan heard the blood rushing through her veins, but his breath caught when another scent came into play; a male in his mid teens, sweet with youth and sexuality.

The boy walked along a path, toward where the seer stood frozen in her garden. When he saw the tall and pale figure standing near her, he ran forward, but fell to his knees, screaming in agony, about twenty feet from Domenico.

"What brings you here, demon?" the seer said, her voice clear and syrupy.

"Your scent," Domenico said. "And your delicious blood." He circled her, slowly moving in for his attack.

"Let him go," the seer cried out.

Domenico chuckled, but kept his cold stare on the witch. "Kenan, take the youth now while he is rich with fear."

"No!" the seer screamed.

Kenan leapt down from the ridge, and knelt beside the boy. As he drew in the aroma of adolescence, lust and hunger gripped his mind. The youth trembled with fear. Kenan ripped off the boy's clothes, freed himself, and emptied his seed into the boy's tight ass.

"Stop!" the seer begged, as the youth's screams tortured her ears. "Please?" She fell to the ground. Unable to free herself from Domenico's invisible hold, she cried out in horror.

The victim's screams were shortened, as Kenan plunged his fangs deep into the boy's bulging jugular vein. He drank until the body beneath him ceased to bear life.

The seer pushed herself up from the ground, and faced Domenico. "I know who and what you are, Domenico! And I know who you murdered for your power. You are a foul creature!" She spat in Domenico's face. The stench of sulfur made her gag, but she held his gaze. "Your end is near!"

Domenico slapped her hard across the face. He fought his anger, but to no avail. "You lie," he said. "You and your kind know nothing of my history or my fate!"

"The sands on the beaches of Lazio have run through my fingers," she said. A smile brushed the corners of her rosy lips as she spoke her final words. "You have the curse of Vinicio."

Domenico tore into the seer's neck like a rabid dog. Moments later, parts of her mutilated body were strewn across the ground. The vampire rose. His gnarled claws retreated, and the film of blood disappeared from his eyes. He grabbed Kenan and vaulted into the night sky. Kenan tucked the seer's final words deep into his memory.

*The curse of Vinicio.*

On the outskirts of Rome, a sickly odor tainted the air. Bodies lay in different stages of putrefaction. Faces of the dead were tinged with green, their tongues and eyes protruding. Corpses of Swiss Guards rested on the bloodstained steps leading up to St. Peter's. Soldiers, drunk with war, raped and killed innocent victims, and destroyed religious buildings, statues, and artifacts.

An image caught Kenan's attention: the red silk of a holy man's robe draped over black shoes. He knelt beside the dead man and rolled him over. His face was unrecognizable, smashed in and covered with blood—blood that held no memory of recognition.

"Hoping to find your father?" Domenico said. He yanked Kenan up. Kenan pushed back and stared into his maker's dark eyes. "Tell me who he is!"

"You are not worthy to whisper the name of your father," Domenico said, as he turned and took off down the steps.

Kenan knew he must find a way to escape from Domenico. He would be more observant of his maker. Domenico showed no mercy to those who betrayed him, and seldom granted absolution to anyone who dared question him. But like all men, he must have a weakness, and Kenan would make it his duty to discover that flaw.

# 29

*Tuscany, Casa della Luna Crescenta*

PRUDENCE STOOD IN Gabriel's study, and stared at the icon of the Lady and the Rose embedded into the wall. It was not often that she called upon the Lady for assistance or advice, but because of the visions that haunted her of late, she knew she needed to ask the goddess for help.

She stretched a hand toward the icon, and a gentle breeze drifted around her, bringing with it the scent of rose and frankincense. Red and pink rose petals appeared and twirled in a spiral that grew to Prudence's height. A woman, dressed in a long shift of white gauze, stepped out from the curtain of fragrant color. Her skin imitated the translucent alabaster of her sculpture, and the ivory white of her irises were framed with a background of flowing ice-blue water.

"What is it that troubles you, Prudence?" the woman said. Her breathy voice whispered around the room.

"I have seen two deaths," Prudence said, her words caught for a moment in her throat. "One is my son's. I am here to ask for his protection."

"Gabriel…" the woman said. "Yes, I have also seen his death."

"I will not be with him as my mother has called for me."

The woman stepped toward Prudence. "I shall watch over him in your absence." She held Prudence's hands in hers. "A mother's love…" she said.

Prudence gazed into the woman's eyes. "And his beloved, what of her?"

The woman squeezed Prudence's hands, and then released them. "Only Gabriel's love can save her. This is *their* story, dear one. Neither you nor I can change what they have already written. They chose their own lessons before they entered this world."

The woman walked with Prudence toward a window, and gazed out across the fields to the farmhouse in the distance. She hummed a haunting melody that Prudence remembered from her childhood. "I see you surrounded by the dead," the woman said. "So much sadness and pain. I sense you are anxious about seeing your parents after so many years apart, but I can assure you that your parents feel the same. They want to help you, but let them do so in their own way. Listen to your father, for he is wise and kind."

The woman embraced Prudence.

"At times, I feel they are a dream," Prudence said. "Something I created from my own loneliness."

The woman ran a hand over Prudence's long hair. "They are real, Prudence," she said. "You are weary, an understandable trait even for one such as you. Use your time with your parents to infuse your energy, for you will need strength to endure the dark days ahead." She kissed Prudence's forehead, smoothed her hair, and stepped back toward the wall.

Petals rose from the floor, and then swirled and danced around the woman in orchestrated wonder. In Prudence's hand appeared a dusty pink rose in full blossom. She placed it in the alcove beside the icon of the Lady and the Rose. She caught the edge of her long satin dress in her fingers, and when she turned she was standing at the top of a set of stairs at *Casa della Pietra*.

Over the centuries, *Casa della Pietra* had always been a safe haven for members of the Allegiance. However, only those closest to Prudence knew the exact location of the fortress. During onerous times, she had offered shelter to many whose fate would surely have been death. But once they vacated the grounds, the memory of *Casa della Pietra's* location would be erased from their memory, and caught in the web of her magic.

With her foresight, Prudence had seen the necessity to divide the fortress into apartments for her family, friends, and closest allies, while also providing rooms for refugees needing shelter. She was grateful to have those she loved close to her, and now, as she walked by Christopher's rooms, and toward the library, the life Layla carried in her womb reached out to her, bringing a wave of joy to Prudence's heart. Prudence stood at the doorway and looked around. Christopher was at his desk, reading over files and scribbling notes onto a yellow legal pad. Jeremy seemed busy matching each of the missing girl's profiles with police records and photographs he had obtained from their social media pages.

Prudence mentally scanned the photographs of the six teenage girls spread out across a table. "Any luck finding images of tattoos on these girls?"

"A few," Jeremy said. "It takes a long time to weed through all of the social media pages in the hopes of finding a bikini shot. But Layla's been helping, which is great."

Prudence picked up one of the photographs, and ran a hand over the image. She repeated this action with the remaining photographs. "These girls do not have long," she said, "we must find them quickly."

Christopher looked up from his notes. "We're working on it. I have pages of names of missing girls who fit the profile we've put together, but I haven't begun on other countries yet."

Prudence placed the photograph on the table and turned to Jeremy. "Do you have any questions about Katja's diaries, or your father's letter?"

Jeremy shook his head, and Prudence sensed a slight resistance to discuss the information. She rested a hand on his arm. "I am here for you," she said.

"Maybe it'll be easier once more time has passed," Jeremy said.

"Time does help with loss," Prudence agreed. "Kishu asked if there is something he can do to assist, and he is particularly efficient on a computer. He is in the kitchen right now, perhaps you could go and ask him to help you?"

Jeremy looked over at Christopher.

"Go," Christopher said, "and ask Kishu to bring some of his tea with him, the good stuff."

Jeremy walked toward the door and turned back to Prudence. "Can I get you anything, Prudence?"

Prudence smiled. "Thank you, but no."

Christopher waited for Jeremy to leave, and then sat back in his chair.

"What can I do for you, Prudence?"

"Is Layla resting?" she asked.

"Yes," he nodded. "Watching me recover from being shot must have been difficult for her. I'm not sure I'd have done so well if the tables were turned."

"Women seem apt in such situations," Prudence said. "Centuries of attending to loved ones during times of war are ingrained in our collective memories. Like a lifeline, these threads are there when we need them. Layla comes from a long line of strong women. Her mother, Antonia, is perhaps the most intellectually savvy mediator I have ever had the pleasure of working with, and she hides her talents well behind a mask of eccentricities," she grinned. "No one can say no to her."

She sat in a chair near Christopher's desk. "I shall be leaving shortly to meet with my parents. With this in mind, there are legal matters I must secure before we depart, and I feel the need to plan ahead should my darkest premonitions arise."

"Of course, Prudence." Christopher unlocked a drawer on his desk, took out an aged leather-bound book, and placed it in front of her.

With a wave of a hand, Prudence commanded the door to the library to silently close. The book opened to a blank page, a fountain pen magically appeared, and she began to write. When she had finished, she turned the book toward Christopher and handed him the pen. He read over her notes, and as he did she noticed a slight emotional shift on his face.

"Remember, Christopher, you are under the oath of the Allegiance. Not a word must you whisper until deemed absolutely necessary," she said. "One more thing, if there is danger here, you must take Layla, Isabel, Maria, and Eduardo to the inner stronghold where Louisa lies."

Christopher frowned. "But you've always said the fortress is secure."

"Correct," she said, "however, Kenan's power has amplified. He may not find the exact location, but if Freyja were close enough there is a chance she will pick up a trace of my magic. That is why I have protected the inner stronghold with complicated spells. Do not be concerned for the twins and Coco, I have spoken with Chantal regarding their safety."

He returned the book to the drawer and turned the key in the lock. Prudence rose from her chair. "Layla is stirring," she said. "I will leave you now." At the door, she turned to Christopher. He rested his head in his hands.

"Do not forget, Christopher...to find the light we must endure the approaching darkness. *Sine virtute omnia sunt perdita.*"

# 30

THE VICE-LIKE GRIP on Coco's upper arms caused a surge of panic to rush throughout her body. Two men stood either side of her, both over seven feet tall. Metal plates of armor covered their torsos, leaving their broad shoulders, and thick arms, free from restrictive armament. Coco was trapped.

She watched as two hulking men dragged a young man across a stone floor before her. His frantic screams rang in her ears. He struggled as he was forced to stand in front of a figure, whose features were concealed beneath the hood of a long dark cape.

The young man screamed. "No!" His pleas for release went unheard. While one of the men held him securely, the other yanked the young man's right hand forward and spread his fingers out on top of a thick block of stone before him. The hooded man set a short, sharp blade above the young man's middle three fingers, and then quickly sliced through skin, flesh, and bone.

A harrowing howl tore from the young man's mouth. As he was dragged past Coco, she stared at the blood dripping from his hand. She noted the absence of his middle three fingers. Her breath burst in and out of her mouth in frenzied gasps. Cold fear snatched what was left of hope from her mind, when she realized the same act of horror was about to be done to her. She screamed, as she twisted her body and kicked out at the men holding her.

"Please, don't do this," she begged. "What have I done?"

While one of her captors held her firmly, the other yanked her right arm, and placed her hand on the bloodied stone. He held back her thumb and little *finger. The hooded man set his blade above her middle three digits. Coco's heart pounded. He lifted his head, but the face Coco saw was her own.*

*"Wake up," she screamed. "This isn't real!"*

*She fought the urge to surrender to the terror, and instead hurled her mind through the darkened corridors of her subconscious, and back into reality.*

She sprang up in her bed and clasped her hands together, relieved to find all of her fingers in tact and unharmed. A cold sweat seeped from the pores of her skin. Moments later, six immortals burst through her bedroom door. Gabriel grabbed Coco, and held her shaking body. "What happened?"

"A nightmare," Coco said.

Chantal sat on the bed and placed a hand on Coco's back, while Alessandro stood beside her. She eased herself back from Gabriel, and stared up at the concerned faces staring back at her. "I'm okay, really," she said. "It was just a hooded man…he was going to slice off my fingers."

"You were caught in a dark place," Chantal whispered. "But you proved yourself stronger than the darkness."

Gabriel kissed Coco's forehead, cupped her chin, and looked into her eyes. "Darkness is not always bad, Colombina," he said.

"It felt pretty bad to me," Coco said.

"Better for our deepest fears to be played out in our dreams, rather than our reality," Gabriel said. "Dreams are Mother's specialty. We'll leave you in her capable hands."

Coco noticed Stefan rest a hand on Prudence's shoulder. "Dreams awaken the truths of our existence," he said, "and remind us to honor our life's purpose." He turned and joined Caprecia, who was standing by the door. "We shall be near if you need us."

Gabriel kissed Coco's hands, and then rose and exited with Stefan, Alessandro, and Caprecia.

"Do you want to share your dream with us?" Chantal asked.

Coco replied with a nod.

Prudence walked across the room and built up the dwindling fire. "The night is cold," she said.

Chantal picked up Coco's robe and draped it over her shoulders. "Would you like me to make you some chamomile tea?"

Coco nodded, and Chantal headed toward the kitchen.

Coco made herself comfortable on the sofa by the fireplace. "Do you ever have nightmares?"

"Yes," Prudence said.

"Do they scare you?"

"I have trained myself to listen and watch in earnest," Prudence said. "I often beckon forth nightmares, for they yield hidden gems."

"You encourage bad dreams?"

Prudence eased herself into an armchair across from Coco. "Always," she said.

Chantal returned with a cup of tea, placed it in Coco's hands, and arranged a blanket over her daughter's legs. "I have years of mothering-time to make up," she said.

Coco patted the sofa, beckoning her mother to sit beside her. When Chantal was settled, Coco gazed at the crackling fire, steadied her breath, and shared her nightmare with Prudence and Chantal. "Looking back," she said, when she had explained the entire dream, "the whole scene felt inquisitional."

"A committee of men," Prudence observed.

"Yes," Coco agreed, "judgment without jury. But what does that have to do with my current reality?"

"Each of those men symbolize a part of your psyche," Prudence said. "For instance, the young man, he struggles to keep his signature, his uniqueness as an artist...he is an aspect of you. And the men holding him back are repressed; bland followers stripped of their individuality. Perhaps they are a reflection of the person you would be, had you chosen to stay in your old life."

"So you're saying that everyone in my dream is a reflection of me?"

"Correct," Prudence agreed. "Did you say the blade sliced through the young man's middle three fingers?"

"Yes," Coco said. To demonstrate, she wrapped her left hand around the middle three fingers of her right hand. "A perfect cut."

A slight frown passed across Prudence's face. "The hooded man hoped to strip you of your ability to paint," she said. "To leave you with just your thumb and the opposing digit—your little finger—forcing you to give up your work as a Creative. The semi-darkness of the room and dark clothing the men wore represents *nigredo*, the *mortification*...death in the metaphorical sense, and a vivid reminder to be true to your *Self*, and to do what is right. Were any of the men familiar to you?"

"I couldn't see their faces," Coco said, "but the hooded man frightened me...just as I remember feeling when I first saw Kenan."

Prudence closed her eyes for a moment, as if visualizing the scene Coco had described. "For women, our darkest fears are often portrayed in our dreams by an animus, meaning our *Self* is reflected in a familiar masculine form. This is to guide us away from inflicting self-sabotage in our waking life. A way of holding us back from doing something we may regret." She took a moment and then looked into Coco's eyes. "As frightening as it may have seemed at the time, the men in your dream gave you a gift. And the fact that you woke yourself up before you lost your fingers, shows you have a healthy psyche. The men saved you from a life of eternal repression. May I ask what you were thinking about just before you fell asleep?"

Coco's gaze drifted back to her hands. "I was thinking about Gabriel. When I saw him near death on Lopez Island, I had the realization of his place in my heart. Life without him frightens me."

"Perhaps this is a complex that you carry, Colombina. You have a history of seeing those you love violently torn away from you." Prudence waved a hand, and the notepad and pencil that sat beside the bed landed in Coco's lap. "Can you draw the formation of the men in your dream, while the image is still fresh in your mind?"

"Sure." Coco sketched quickly, and then handed the notepad to Prudence.

Prudence traced over the image with a finger, while she explained the importance of the formation. "Do you see how these five points, the position of the men: the hooded man, the two men holding the young victim, and the two men holding you, form one large triangle?"

"The *quintessence*," Coco said.

Prudence smiled. "Yes, and the triangle you have drawn stands erect, as opposed to the open vessel of femininity. We can call this triangle male in gender."

Chantal leaned forward and peered at the drawing. "At one point, you mentioned there were seven people in the room…and you went to sleep thinking of Gabriel." Coco nodded, and Chantal continued. "G is the seventh letter of the alphabet. Also, the triangle in the world of art is connected to the Golden Ratio, a significant foundation of art in the Medieval and Renaissance eras. Your life is drenched in art."

"So what does this all mean?" Coco asked.

"Many things," Prudence said. "But this is your dream, so you must take what feels relevant to you. Remember, every person in your dreams represents an aspect of your *Self*. Perhaps, in this case, Kenan represents your shadow, the dark aspect of your psyche. After all, he stole Chantal away from you, and then your father left to search for her. This separated you from your family. And Kenan is hell-bent on destroying all Creatives."

"Why?" Coco asked. "Why does he want to destroy us?"

"Kenan is frightened of what we have," Chantal said. "He sees Creatives as heretics, tools to destroy the archaic vein of Catholicism he was raised to believe. He sees Creatives as yielders of magic, a form of blasphemy. There were moments during my captivity when I saw sadness in his eyes, a longing of sorts. I wondered about his own past; his parents and his maker."

Prudence cut in. "Over the years, Stefan, Gabriel, Alessandro, and myself have managed to piece together parts of Kenan's life," she said. "We know that he lived with his mother at a cottage located in the foothills of Florence. His uncle was the local priest, and loved by his parishioners for the kindness he showed others. He had a deep passion for the written works of the early Greek thinkers. But this devotion was not reciprocated by the local cardinal, who threatened him with excommunication if he did not adhere to the mass in its strictest form."

"What about Kenan's father?" Coco asked.

"We believe Kenan is the product of his mother's liaison with a high-ranking member of the Catholic Church," Prudence said. "Sexual misconduct among clergy was not unusual at that time. Mostly kept under lock and key, and behind closed doors. When women gave birth to these illegitimate children of faith, or *bastardi di fede*, their mothers were given money in exchange for their silence. But Kenan's mother's deal seemed somewhat sweeter than others. Her brother, who at the time was a student of the Church, was placed at the small chapel upon completion of his schooling in theology. From all accounts, he loved Kenan, and treated the boy as if he was his own son. Apparently, he went missing one evening, and it was at this time that Kenan and his mother were forced into poverty. Coincidently, this marked the time of the local cardinal's rise in position to be closer to the Pope. When Stefan and I first met Kenan, we traced his heritage and found the remains of his uncle buried away from the grounds of the church, on unhallowed ground."

"How did he die?" Coco asked.

The fire hissed as Prudence poked at the wood with a fire iron. "His body had been drained of blood, and carried the stench of an immortal, the same vam*pir* who changed Kenan. I can only surmise that the cardinal felt threatened by the priest's increasing numbers at his parish and their dedication to his sermons, sermons that apparently were laced with humanism. We were told that neighbors often heard Kenan's mother screaming at her brother, telling him to conform to the cardinal's wishes and read the sermons he dictated, rather than risk the consequence. One point was clear, Kenan was the joy of his uncle's life."

"And Kenan's maker?" Chantal cut in. "Is he still alive?"

Prudence shook her head. "No," she said. "Some believe Kenan killed him." For a few moments, the crackling of burning wood was the only sound in the room.

"What do you believe?" Coco asked.

"To kill another creature unless it is in self-defense, or the defense of others, is punishable by death under our law," Prudence said. "I have wondered for many years if perhaps Kenan realized that what he was doing was wrong."

Coco noticed the witch's golden eyes seemed full of sorrow. She stood, as if to gain her composure, and then rested her hands on the mantle. When she spoke, Prudence's voice was lilted sadness. "Domenico preferred to drink the blood of seers. He lived during the time of the Inquisition, and was singlehandedly responsible for the deaths of thousands of innocent women. Most were peasants who survived on poor diets; a fact later proved by physicians to cause brain deficiencies, and in some cases bodily disfigurations, but members of the Inquisition saw these abnormalities as being linked to the devil himself.

"Domenico sniffed out the honeyed scent of seers and kept them for himself, barely keeping them alive so he could continue to drink their life force. He handed over the weaker peasants to the Inquisition, calling them heretics. Weak from starvation, and unable to defend themselves in the Inquisition's so-called justice system, many were tortured until they relinquished to a forced confession. During the latter part of the fifteenth century and first quarter of the sixteenth century, thousands of innocent people, mainly women, were tried. Hundreds were burned at the stake."

Prudence returned to her chair. "I heard that Kenan despised Domenico's addiction to the blood of seers, or 'witches' as the clergy preferred to call them. His youth had been soaked in the strict Catholic beliefs of his mother, with whispered rumors of Inquisitional hearings among his uncle's parish. Living under the harsh indenture of Domenico must have played on Kenan's Catholic guilt. But the longer Kenan stayed with Domenico, and the more he learned about life as a vam*pir,* his own sense of debauchery most likely began to feel normal.

"While the likes of Domenico carried out witch hunts, the Allegiance searched for children born from seers. Some carried the lavender eyes of Creatives. Their mothers were prime targets for the Inquisition, and were often given to bishops, cardinals, and popes for their personal form of retribution. If they were lucky enough to survive the abuse of religious piety, their infants were thrown in the garbage... *bastardi di fede.*

"By the beginning of the eighteenth century, the words of physicians and men studying law were taken seriously. This had begun to transpire earlier, during the Italian Renaissance. Once those in power realized that education had spread from the wealthy, into the other classes, life for European seers seemed somewhat lighter. Many were respected healers, and were often called upon by nobility. But others stayed in hiding and, to this day, children born from seers have no idea of their family lineage."

"But I thought the Allegiance protected all Creatives," Coco said.

"We do not hold Creatives hostage, Colombina," Prudence said. "Creatives, more often than not, are human. You are an exception. When a Creative falls in love with another human and chooses to live in the world they know, we do not challenge their decision. We believe in the freedom of choice."

Coco reached once more for Chantal's hand. "What about you, Mother?"

"I chose to move from Hawaii to Tuscany specifically to study with Prudence," Chantal said. She peered up at Coco, and smiled. "When I met Alessandro, I made the decision to stay in Italy and continue my work as a Creative. Alessandro insisted we buy a home of our own, something we could give to our children. I'd been staying at the farmhouse, but after Alessandro threatened to move us further away, Gabriel sold us the house and surrounding land, including the lake. He enjoyed having Alessandro nearby. When I had the vision of what would happen to me, I entrusted Prudence with part of my secret. She promised to keep you and Christopher safe, no matter what happened to me."

Prudence looked over at Chantal. "I am not sure Alessandro will ever forgive me."

"He's more upset with me," Chantal said, "but I did what I knew had to be done. And now, because of my immortality, we shall be together for many years to come. For this, both of us are grateful. The fact that I am tied to Kenan is unfortunate."

"Prudence, you mentioned that under the law of our kind, killing another unless in defense is a crime punishable by death," Coco said. "So why is it that Kenan is still alive?"

"Greed and power," Prudence replied.

"Then this world is no different from that of humans," Coco said. "Delirious lunatics running on lies and broken promises, agreeing to the people's needs only to win votes, and then tossing the rights of the people out with the tarnished promises of change. This is wrong!"

"Yes, it is," Prudence said, "and it is time I asked others for help. We cannot take on Kenan and his supporters alone. They have become too strong, and have infiltrated their immoralities into the human world." She rose, and reached out to Chantal and Coco. The three women stood together, and Prudence kissed their cheeks. "Stefan is waiting for me," she said, and turned and left the room.

# 31

GABRIEL STOOD WITH his parents in front of the fireplace in the main living room at *Casa della Pietra*. He was aware of a slight aura of anguish pulsing beneath his mother's normally poised demeanor. There was sadness lingering in her eyes, as if she was hiding something from him. "What's going on, Mother? You seem distracted."

Prudence looked up at her portrait that hung above the mantel; the painting Botticelli had created centuries ago. The edges of which had been singed during the Florentine Bonfire of the Vanities, in 1497. The painting that ironically, Kenan had pulled from the raging fire, and was later retrieved by Stefan and Prudence.

"When you were a little boy, you asked so many questions," she said. "Some I could answer, others I could not. Do you remember what I used to tell you?"

Gabriel smiled. "Of course," he said. "You told me to search where before I had not found answers."

Prudence turned to Gabriel, and nodded. "Yes, that is correct." She turned her gaze back to the portrait. "Perhaps one day, this painting will speak to us, not just of my journey, but of yours too."

Gabriel frowned. "Perhaps."

"Ignacio and Caprecia will be here shortly," Stefan said.

Prudence gave her son a motherly embrace, but he sensed her apprehension. "Is there anything you need to tell me?" he asked.

"Only that I love you." She kissed his forehead. Gabriel held onto her hands, hoping to sense what troubled her, but she hid her emotions well.

"I love you too, Mother," he said, then turning to his father to embrace him.

"We shall return soon, Gabriel," Stefan said. He kissed Gabriel's cheeks, and then clutched his elbow. "I love you, son."

"And I love you," Gabriel said.

They bowed their heads together and whispered. "*Sine virtute omnia sunt perdita.*" Once again, Gabriel tried to read his mother's emotions, but his thoughts were interrupted when Ignacio and Caprecia entered the room.

The glint of knives was visible beneath Ignacio's long black leather coat. Caprecia wore two knives strapped to her hips, and the handle of another could be seen emerging from one of her boots. Stefan helped Prudence strap sheaths to her arms, both of which held her weapons of choice: Venetian stiletto daggers. At close range, when thrust precisely, the needle-like point could cause irreparable damage to internal organs. Prudence squeezed Gabriel's hand one last time, and then Stefan guided her to the center of the room, where Ignacio and Caprecia joined them.

Prudence lifted a hand to her mouth. "Raido," she said. She unfurled her fingers, and a small glass ball appeared on the palm of her hand. She drew in a breath and then blew across her hand. The glass ball rolled to the tips of her fingers, and stopped.

"Mother," Prudence said.

Mist rose around Prudence and extended outwards to encompass Stefan, Ignacio, and Caprecia. The four immortals disappeared into a swirl of dense fog.

# 32

## Northeastern Norway

WHEN THE AIR cleared, Prudence saw that she stood before an elegant woman dressed in a white *chiton*—the dress of the goddesses—and a matching cloak trimmed with gold brocade. Her golden hair hung in gossamer curls around her face, and cascaded like a champagne waterfall down to her waist. Her eyes, the color of forest green, glistened in the light. The woman held out her hands in welcome. "My brave and beautiful daughter," she said. "How I have longed for this moment."

Prudence stepped forward, and into her mother's loving embrace. A tall man with white hair, and eyes that mirrored the golden hue of Prudence's, stepped out of the mist behind the woman. From the corner of her eyes, Prudence saw Stefan and Ignacio take up a defensive stance on either side of her. Stefan laid one hand protectively on her shoulder, as the other reached for his sword.

The tall man smiled. "There is no need of weaponry, Stefan," he said. "You are family, therefore you are under my protection, as is my daughter."

Prudence looked up and caught his gaze. A surge of fatherly love poured from him to her. She reached out to him, and he brought her hand to his heart. "At last, we are together again," he said. He looked at Stefan, Ignacio, and Caprecia. "Welcome. I am Hakon, and this is my wife, Sonja."

Stefan removed his hand from the hilt of his sword, and lowered his head to Hakon. "Forgive my impulsive behavior," he said.

Hakon stepped forward. The two men clasped each other's forearms in a show of trust. "I honor and appreciate your protectiveness with my daughter," he said, "and I thank you for giving her sanctuary when my wife and I were not able to do so. We have much to discuss."

Prudence looked around her. They were in a vast cavern, where stalactites hung from the ceiling, some of them connected with stalagmites as thick as aged trees. Everything glistened with flecks of gold and light. She heard a familiar sound, and turned to see a stream of water, falling from a rocky ledge about sixty feet from the ground, where it continued over a marble-lined riverbed. Further along, the clear water stilled and formed a large pond that mirrored the crystal formations hanging from above. A thin ray of light filtered down from the ceiling, and caught the needle-like formations of calcite growing throughout the cave. Prudence admired the kaleidoscope of illumination, and noted various stairways carved from rock, that led up to other chambers.

Sonja guided Prudence down a few steps to an area that resembled a living room, where white pillows lined numerous outcrops of limestone rocks. Once they were all seated, Prudence spoke. "I am here because you called for me in a dream, Mother, and handed me the rune, Raido." She reached for Sonja's hand. "I believe you are both aware of the current situation of my family, and of the abduction of one of our own. A human, Louisa." She felt a tremor of anxiety from Ignacio. "Freyja left a trace of her essence upon Louisa's body, this was how I knew she had stolen her soul. We need your help to find her, and Freyja's realm is not one I can enter without your help."

Hakon rose and walked toward the indoor waterfall. "Darkness has fallen once again upon your world," he said. "Those with power feed fear into the minds of the weak and desperate." He shook his head. "They are blinded by hope concealed behind lies and ignorance. They place their faith for a better life in the hands of greedy hypocrites. Kenan is a demon, and Freyja is lonely and craves to be loved."

"How do you know what she craves?" Prudence asked.

Hakon turned to Prudence. "She came to me once, a long time ago, and made a bargain with me," he said. "Freyja gave me the life of my beloved, and, in exchange, she asked to experience love as a human."

Prudence went to speak, but Sonja caught her hand. "Before we take this journey, you must know what you are up against."

"We made a deal," Hakon said. "I kept my word, but the one Freyja chose to love broke her heart, and she forgot about her own world. You see her as a destructive force, but she was not always this way. In human form, she was too frail to survive a broken heart, and so I stole the memory of her heartache away from her. With it, she would have ceased to exist." He stared at Prudence. "But even with the memory of love gone, Freyja constantly searches for something to fill the emptiness in her soul." His gaze met Ignacio's. "You know this emotion only too well, Ignacio. I can sense your sadness."

"Will you help us find Louisa?" Ignacio asked.

Prudence rose and walked over to Hakon. "It was Kenan she fell in love with, wasn't it?" Prudence took hold of Hakon's hands, and a flood of his memories washed over her. "Freyja caught a flicker of recognition around Kenan, but she does not know from where this emotion stems. She is holding Louisa hostage...Louisa's life in exchange for a memory." She dropped his hands. "During my abounding life, I have found the tenacity of the human spirit to be dauntless when it comes to protecting those they love. These three immortals standing beside me were once human, and as such, they are empowered with immense courage and compassion. We are not pawns to move as bargaining chips in a game between you and Freyja, Father."

She caught a breath. "Do you know how difficult my life has been? How many loved ones I have had to watch die over the past twelve hundred years? And now, because of the bargain you made with Freyja, everything I love is in danger of being destroyed." She turned to Sonja. "If you know what haunts me, then you must understand that not only is my son's life in danger, but also the Allegiance. How do I end this? How do I kill Kenan?"

Hakon glared at Prudence, his gaze penetrating through her golden irises and into her soul. Prudence could sense his frustration. After an eternal couple of seconds, however, she felt something within him crumble. "If I knew how to kill Kenan, I would have done so long ago,"

Hakon said. He turned to Sonja, and stared for a moment into her eyes. She nodded to him, answering his silent question.

"Your words remind me of the young man I used to be," Hakon said. "Yes, I will help you find Louisa." He turned abruptly, and as he did, his white and golden robes swiftly morphed into the garb of an elfin warrior: A leather tunic embedded with chainmail lay under a floor-length leather coat adorned with wide wrist cuffs, along with shoulder pads made of intricately engraved metal plates. Dark leather straps wrapped around his long boots, and continued up over his leather pants. A thick belt hung on his hips, and a baldric held the scabbard that bore his sword, its hilt emblazoned with the warrior rune, Teiwaz. Over a shoulder hung a yew bow. Arrows with shafts marked with runes flickered in the light, and waited in readiness in a well-worn quiver.

"Come," Hakon said, "it is best we approach the boatman before the light of dawn is upon us." He turned to Ignacio. "As it is *your* beloved we are to rescue, you must be the one to pay Charon." With these words, Hakon flipped a coin into the air, where it hovered momentarily before falling into Ignacio's open palm.

# 33

*Casa della Pietra*

COCO SEARCHED THROUGH the playlists on her iPhone, pressed shuffle, and stepped into a hot bath. She stared at the cloud of bubbles surrounding her naked body. She scooped up a handful, and then listened to the faint crackle as one by one the bubbles burst, until only a few puffs of foam remained in her palm. She eased herself below the waterline and her hair caressed her face. The sound of the music seeped into the water, and a wave of sadness washed over her. She imagined Gabriel's arms around her, but for some reason this made her sad. She pushed her body up again, and listened to the lyrics as if for the first time.

*Catch my hand when I'm falling,*
*And my tears have left me blind...*

Each word resonated through Coco like déjà vu, but she had no idea why. She crossed her arms, but that did nothing to shed the terrible sense of foreboding and loneliness that clung to her. The music stopped, and after a time she realized the water had chilled. She dried off, grabbed her sketchbook, and slipped under the quilt of Gabriel's bed. Pencil in hand, she closed her eyes for a minute. When they opened, she began to draw.

A door opening and closing alerted her that Gabriel had returned. She looked at her phone, and saw she'd been drawing for over an hour. The sound of running water told her he was in the shower. She looked at her drawing, and wondered what it meant: a self-portrait of her, floating in water. The picture conveyed sadness, and yet her face seemed at peace. Underneath, she had written a line from the song that she'd listened to earlier.

*Be my anchor when I'm drifting,*
*And bring me home, when life's unkind...*

Coco shivered in response to Gabriel's presence. A narrow stream of moonlight flowed from a gap in the curtains to his face. She followed his eyeline as his seductive gaze caressed the folds of the sheet covering her naked body. A hollow-bodied guitar bass line drifted down from hidden speakers, and filled the room with music. Coco placed the sketchbook and pencil on the bedside table.

Her breath quickened and her body flushed, as she watched water drip from Gabriel's dark hair and gather like dewdrops on his sculpted shoulders. *Even without your clothes, you have an air of sophistication, balanced with an element of hip.* A corner of his mouth lifted into a suggestive smile as he sat on the bed beside her.

"I heard that," he said.

"I figured you would."

He brought his lips to hers, and she reached for his shoulders. The towel fell from his hips as he eased himself on top of her. He lifted her hands from around his neck and tucked them beside her body, then cocooned her within the bed sheet.

Gabriel's hands traveled slowly over the fabric that held her form captive. A murmur of satisfaction escaped her lips, while the warmth of his mouth lingered between her thighs. Imprisoned beneath him, she couldn't move. The music was slow and bluesy.

"Gabriel," she moaned. But he ignored her words and kept up his impassioned kisses, massaging her breasts until her nipples hardened and strained against the silk. Heat spread throughout her body as he moved his lips over her stomach to between her legs, teasing her with his warm breath. She tried to move, but this evoked more pressure from Gabriel.

The sheet clung to her, moist with her excitement. Her screams of pleasure broke out, and he covered her mouth with his.

Gabriel gave one quick tug on the sheet, and it was gone. He moaned as he entered her. Coco wrapped her legs around his body and he lifted her off the bed so she rested on his thighs. She moved in rhythm with him, running her hands over his shoulders, down his back, and through his hair. His breath caught, and her muscles clenched around him as they climaxed.

They lay together in the cooling minutes that followed, listening to a woman singing the blues. Coco snuggled into Gabriel, whose arm was locked around her. "Will our lives always be like this?" she asked. "You going off to fight, me painting horrific images, and then sharing precious time together whenever we can?"

He delicately stroked her forehead. "I guess that's why it's important to make the most of every moment," he said. "Throughout history, good and evil have fought incessantly, each hoping to unbalance the scale in their direction."

"Did you find any of the missing girls?" Coco asked him, suddenly.

"Yes."

"Were they okay?"

"Are you sure you want me to answer that question?" he asked.

"Yes."

Gabriel sat up. "A Georgetown mansion was being used to administer archaic forms of torture. The girls were kidnapped, and then taken back to the house. One bedroom was set up with a device similar to those used by the Inquisition during the witch hunts." He turned to Coco. "Shall I continue?"

Coco sat next to him. "I need to know," she said.

"The girl's hands had been tied tightly behind her back, and then she was suspended into the air using a chain and pulley device. Dr. Fiore said when he released the girl, her shoulders were both dislocated, most likely from being jerked up and down in the air quickly by her torturer. He probably forced a few drops of his blood into her mouth, just enough to heal her wounds before the process was repeated. She'd been forced heroin, raped and beaten multiple times over, and was barely alive when Alessandro broke through the door. Dr. Fiore was able to save her."

"Did my father kill her attacker?"

"No," Gabriel shook his head. "*I* did."

"And the other girls?" Despite what she had said a moment ago, Coco had almost heard enough.

"They were being drained of their blood," Gabriel concluded. "But from the horrors their memories held, they were all, at some stage, put through the hell and pain of *strappado*."

Coco sighed. "What happens to the girls now?"

"Dr. Fiore attended to them," Gabriel said. "She wiped their memories clear of the trauma they had experienced, and then members of the Allegiance returned them to their families."

"I needed to know they were okay," Coco whispered.

"I know," Gabriel said.

She lifted her eyes to him. "Aren't you tired?"

"No," he said, "When Kenan's dead, I'll sleep. Not before then."

# 34

GABRIEL WAITED UNTIL Coco's breathing slowed, and the slight flutter behind her eyelids showed she had entered a heavy dream state. He dressed, turned to look at his beloved once more, and then silently went downstairs to his study. He sensed Pelayo's presence just as he was about to toss a rune into the air.

"Going somewhere?" Pelayo asked.

"Yes," Gabriel said.

"On your own?"

The door opened and Dr. Fiore entered. Absent of her white lab coat, she instead wore a skintight black spandex suit, thigh-high black boots, and shoulder straps carrying a variety of silver-bladed daggers. Below her right hip, resting in an Italian-style hanger, was her favorite weapon, a swept-hilt rapier sword.

"Of course he's not going on his own, are you, Gabriel?" she asked.

Pelayo eyed Dr. Fiore's clothing. "Is that the latest look in women's office apparel?"

"What do you suggest?" she quipped. "A navy blue two-piece business skirt suit? And perhaps a beige silk shirt, tied into a bow at the neckline? I *never* wear beige!"

Gabriel glared at her. "I'll be quicker, solo. I want to track the vampire I saw in Manhattan while his scent is still fresh in my mind."

"I'm faster than you, Gabriel, and if you find the girls, they'll need my help," she said. "I'm ready when you are. And while my lab coat is off, please use my warrior name."

"Hopefully, there will be no need for fighting tonight, Sabine," Gabriel said.

"Don't be a fool, Gabriel, and drink this," Sabine said. She tossed him a bag of blood. He caught it, ripped open the bag, and drank the contents.

"Ahhh!" he exhaled. "Nothing quite like a good A positive!"

"Does Coco know you're leaving?" Pelayo asked.

Gabriel shook his head.

"What do I tell her when she wakes, and finds you gone?"

Gabriel looked at Sabine. He was not about to argue with her raised eyebrow and fiery temper. "We'll be back by then," he said. "I'll track the vampire from Midtown, where we saw him, but I have a feeling he's lurking on the Upper West Side."

"Did Ignacio give you the location?" Pelayo asked.

"He didn't have the exact address, just that he'd heard Kenan kept an apartment near Central Park." Gabriel noticed Pelayo staring at the silver knives tucked into his boots, and the gleam of a sword beneath his long dark coat. "Purely out of habit, I need to leave. You know what you must do."

"Take care, *amigo*, even your magic cannot help if you are outnumbered."

"I won't go in alone, but I need to know who's helping Kenan," Gabriel said, "and preferably before he surfaces again."

"If Coco wakes up and you're not back, I'll come searching for you," Pelayo said.

"We'll hold you to that." Gabriel tossed a rune into the air and disappeared with Sabine.

○

The streets of Manhattan were slick with a thin layer of snow. A few pedestrians in need of transportation huddled under coats and hailed cabs or headed for the subway, eager to get home and out of the cold. Gabriel and Sabine emerged from a cloud of mist on the rooftop of the Algonquin Hotel.

"I wish I could do that," Sabine said.

Gabriel grinned. "It's awesome, isn't it," he said.

"Your warlock talents would have come in handy during the 8th century B.C."

Gabriel stood still for a moment and turned to her. "Seeing the brutality committed upon the girls at the Georgetown house must have awakened horrific memories for you. Are you sure you want to be here?"

"What else would I do, Gabriel?" she said. "My name speaks of a time long passed, of abduction and rape. Unlike my sisters and friends, I had escaped my kidnapper's clutches. But, in the chaos, I was struck by my enemy's sword."

Gabriel sensed the pain she had buried deep within her psyche. "The paintings depicting the rape of the Sabine women do little to impart the terror, and injustice, they must have experienced."

Sabine nodded. "For many years, I had been sought for my knowledge of healing, but that day the soldiers had walked by, and considered my injuries and impending death a burden." She paused for a moment. "When the light of day had passed, I staggered away from the melee… blood dripping from my open wound. Close to death, I collapsed, and fell into delirium. When I awakened, it was with a thirst for blood and a renewed strength. The one who gave me immortality also taught me the way of the warrior. He gave me a sense of purpose, and taught me to fight with multiple weapons. But, more importantly, he taught me to keep my hunger for revenge under control, and to forgive…but never to forget."

They walked toward the edge of the building.

"When I awakened in this immortal body, I vowed to protect women who are subjected to violence in any form. The memory of that day—hearing my sister's scream as they were torn away from their families—is embedded in my soul. But Romulus paid for what he did." She turned to Gabriel. "Now, enough reminiscing, we have work to do."

Gabriel pointed along the street to the next intersection. "That's where I saw him."

Without delay, they leapt across rooftops, and jumped down onto the street at the corner of 44th and 5th where Gabriel quickly picked up the scent of the vampire.

"He's a young one," Sabine said. "His blood lust is governed by sex. Ignorant fool."

They sprinted along Fifth Avenue to Rockefeller Center, where cultural mythology beckoned to those who would listen in the form of Atlas, bearing the Earth upon his shoulders, and the glistening spires of St. Patrick's Cathedral. Gabriel sensed a moment of hesitation in the vampire's journey. He looked up at the ornate spires, glistening like quartz crystal, as snowflakes brushed the Neo-Gothic church. Perhaps the vampire had done the same, a momentary pause to repent his sins. From here, Gabriel knew that the vampire did not stop again until he entered Central Park.

A strong wind blew what was left of browned leaves onto the ground, where they would stay hidden under a white blanket until winter became a memory. Verdant bushes, trees, and grass transformed into ghostly images around him, and thick earth-colored tree trunks stood as they had in decades past, with their outstretched limbs beckoning small animals to take shelter.

Gabriel welcomed the surreal silence the snowstorm offered. He sensed ten creatures in the park, eight of whom were vampires, and one of them was the vampire he had been tracking. With a quickened pace, they sprinted along a pathway and under a bridge built of redbrick and sandstone. From here they left the main path, and sprinted past the Loeb Boathouse toward the Metropolitan Museum of Art.

They came to a sudden halt when they noticed the bitter smell of human fear permeating around them, and followed by the sweet and salty bouquet of fresh human blood. Another scent drifted nearer. It was the vampire Gabriel was tracking.

"Show yourself," Gabriel said.

A throaty chuckle, followed by the smacking and licking of lips filtered through the air. A tall and muscular vampire stepped out from a flurry of snowflakes, his amber-colored hair clung to his head as he lifted his forearm, and wiped his mouth.

"You interrupted my breakfast," the vampire said.

"There was no need to kill her," Sabine said.

"Who are you to tell me how to eat?" he asked.

In a flash, Sabine had the vampire on the ground.

"What can you tell me about kidnapped girls?" Gabriel said. "Each one bears the same tattoo."

The young vampire squirmed under the doctor's hold. "Girls go missing all the time in this city. Who gives a fuck if they have a tattoo?"

"Kenan, your boss," Gabriel said. "He gives a fuck about their tattoos." His tone remained calm. He noticed the slight tensing of the young vampire's neck when he mentioned Kenan's name.

"Let me up and I'll talk," he said.

Gabriel gave a quick nod to Sabine, and she released her hold. If the vampire fled he could outrun Gabriel, but not Sabine. She came from ancient blood. Her speed and temper were notorious.

The young vampire sprung up, lingered for a moment, and then made a break for it. Sabine raced after him in a blur of black and silver. Gabriel caught up with her under a cast iron bridge close to the reservoir, where she held her captive securely on the ground. He fought to turn his head away from Sabine's deadly grip. Gabriel had witnessed her wrath numerous times and knew she had no tolerance for vampires who killed and tortured the innocent...especially women.

Gabriel stood by the vampire's head. "Tell me about the girls and where they are being held prisoner," he said.

"What girls? I don't know—"

The sound of bones popping met the darkness, as Sabine slowly crushed one of her victim's hands. "The girls!" she growled, releasing his mangled appendage.

The young vampire gritted his teeth as his bones began to heal.

"We asked you a question," Sabine said. She waited a few moments for him to answer. When he didn't speak, she ripped open his shirt and slowly undid the buttons of his jeans. Her cold fingers stroked his penis. He gasped as the urge for sex overtook the pain coursing through his crushed hand. Sabine wrapped her fingers around his erection, squeezing firmly, and watching the horror in his eyes. When he went to scream, she slapped him hard across his face. "Where are the girls?" she demanded.

Gabriel decided to try an alternative solution. He pulled a rune from his pocket and tossed it in the air just above the vampire's head. "Show me where the girls are being held prisoner," he whispered. The rune spun in mid-air. Gabriel closed his eyes, and felt a familiar thrust of energy enter his body, as scattered images from their captive's memories played like a film in his mind.

*The young vampire carried an unconscious girl out of a car. He walked through a private garage and into the kitchen area of an apartment. Gabriel searched the room for a clue to the location. On a granite counter, were assorted real estate flyers, showing properties on the Upper East Side of Manhattan. He followed the vampire up two flights of stairs and into a bedroom, where he laid the girl across a bed and drank from her neck, fondling her breasts as he sucked her blood. When he was done, he licked the girl's breasts and undid her jeans. Gabriel noted that the girl had the same tattoo as the other victims. The vampire's phone vibrated. He looked at the name on the screen, cursed, and then let go of the girl and exited the room. Gabriel went to the window and regarded the view. He knew exactly where this place was.*

Gabriel opened his eyes, and caught the rune as it fell. "Found them," he said. "I don't care what you do with him, but we need to leave now."

The young vampire's eyes grew wide, and he began to shake his head from side to side. "Please, I just wanted the money—"

"Don't lie to me!" Sabine sneered. "A destitute vampire is an oxymoron." She looked up at Gabriel. "Did he do anything without the girl's consent?"

Gabriel's silence was her answer. With one quick movement, Sabine ripped the vampire's penis from his body. His screams were silenced when her rapier sword sliced through his neck. "Let's go," she said. "The girls will be frightened."

They moved across the park toward the Natural History Museum to 74th Street, and stopped outside a row of Brownstone buildings. Gabriel noted a private garage door painted gloss black. He looked up at the third floor, and nodded to Sabine. Together they sprang up and landed on the roof. They listened for a moment. Gabriel held up a hand indicating he'd heard five vampires. Sabine nodded. Moments later, they both stood in the bedroom Gabriel had seen in the young vampire's memory.

A girl was huddled on the floor in a corner, her body bruised and shaking. She rocked back and forth, and started to scream when she saw the two strangers in the room. With a wave of a hand, Gabriel silenced her. Sabine grabbed a blanket from the bed, wrapped it around the girl, and then stared into her eyes.

"Hush," she whispered, "we're here to help you." She kissed the girl's forehead, and lifted her onto the bed, where she fell instantly to sleep.

From outside the door came a muffled scream. Gabriel bolted for the hallway, and tore a door to one of the bedrooms off its hinges. The vampire raping the young girl was dead in seconds, and soon Sabine held another shell-shocked girl in her arms.

"They're the only two humans I sense here," Gabriel said. "Take them to Prudence's apartment, and then call Pelayo."

"Yes, but—"

"Go!"

With the girl in her arms, Sabine raced past Gabriel to the other bedroom. Seconds later he heard glass shatter. He knew a window was not a deterrent to a vampire as strong as Sabine, who, by now was probably half way to his mother's apartment. The first knife he cast caught an approaching vampire directly in the heart. Gabriel grabbed his sword and in one clean slice, the vampire's head was removed, and rolled down the stairs leaving a trail of blood.

Gabriel stood on the landing, feet slightly apart, sword raised and his mind calm. He sensed the three remaining vampires waiting for him on the rooftop. They were young, nothing too powerful. He turned, and was about to lunge up the stairs when he heard the unmistakable click of a timer. He waved a hand. A deafening roar boomed around him, followed by silence.

# 35

*Svalbard Island, Arctic Ocean*

PRUDENCE FELL TO her knees, gasping for breath. Her mind flooded with the vision of a huge cloud of dust and debris rising up from the ground, and engulfing a collapsing brick building. Stefan knelt beside her. They clung to each other, unable to speak. The rise and fall of powerful waves breaking against a fierce offshore wind carried sprays of saltwater into the night. The cold drops of water on her face brought Prudence back to reality. She clung to Stefan, while adrenaline coursed throughout her body. "Do you feel Gabriel's essence?" she asked.

Stefan brought his grief-stricken face close to hers, and whispered. "I feel only pain."

Sonja reached out to Prudence, and placed a small piece of silver thread in the palm of her hand. "Keep this near your heart," she said. "Your son's spirit is fighting for life. This will help guide him back to his beloved."

Hakon rested a hand on Stefan's shoulder, and motioned to two crescent moons that appeared between dark clouds. "We must move forward," he said. Stefan nodded, and with his arm around Prudence, he stood and followed Hakon as he led the group along the beach and toward a wooden boat anchored at the shoreline.

A figure emerged from the shadow of the boat. His taut, muscular body was draped only in a piece of roughly woven crimson fabric. Silver hair billowed around his face like a mane of strength, and matched his wiry moustache and beard. He lifted his head as they approached, staring at Hakon with eyes devoid of emotion. The only color his irises bore was a ghostly white. Charon had arrived.

He held out an open palm, and Ignacio dropped the coin into its center. The group watched as Charon's bony fingers clasped around the coin. Hakon urged them all on board. Seconds later, Charon stood at the bow, guiding the wooden boat away from the shore with a single oar. The gentle lapping of the waves soon changed as the boat's course took it deeper into a trough of inky water. The bow sank down as it rode the crest of gathering swells that would carry its passengers across the River Styx, to the Svalbard Islands.

Thunder boomed, off in the distance. Lightning flooded the angry currents and shed light upon empty souls, emerging from the ocean, reaching their white arms out for help. The foreboding sound of heavy waves crashing onto rocks meant the shoreline was near. Charon guided the boat over the wash, finally bringing it to rest at the end of a long wooden jetty. He lowered his head, and Hakon led the others off the boat.

As they walked along the aged wooden planks the clouds of air that escaped their mouths drifted into the frigid night. Soon the sound of the waves crashing dissipated, and a quiet eeriness surrounded the immortals. The jetty ended at the mouth of a cave. Hakon held up a hand to the others and they gathered beside him.

He faced the entrance and whispered a verse in ancient Norse. When he finished, the entrance to the cave began to glow, and a tunnel lit with torches appeared ahead. "Stay close to me," he said, "do not stray, and do not dare to answer the pleas of the dead if they accost you. You cannot help their souls—they are beyond redemption." He took hold of Sonja's hand and together they led the group into the heart of Freyja's realm.

Gradually, the surface of the tunnel changed from gray rock to limestone. Glow-worms glistened in the dim light, and the tinkling notes of water dripping onto the creamy stones ebbed from pitter-patter to splashes that echoed back and forth along the path. But when the organic smell of the cave shifted, and a hint of geranium seeped into the air, Ignacio reached toward Hakon. "She is near," he said.

Caprecia grabbed his arm, quickened her pace and began to run ahead of the others. "Caprecia, you must wait!" Hakon said. He reached out to her and a flash of light extended from his fingertips and caught Caprecia around her waist.

"Please," she cried, "let me go."

Prudence embraced her. "Caprecia, we must be cautious. We do not know if Kenan is here," she said. "Please, we are stronger together."

A woman's voice, dripping with sexuality and allure, echoed along the chamber. "Who are you who wander this path?"

Six ghost-like women appeared before them and blocked their way. They were dressed in long black garb. Each wore a black cornette that sat like a butterfly upon their heads. Their faces were gaunt and pale with sunken gray eyes, framed with long black hair, slick with oil. They all stared at the ground, never moving their line of sight, and only parting to make way for the woman who had spoken. She was dressed in a similar style to the other women, who now formed a semi-circle around her, the only difference being that her face was covered by a black veil. Her gloved hands tossed stones into the air, and as they descended, all but one froze. She held out a hand and it landed in her palm.

"Kano...reversed," she said. "Darkness looms..."

The women around her repeated her words, although none opened their mouths to speak.

Hakon stepped forward. "We are here to collect the soul of a woman that is ours," he said.

The sound of the women's laughter rang through the air.

"Louisa," the veiled woman said. She pointed to Ignacio. "I can feel your need for her." She turned and walked away.

The group of women followed. "There is always a price to pay," they said in unison.

Hakon pulled six arrows from his quiver. He loaded one and pushed Sonja behind him. Stefan stood poised with his sword in hand. Ignacio positioned himself on the other side of Hakon, armed with multiple knives.

What began as a single high-pitched note quickly morphed into a chorus of shrill screams. A cloud of black hurtled along the tunnel toward the group. Hakon released six arrows into the mass. The screams grew louder and angrier. Ignacio cast two knives into what looked like flailing arms. A sickening screech erupted. An elongated face burst through the cloud of darkness toward the three men. Stefan reared to his full height, and slashed at the face with his sword. This time, laughter tore through the tunnel. The three men fought together. Caprecia struck out at the howling hags with kicks and knives, but the more the immortals fought, the more strength the hags gained, as if feeding from their courage.

Prudence saw Sonja close her eyes and fall to her knees. When her eyes reopened, Prudence shared her vision, and instantly knew what she had to do. She spun around, and unleashed a keening cry. She raised her arms above her head and muttered a spell.

A thin layer of metal covered the immortals like a cone. Howls of pain erupted from the hags as they saw their distorted reflections staring back at them. Curses followed. And then silence. Stefan dropped his sword and caught Prudence as she collapsed.

"*Tesoro*," he whispered. "Come back to me."

She gasped. Her eyes opened, and she saw the angst that welled in Stefan's eyes. "I am here, *il mio amore*," she whispered. "Have they gone?"

Stefan nodded.

Prudence looked over at Hakon. He lifted Sonja into his arms and brought her to Prudence. "Thank you both," he said.

Sonja reached out to Prudence. "You saw my vision," she said.

"Yes," Prudence said, "I saw mirrors and the hags' reflections burst into flames." She waved a hand and the dome disappeared. She saw Ignacio crouched on the floor next to Caprecia. Both were splattered in blood.

Ignacio looked up. "What the fuck were they?" he asked.

"Succubi," Hakon said, "they do not like mirrors."

"Reason enough to have a mirror above one's bed," Ignacio said, as he jumped up and held a hand out to Caprecia.

Stefan chuckled. He helped Prudence to her feet, reclaimed his sword, and then addressed Hakon. "Shall we move forward?"

With a quick nod, Hakon kissed Sonja's hand and resumed the lead. "Yes," he said. "Best not to stay in this place for too long."

# 36

*Casa della Pietra*

COCO AWOKE WITH a start. She turned her head, hoping to see Gabriel, but he wasn't beside her. Thinking she would find him in his study, she showered and dressed, and then went downstairs to look for him.

When she opened the door to the study, she immediately sensed something amiss. Her mother, father, and Pelayo looked up at her as she entered, and none of their faces looked hopeful. She gazed around the room and didn't see Gabriel, but the angst in Chantal's eyes confirmed that something was not right.

"What's happened?" she asked. "Where's Gabriel?"

Chantal walked toward Coco. "We don't know," she said.

"But I thought this fortress was impenetrable," Coco said. "Where are the twins?"

"This fortress is safe and the twins are fine," Pelayo said. "Gabriel left here hours ago, and on his own accord. He wanted to track a vampire we saw while monitoring Arianna at the bank in Manhattan."

"He's in New York?" Coco asked.

Pelayo nodded. "Yes."

"He went alone?" Coco shouted. "Without telling me?"

"Dr. Fiore went with him," Pelayo said.

"The doctor called a while ago," Alessandro cut in. "She told us Gabriel is missing."

Coco pulled her phone from her pocket and went to call Gabriel, but Chantal caught her hand. "Christopher's been calling Gabriel's number for hours," Chantal said. "We've all called, but no one answers."

Alessandro strode across the room, and placed his hands on Coco's shoulders. "Members of the Allegiance are searching for him," he said.

Coco glared at her father. "What else?" she asked.

"There was an explosion at a building," Alessandro said, his voice emphatic. "We think he may have been inside."

Coco lowered her head, stared at the well-worn Persian rug on the floor, and fought the flight or fight primal response rising in her body. Alessandro stepped back. Coco reached for her mother's hand, and then evened her breath, and quieted her mind. She closed her eyes and reached out to the emptiness and found something, a silver thread. She gasped, her eyes opened, and she stared at Chantal. "I feel him, Mom," she said. "He's alive. I know it."

"Then you must find him," Chantal said.

Coco turned to Pelayo. "I need an image of the place where Dr. Fiore last saw Gabriel. I can get us there."

"I promised Gabriel I would keep you safe," Pelayo said. "He wouldn't want you away from here, it's too risky."

"If you don't take me, I'll go by myself," Coco said. "But I'd feel better if you were with me, and so would Gabriel."

"Christopher and I will be with you too," Alessandro said.

Christopher entered the room and handed Coco a photograph of a Georgian styled building.

"This looks familiar," Coco said. "I've admired this building for years. It's opposite the Met."

"Yes," Christopher said. "The building is owned by Prudence and Stefan."

Coco looked at Christopher. "And it was blown up?"

"No," Christopher replied. "This is where we're going to meet with Sabine, then go from there."

"What?" Coco asked. "Who the hell is Sabine?"

"Dr. Fiore minus her white lab coat," Alessandro said.

Coco frowned. "I don't understand."

"Sabine is an ancient vampire," Alessandro replied. "When she's not working as a doctor, she dons the clothing of a warrior. She is a force to be reckoned with, and no better fighter to have at one's side."

Coco looked at the photograph in her hands. "So, this is where we're headed first?"

"Yes," Christopher said. "It's up to you and Mom to get us there, just like you did when we traveled from Tuscany to Washington State. Use your innate talent as a Creative to transport us there quickly."

Coco nodded. "Okay."

"Let's go to the main studio" Chantal said. "You paint the apartment in the photograph. I can paint the image you'll need to return here." She turned to Alessandro. "Give us thirty minutes." She clasped Coco's hand and led her quickly out the door, and toward the stairs.

○

In the darkness, Gabriel became aware of a faint silver thread. A blaze of pain seared over his charred body, but he kept his focus on the thread and willed it closer. He didn't know why he cared about it, or what it meant, only that it called out to him. His breath caught in a whistling rattle as he inhaled. The thread lingered for a moment, and then a cascade of small stones engraved with symbols fell toward him. They hung momentarily in the darkness just inches from his face, until one stone broke away and rested upon his forehead.

More pain.

Exhale.

A muted gag, that fell in a puddle of misery.

A hushed whisper fluttered by his form and brushed across his memory.

Othila…the rune of radical severance.

The sound echoed before it dissolved into silence.

In his mind, he reached out and caught the end of the silver thread. An ivory glow pulsed beneath the layers of torn and burned muscle, and a faint ripple of hope flickered over what remained of Gabriel's face.

# 37

## *Italy*

AFTER THE SACKING of Rome in 1527, Domenico loosened his tight hold on Kenan. But experience had taught Kenan to be wary of this new development, and he knew better than to let down his guard. He decided to divide these short periods of freedom into two main areas. In order for him to overcome Domenico, he would need to become a stronger warrior.

With this in mind, he sought out hidden places where men fought each other like gladiators of the past. These places were for the destitute. Men who had lost families, loved ones and land to war and disease. Men insane with anger, deprived of dignity and angry as all hell. These were the men who taught Kenan how to fight.

Any remaining spare time he had, Kenan used to discreetly uncover the final words the seer had spoken, moments before Domenico killed her. *The sands on the beaches of Lazio have run through my fingers. You have the curse of Vinicio.*

The fighting came easy to Kenan, and gradually he grasped the importance of strategy, whether fighting one-on-one, or with an army. He understood why men fight and why so many choose to go to war. For some it meant camaraderie, others craved the strength of a fighter, and, for many, war meant escape from the monotony of their day-to-day lives. But what Kenan found difficult was obtaining information about *Vinicio*.

Decades became centuries, and degradation from Domenico became normal. Kenan's survival depended on being at the brunt of Domenico's anger, which, when it happened, was brutal, but quick. This was Kenan's saving grace, until the day he saw Ravinka.

Kenan pulled up his horse, and watched a woman who stood at the edge of a cliff. The first image was of her long black hair dancing in the wind as if it was a separate entity. A squall gathered strength on the horizon, and a blast of wind tore at her cloak, whipping the fabric away from her body and revealing her flesh beneath a thin white dress.

Hoping to breathe in her scent, Kenan inhaled deeply, but the salty ocean was all he caught. Intrigued by the fact he could not detect her scent, he watched as she walked along the edge of the cliff, and then continued on a road that led to a nearby village. He wanted to follow her, to taste her, but Domenico's call was louder. Kenan willed his mind clear of her image, to hide all trace of her from Domenico, a trait he had taught himself over the years, and an invaluable tool against his maker. He contemplated the woman one last time, and then turned his horse in the direction of Rome.

Whenever possible, Kenan returned to the cliffs, hoping for another glimpse of the dark-haired woman, but to no avail. He did not understand his attraction to her, but wondered if it was more the image of freedom she portrayed, a detachment of sorts, that appealed to him. He knew nothing of relationships, either with a male or female, and in truth he didn't feel comfortable in the presence of women. But there was a draw to this bohemian-like woman, one that he'd not experienced prior.

As Domenico's charge, it was Kenan's job to gather payments from mortals who required the services of his maker; services that included gathering secret information, stealing, or murder. And so it was for this reason that Kenan found himself one afternoon in a village, by the cliffs where he'd last seen the woman who teased his mind.

He dismounted his horse, and tossed a young stable-hand a few coins, and then strode through the village amidst the throng of market-goers and merchants selling their wares. The smell of overripe fruit and burnt meat hovered over the town square making it easier for Kenan to ignore the distinctive sapid scent of the blood of gypsies.

He made his way across the square just as the setting sun caught a glimmer of familiarity. He turned, and saw a mass of long raven-colored hair near the edge of the market. The woman leaned her head back, and brought two kittens up to her face. She kissed them and caressed their soft fur over her lips, neck, and collarbone. Then, as if she knew someone was watching her, she turned and smiled at Kenan.

A strange feeling washed over him, almost a sensual reaction, but much more than that. This pull to another was an emotion he had not encountered until this moment. Something batted his boots, and when he looked down, a large cat sat beside him. He leaned over and stroked its back, and as it arched a vision of the woman with the long black hair flickered through his thoughts. He stood and looked once again in her direction, but she was no longer there, and when he peered at the ground, the cat had also disappeared.

Kenan pushed his way through the crowd to where the woman had been standing. He strained his neck, and looked above the throng of people, and in the distance he saw her disappear around the corner of a building. He raced along the cobblestone street and turned the corner. A smile touched his lips when he saw her beyond the village, standing alone in a field of golden wheat. A second later, he stood behind her.

He wanted to touch her hair, to confirm she was not a figment of his imagination. "Who are you?" he asked.

The woman turned, and in that moment bliss filled his heart. He sank into her blue eyes, and was reminded of the azure blue of the ocean.

"My name is Ravinka," she said. "I saw you once. You watched me on the edge of the cliffs." She handed him one of the kittens. "Be gentle, it would not be good if you hurt her."

Kenan accepted the kitten, although he found it difficult to hold such a delicate creature. He wondered if in some way she had given him the kitten as a test of sorts. The tiny creature licked his fingers, and he smiled. "I did not think her tongue would be so rough. She is so tiny and fragile."

Ravinka eased herself onto the ground amongst the flaxen grass, and beckoned to him to do the same. She released the kitten she had held, and watched it explore the area close by. Kenan sat next to her, and placed his kitten on the ground and grinned as the small ball of black fur jumped over its litter-mate.

"They are so sweet and gentle," Ravinka said, "why would anyone want to harm such a creature because of its color?"

Her comment made Kenan uncomfortable, and yet he did not want to lie to this woman. "There are those who once thought black cats communed with the devil," he said. "That is all."

Ravinka lay down, and looked up at the billowing clouds gathering in the sky. Kenan wanted to have her, to savor her blood and lose himself in the sweet caress of her womanhood. Instead, he stood. "Be careful," he whispered, "you walk too closely to the edge of the cliffs." He strode away and did not look back.

Two days later, Kenan rode with Domenico into Rome, where they went directly to the Vatican. A solemn-faced man wearing a knee-length priest's dress and britches greeted them. He led the two vampires across the piazza to a large stone building. They entered, and continued on through a series of wide hallways, each decorated with elaborate frescoes on the walls and ceilings. Statues carved from marble stood guard along the way, until they entered a long narrow room where two shining suits of armor were positioned either side of a heavy wooden door. The priest turned and bowed his head to Domenico. He removed his sword. Kenan followed suit.

The priest reached for a large brass key attached to a cord around his waist, and slipped it into the lock. The door creaked open and they entered, leaving their swords by the door. A stone platform branched out onto a narrow walkway made of bricks that spiraled into a steep descent. Kenan looked over the edge to the void hundreds of feet below, and noted the drop in temperature, and the smell of mold that emanated from the cold rock walls.

When the path ended, the priest guided the two immortals along a narrow row of stones that framed a section of roughly hewn planks of wood. Strips of aged leather bound the boards together that sat in rusted hinges. This was a door, and by the aura of death seeping up through the cracks in the wooden planks, Kenan surmised this to be either an oubliette or a cell. Either one meant a slow and terrifying death for the occupant.

Beyond the oubliette stood an iron gate. The priest pushed down on the handle and the gate squeaked open. He ushered them inside and then pulled the gate shut. The click of the lock brought a sense of unease to Kenan. He turned to Domenico, whose face remained expressionless. "This place has been the epicenter of the true Catholic Church for centuries," Domenico said. "What lies above us, in the Vatican, is for humans. Only the Pope, and a few mortal allies are familiar with the immortal world, and our Holy Father. He walked up to a font built into a rock wall, paused for a moment, and then dipped a finger into the water, and made the sign of a cross. "*In nomine Patris, et Filii, et Spiritus Sancti.*" He stood for a moment with his eyes raised to heaven, and then stepped back. Kenan noted red blisters forming on the finger Domenico had dipped into the holy water. This act of mortification was done in gratitude to God. Domenico believed that sufferance guaranteed him entrance to heaven when his time on earth ceased to be. Kenan duplicated Domenico's actions, relishing in the pain the holy water gave to his vampire body.

They walked side by side along a dimly lit tunnel carved out of earth and rock. Domenico stayed silent and Kenan did likewise, although his mind was full of questions. They were headed somewhere deep below the Vatican, to an area open only to a select few. Every now and then, an archway formed another tunnel, and it seemed to Kenan that Domenico switched direction without hesitation, as if drawn by a magnet to a specific destination.

Kenan memorized the route, not realizing at the time the benefit of this simple act. When Domenico stopped abruptly at an archway blocked off by another gate, Kenan marked this spot on a map tucked away in his memory with other important facts. This door, unlike the others, was locked from the inside. Moments later, a priest, dressed in a black cassock and sash, opened the gate and directed them inside.

By the long coat the priest wore over his cassock, Kenan knew he held a position in higher education. But this priest was like no other Kenan had met before; he was a vampire, and he was ancient. His angular features and pallid skin resembled the marble busts of ancient Roman men. Tousled black locks and well-trimmed facial hair flecked with dashes of charcoal offset a pair of deep-set obsidian eyes.

The priest chuckled, and his tone sent a warning to Kenan, made more ominous when he found himself up against a wall with the priest's hands on either side of his face. "Yes, I am ancient," the priest said, "In our world of immortals, I am known as the Holy Father. And you must learn to do better at hiding your thoughts, young Kenan." He dropped his hands, but not before taking a deep inhale along Kenan's neck, and whispering in Kenan's ear. "I know your intentions."

Before Kenan could react, he found himself standing alone. He looked up, and saw the Holy Father was in deep conversation with Domenico on the other side of a vast library. He wondered if Domenico had heard the words the Holy Father had whispered to him. As soon as that thought entered his mind, the Holy Father turned to him, and while still talking to Domenico the word *no* echoed in Kenan's mind. It was the voice of the Holy Father.

With his curiosity aroused, Kenan thought of a question he wanted answered. *Did you know my father?*

*Yes, and he paid for his sins.*

Kenan dared not move. He had not been ready to hear this answer. The Holy Father continued, all the while conversing with Domenico. *He was a man of God and therefore sworn to celibacy. In my world, there is no room for deviation from the Holy vows. Men who wear garments of the Catholic Church know this.*

The Holy Father's words rang in Kenan's head. He was so close to finally knowing his father's name, yet another question tugged at him. *Who is Vinicio?* The moment the words left his thoughts, something clamped down on his mind. He stared at the two vampires. They looked angry. Domenico seemed ignorant to the silent conversation between the priest and himself.

The Holy Father relaxed his grip on Kenan's mind, and his next words slid into Kenan's thoughts in the form of a warning.

*Vinicio is the devil!*

Kenan remembered the seer's words: "You have the curse of Vinicio... *la maledizione del diavolo.*" It occurred to Kenan that during his silent communication with the Holy Father, he had missed Domenico's entire conversation. He glanced toward his maker and noted that he did not look happy. He appeared to lack the reverence for the Holy Father that he had when they'd first arrived. Domenico stormed toward the entrance, and Kenan knew that he must follow. He turned to the ancient priest, knelt on his right knee and gave the sign of the cross, and then hurried after his maker.

The gate to the underground tunnels flew open. Domenico fled up the spiral path, and waited impatiently for the door to be unlocked by the priest. The two vampires sheathed their swords, and Kenan strode briskly beside his maker, along the frescoed hallways to the open courtyard, where a member of the *Guardia Svizzera* stood with their horses.

Since returning from the Vatican, Domenico chose more often than not to be alone in his private underground quarters beneath the small villa he owned on the outskirts of Rome. This meant Kenan had fewer demands on his time, and he found himself straying further away, closer to the cliffs where he had first seen Ravinka. He waited for two days, hoping to see her. When she didn't show, Kenan rode into the village where they'd conversed, but there was no sign of her. Filled with disappointment, he decided to ride to Domenico's coastal villa a few miles south.

Kenan had never been emotionally drawn to anyone, and his continual thoughts of Ravinka confused him. In truth, he knew it would be impossible for anyone to ever love him. Ravinka had a gentleness that seeped from the pores of her skin, and, in retrospect, she was the opposite of him.

Kenan had not grown up near the ocean; he'd not even seen waves or sand until he had met Domenico. And so, on this day, without the shackles of his maker pulling at him, he released the reins and gave his horse unbridled freedom. As they approached the sandy road leading down to the beach, he saw in the distance a familiar figure sitting alone on the sand. He knew at once who it was.

He pulled up his horse and dismounted. Ravinka turned to him, and he saw tears in her eyes.

"Why are you crying?" Kenan asked.

Ravinka turned away, and shook her head. "You must leave this place," she said.

Kenan knelt beside her, and lifted a hand to her face. "I cannot leave," he said. "I have a master, it is complicated."

Ravinka touched the palm of a hand against his cheek. "Your skin may be cold," she said, "but I know there is still warmth somewhere deep in your heart." She kissed his palm.

Kenan's mind flooded with an unknown emotion. Ravinka looked up at him, and a smile broke through her tears. "This is love," she whispered.

He brought his lips to hers and fell into the abyss of insecurity that she called love. He had never kissed anyone so gently, and had never been kissed with such passion. Ravinka eased her body onto the sand, and Kenan lowered himself over her, aware of his strength and willing himself not to hurt her. Their tongues explored each other's mouths, tasting each other's passion, lost in the throes of love.

Kenan had never thought of kissing as a sacred experience, but Ravinka made it so. And when she was done tasting his mouth, she kissed his cheeks and forehead and down his neck. His fangs emerged, and he pushed himself up and lowered his head.

"I know what you are," Ravinka said. "I know that loving you is dangerous for me, but I had to see you again. Please, do not push me away, for then I will die of a broken heart."

He leaned forward, resting his hand on his knees. He forced himself to gain control, wanting desperately to calm his killer instinct. "I do not want to hurt you," he said, "but this is what I am. I want you completely. I want your heart, your body… and your blood." He gazed at her. "But more than this, I want to be loved. I am not good. I am a dangerous creature and I cannot love, for I have forgotten how that feels."

He felt the warmth of her hands on his back, and her lips moving up his neck. "You have my heart and you may have my body, but for you to have my love you must take my blood…but only a little, so that I may live to love you. Can you do this?"

He shook his head. "I cannot answer that question as I have never done this before."

"Have you ever spoken to a woman in this way before now?" Ravinka asked.

"Never."

"Then your will is stronger than you think," she said. "I made my decision to come back and wait for you, and I knew what you were the first time I saw you. I knew this would be dangerous, but my heart pushed me forward."

Kenan stared into her blue eyes. "Whenever I look at the ocean, I see your eyes."

"And whenever I look into the dark of night I see yours." Ravinka laid his weapons on the ground. She removed his jacket and boots, and then loosened the laces of his shirt, leaving a dusting of kisses over his muscular chest and taut stomach. Kenan undid the clasp of her cape, and watched it fall to the sand, revealing a dress of sheer white linen. Kenan pulled at the ribbons gathered beneath her breasts, and watched the fabric fall in a stream around her feet.

The sun dipped lower on the horizon, leaving a burst of pink and orange in its wake. Kenan's gaze took in the beauty of Ravinka's naked body. He removed his pants and drew her to the ground beneath him. He kissed her neck and shoulders, grazing her skin with his fangs. His fingers slid between her thighs and into her wetness while he trailed kisses over her belly.

A soft sigh escaped her mouth, and she arched her back. Kenan kissed her breasts and sucked each nipple. He increased the depth and speed of his fingers, and just before she climaxed he lifted her up and replaced his fingers with his erection.

He thrust in and out of her, and she wrapped her legs around his hips. As they climaxed, his fangs pierced the skin over her jugular vein. She drew in a breath and her body trembled in ecstasy. As her blood rushed into Kenan's mouth and down his throat, his mind blended with hers. At that moment, he broke away from her and stared into her blue eyes. She brought her lips to his, and her body writhed with pleasure as Kenan emptied himself within her. He realized then that Ravinka was love.

She fell asleep in his arms, and Kenan watched the stars in their myriad colors twinkle in a blanket of darkness. When she awoke, he told her his life story; most of it, anyway, for there seemed to be so much that he could not remember. Ravinka did not run, but chose to stay. When he asked her about herself, she said her family came from the north where they had lived for generations. She went on to explain that one night, she dreamed of a prince with pale skin. When she woke up, she set out to find him. She had almost given up hope, but found herself at the cliffs, where she often sought solace in the sky, ocean, and earth. That was the day she first saw Kenan.

Before the sun rose, Domenico summoned Kenan. He had no choice but to leave. He kissed Ravinka's lips, and her eyelids fluttered open. "You have to go," she said.

Kenan nodded. "I do not know when I can return," he said, "but wait for me at the cliffs. I will come for you."

# 38

## *Casa Della Pietra*

COCO HELD A hand out toward the painting she had just completed. As the pigments of paint drew to her fingertips, the image of an apartment building came alive. Pelayo, Christopher, and Alessandro stepped forward, followed by Coco. They emerged from a shadowed doorway, just off 5th Avenue, in Upper Manhattan.

Across the street, Coco saw the familiar steps leading up to the Metropolitan Museum of Art. Alessandro caught her elbow and guided her through the door that led to a private elevator. Coco noticed a replica of the Lady and the Rose, embedded into a brick arch above the doorway. This told her, this property was protected by the Allegiance.

Coco made sure the leather messenger bag she carried that contained Chantal's painting of Gabriel's study at *Casa della Pietra* was secure, as this was their means of returning to the fortress, once they had found Gabriel. An eight-inch Turkish jewel-encrusted knife and scabbard Gabriel had given her rested in her jacket pocket. She gently ran her fingers over the enameled surface, as if using it as a touchstone to help find him.

Alessandro slid a key into a lock, and the elevator ascended. When the door opened, Coco followed the others into a small glassed-in foyer that led into the top-floor penthouse apartment. They entered a spacious rectangular room, lit with a soft hue that glowed from three crystal chandeliers. At one end of the room was a grand fireplace with a carved wooden mantle, surrounded by two matching hand-carved loveseats. The opposite wall encased a floor-to-ceiling bookshelf graced with antique folios of classic literature.

Coco surveyed the room and then walked over to one of five windows. It was 2 a.m., and Central Park seemed like a deep abyss, outlined with the muted night lights of Manhattan's Upper West Side, shrouded by flurries of snow. Alessandro stood beside her. "Dad," Coco said. "Where would Gabriel go if he was injured?"

"I'm not sure," Alessandro answered, "but if he knew vampires escaped from the building, then he'd stay away from our safe-holds."

"Why?" Coco asked.

"Because he'd want Kenan to believe he's dead."

"You're his best friend," Coco said, "do you think he's dead?"

Alessandro shook his head. "At first I was unsure, and my mind was clouded with emotion."

"So where is he?" Coco asked.

"We're hoping you might know the answer to that question," Christopher said.

Coco turned to her brother. "But I don't know!"

"Gabriel wouldn't have left you without leaving a clue, that's how the Allegiance works, Coco," Christopher said. "Clues are never written down, they're spoken or represented by an object, something related to the interests of the receiver. You need to revisit the time you spent with Gabriel since he returned from New York."

Coco nodded and sat in a chair. She placed her elbows on her knees and rested her forehead on the palms of her hands.

A few minutes later, Sabine entered the room. Her black spandex suit was covered in a thin layer of dust, and a few splinters of debris were entangled in her hair. The handle of her swept-hilt rapier sword was splattered with dried blood. She sank into a chair, and took a moment to gather her thoughts. "Jason called," she said. "Jeremy found the names and last known addresses of the girls we rescued. I've wiped their memories, they won't remember anything since the moments before their abductions." She looked up at Alessandro. "I had envisioned that by this century societies would be above treating women like garbage. What Kenan is doing to these young girls stems from his inability to accept those who are different from him. He refuses to acknowledge social equality for women or anyone else who does not fit into his archaic form of Christianity. How many more of these houses does he have scattered around the world? How many young women, who choose not to accept religion—*his* religion— are to be tortured and killed by his league of pathetic disciples?"

Pelayo clasped her shoulder, and she reached up and placed a hand on his.

Christopher looked over at his father. "With Prudence and Stefan absent, and Gabriel missing, leadership of the Allegiance falls to you, Dad."

"Is that in accordance with Prudence's wishes?" Alessandro asked.

"Yes," Christopher said, "she had me sign a document requesting this prior to her leaving. I can only surmise she had a premonition that Gabriel would be…incapacitated."

Sabine turned to Alessandro. "Allow me to take my warriors and search out as many of Kenan's houses as we can. Rescuing the young girls will be my main cause, killing the vampires involved with their torture will be second. You have my word."

Alessandro stared at the floor for a moment. "You'll need to work closely with Jason and Jeremy. They've been following up on the information Ignacio gave them. But beware: By now Kenan, or at least his closest allies, must know that the Allegiance is aware of what they're doing. Chantal has put together a portfolio of the vampires she saw with Kenan during her captivity, ask her to text you what she has." He turned to Christopher. "What's the news from D.C.?"

"I need solid evidence to bring a case against the congressman," Christopher said. "We know he's been redirecting funds to certain Catholic schools for two years, and this coincides with girls missing in D.C. The question is, do we act now, or go to the Vatican and give the Holy Father a choice? Either he resolves this, or *we* do. Before she left, Prudence came to me and specifically requested Antonia mediate with Rome, as she has history with the Holy Father."

Alessandro was silent while he considered his options. "Contact Antonia, ask her to set up a meeting with our people in Vatican City. Have Frederico choose two other Allegiance members from Rome to accompany her. Sabine, have the girls returned safely to their homes, and have two of our female members keep watch over them." He stood and looked over at Coco.

She raised her head and he noted her red eyes. "I keep going over the conversations we had since Gabriel came here with Pelayo and Arianna, but nothing seems related to this situation," she said. Coco pulled the scabbard from her pocket. "He gave me this, but that was before he came here the first time."

Alessandro walked over to Coco and examined the scabbard. "The twin to this beauty is displayed across the street. It suits you," he said, and handed it back to her. "I want to take you to the site of the explosion. Perhaps Gabriel left something there for you to recognize."

# 39

*Italy, mid 1500s*

DOMENICO ORDERED KENAN to travel to Bologna and receive payment for services rendered. This meant he would be gone for weeks, so Kenan decided to use the time away to plan how he would kill his maker. The journey took him through the heart of Tuscany, and as such he chose to visit the location where he had been forced by his mother to bury his uncle.

The grave was difficult to find, but after clearing away the overgrowth, he found an area that seemed to be more prevalent with wild flowers. He remembered his uncle's deep love of nature, and mused that even in his death he would want to nurture all things. Kenan knelt on the ground and recalled how his mother had ordered him to dig his uncle's grave on unhallowed ground. She had looked so jubilant that night, when she rolled his body into the hole. He remembered the tears he had to hide, as he covered his uncle with dirt.

"I could not help you," Kenan whispered, "I was just a little boy."

It was then that Kenan's love for his mother turned to hatred and yet, in a cruel turn of events, he was bound to her. She had become ill shortly after, as if God had cursed her. His uncle had been the only person to speak to him in an endearing manner, and he could not understand why God took him away.

A breath of wind caught in the leaves of a nearby olive grove, and brought with it a familiar scent. Kenan reached for his sword, but when he looked around he saw nothing. The scent reminded him of his childhood, of days walking back from the city with his uncle, both laden with food donated from a member of his congregation. A ghost from his past had wandered over his uncle's grave. A shiver ran down his spine. Moments later, he was on his horse, choosing to ride around the city of his youth.

On the outskirts of Bologna, Kenan chose one of the many roads that led to the heart of the city. As he rode toward the university where he was to meet Domenico's contact, the sky darkened, bringing forth showers. Piles of manure mixed with the rain created sludge strewn over the stone alleys, and brought with it the stench of excrement and filth. Kenan guided his horse under the high porticos, grateful for the shelter they provided.

Domenico had given him instructions that included a stable where his horse would be attended. From here, Kenan made his way to the library, where tomorrow he would rendezvous with his contact and collect Domenico's payment. But before then, he needed to feed. He watched the throng of people leaving the building, and waited for his prey. He did not need to wait for long. He sensed his victim's depravity before he saw him.

The rain had ceased but left a heavy mist in its wake. Kenan followed the man to the poorest part of the city, where prostitutes with stained red lips, and bruised eyes lined with charcoal, stood on street corners while their children played nearby. Any other time he would have fed on these destitute whores, but he had no wish to be close to another woman since loving Ravinka.

The man he followed chose his victim whose belly was thick with child. Kenan could tell by the look of terror in her eyes that this man was no stranger. He grabbed her by the arm, and dragged her up a set of stairs. Kenan stood inside waiting for him. When he opened the door, Kenan caught his hand just before it made contact with the prostitute's face. She screamed, but quieted when she saw Kenan twist the man's arm behind his back. Kenan emptied out the man's pockets, tossed her the contents, and then slammed a knee into the man's back. His howl of pain ceased when Kenan's fist met his mouth. Kenan hoisted him over his shoulder and fled. The woman would never need to worry about him hitting her again.

The following afternoon, Kenan lingered outside the library. He had spent the morning gathering information about Domenico's client, a practice which had proved itself invaluable, should a client turn hostile, or try to cheat Domenico out of his payment. Kenan saw the man in question exit the main building. He wore the garments of an academic and was most likely a professor of sorts. Kenan sensed the man's unease as he nervously scanned the portico.

When Kenan stepped out in front of him, the professor froze. "I am here for Domenico," Kenan said, "and will return tomorrow to pick up his payment in full. Is that clear?"

The man nodded; the muscles in his neck corded and his fingers turned white as they tightened around the books he carried.

Kenan turned to leave, but stopped for a moment to deliver a message over his shoulder. "Your son looks so much like you."

The man's eyes widened and his chin trembled. Kenan's threat had been delivered and understood. "I will have your payment tomorrow," the man said.

"Until then." Kenan dipped his head and departed.

As a child, the only book Kenan ever read was the Bible. His mother did not encourage reading outside the tight web of religion, and scorned at her brother whenever he told young Kenan stories, even though they were cast from scriptures. It was not until he became a vampire that reading had become easier for him, like so many other traits, but also it was something he enjoyed. Specifically, he enjoyed reading about incidents he had lived through, and people he had known, like the man who saved him from starvation, Girolamo Savonarola.

This curiosity led him to the library at the University of Bologna. Here, he hoped to find a clue about Vinicio. He searched through books on the famous and infamous, religion and the sciences, but he found nothing. He decided to ask one of the humans for guidance. When he mentioned the name Vinicio or any paintings representing the devil, the old tutor shook his head and said he did not know of the name "Vinicio," but suggested Kenan go to the Basilica of San Petronio. There he would find the devil.

Kenan made his way across the Piazza Maggiore to the front of the

Basilica and entered. He was immediately struck by the sheer size of the building and the gothic arches that soared toward heaven in a maze of geometric shapes. He dipped his finger in the holy water, made the sign of the cross, and offered a silent prayer of thanks to God in gratitude for the burning pain of the mortification.

He stood still for a moment, and looked around the sacred space. Murmurs of priests chatting to one another, confessions from the guilty, and whispered prayers of worshippers filled his head. The late afternoon light filtered in through numerous round windows and stained glass, throwing a kaleidoscope of colors and shapes over the interior. Tiles arranged in mosaic designs decorated the floor of this vast building, and accented the apricot color that trimmed the arches.

He skirted past the small chapels that lined the longer walls, stopping at the Chapel of the Magi with its colorful arched windows and carved railings and gate. In here, the old tutor had said, look to your left and you will see the devil. Kenan stared at the wall, and although the fresco depicted multiple perspectives of life, it was the image of hell that caught his attention. The painting had been created by Giovanni da Modena and depicted Dante's *Inferno*. The devil had been portrayed as a hairy creature, devouring a man in his mouth, while giving birth to another.

Around the image of the devil were men and women being tortured, some were hanging upside down, and others were laid out on rocks. Strange horned animals with wings, oversized rats, and snakes seemed to be carrying out punishments. Some faces showed signs of pleasure while participating in acts of debauchery. A few of the souls seemed to be mirror images of each other but showed different facial expressions; some looked to be welcoming the pain inflicted on them, while others seemed terrified and appalled at the entirety of the scene.

"So, the devil eats his prey and then gives birth to new men…" Kenan whispered, "and I am one of Domenico's children." He walked close to the painting and whispered through gritted teeth. "No more, enough." Kenan strode out of the basilica.

The following afternoon he met up with the professor, who handed over his payment to Kenan without any fuss. With his business complete,

Kenan rode away from Bologna. He stopped at a creek a few miles out of town to let his horse drink.

He heard his attackers before he saw them, and waited until they were close before he lunged at the one nearest, leaving him with a broken neck. Kenan spun around to face his next victim, but five human men surrounded him. Three went down quickly, but the other two men flung silver-tipped knives at his chest and back. The pain slowed him down, but not before he killed one more. He sprung up from the ground and lunged at another attacker, but a blade entered his shoulder. He staggered forward and dropped to the ground.

Ravinka's face flashed in his mind, and he used the last of his strength to yank the knife from his back and throw it at his next victim. But when the man was just a few feet away, a look of horror flooded his face. He dropped his sword, and fell face-forward to the ground. In his back stood an arrow that had pierced through to the man's heart.

Kenan looked up, and in the distance he saw the figure of a woman dressed in a long dark cloak, standing on a hilltop looking down at him. As she turned to leave, a lock of red hair escaped her hood, and blew in the wind. The figure disappeared before Kenan could speak. He had lost a substantial amount of blood due to the multiple stab wounds, so he dragged himself over to the nearest victim and plunged his fangs into his neck. He repeated this three more times, and then mounted his horse and rode toward Florence.

Thirteen hours later, Kenan came upon a small town. His horse needed rest, and so he found a stable, and then went in search of a witch he had heard lived in these parts. In the forest, he picked up a scent similar to that of a seer, and tracked her movements to the entrance of a cave. He crouched down and crawled through the entrance.

The crackling voice of an old woman spoke to him in the darkness. "I have been waiting for you, vam*pir*," she said.

Kenan stood in the semi-darkness. A fire burned in the center of the cave, its smoke drawn upward to a small crack in the roof above. An aged woman stepped out of the shadows. Her face, wrinkled and sagged, was framed with a hood that she pushed back to reveal a bird's nest of silver hair. Her eyes were entirely white, as if she were blind. Her fingers were long and tipped with perfectly manicured fingernails.

"What do you know of me?" Kenan asked.

"I know many things," she said. Her croaky voice cut through the air. "You wish to kill your maker, do you not?"

"I want to know how to kill another vam*pir*," Kenan replied. "One much stronger than I. Can you help me?"

The witch beckoned him closer. "Come nearer," she said. "Perhaps it would be best to ask, '*Will* I help you?' don't you think?"

Kenan took a few steps closer to her. "*Will* you help me?"

Suddenly the witch stood directly in front of him, although Kenan did not see her move. "Are you sure this is what you want?" she asked.

Although her eyes lacked pupils, Kenan knew that the intensity of her stare went beyond his own eyes, and into his soul. "Yes," he said. "This is what I want."

The witch broke her stare. "I shall help you, but the potion I will make cannot be changed. It will be a spell made especially for you, and can be used only once." Kenan watched as she hobbled over to a bench and started opening numerous jars and measuring out ingredients. A thought crossed his mind that she looked as if she were making supper. The vision seemed almost comical.

The witch chuckled. "It *is* something like making supper," she said. "You must learn to guard your thoughts, young vam*pir*, for it is not only your maker who hears them."

He walked over to the bench. "You can hear my thoughts?"

The witch ignored his words, seemingly immersed in her work. "Almost done," she said. "Hand me the dead mouse. You will find him on the floor by the entrance."

Kenan walked over to the entrance and raised his eyebrows when he saw a dead mouse. He picked it up by the tail, delivered it to the witch, and watched as she plucked a single hair from its coat and put it into the bowl with the rest of the ingredients. Then, without looking, she tossed the rodent over her shoulder and into the fire. Kenan couldn't help but chuckle. The witch turned on him. "You should not laugh at the mouse," she said. "He gave up his life for you. Animals do this often without ever receiving thanks from humans and other creatures." She returned to her work. "Sit by the fire and tell me why you want to kill your maker."

Kenan walked over to the fire, and leaned against a rock. "I have found a woman," he said.

Flames shot up from the fire. "It is strange that it takes meeting a good person before a bad person, like yourself, chooses to change," the witch said.

"I was not always wretched," Kenan said, staring into the fire. "But yes, I have done terrible deeds that I am not proud of. My life has been about survival. Is that such a bad thing?"

The witch brought the bowl and a large wooden spoon over to where Kenan sat. She eased herself onto a rock. "The situation is irrelevant," she said. "It is what you do in your life that matters. But soon, that will all be behind you, and you shall be free of the burdens your maker holds over you." She held the bowl and Kenan watched the spoon stir the ingredients without the help of the witch.

"How do I administer the potion?" Kenan asked.

"You shall dip your blade into it," she said, "and then stab your maker. Only then will you kill this vam*pir* of yours. But you only get one chance, so you must aim for his heart. If you miss, then you will die. Do you understand, young Kenan?"

He looked at her, somewhat startled. "You know my name?"

"Of course I know your name," she said, "I am a witch!" The spoon stopped its motion and the witch sniffed the contents of the bowl, before rising to place it in front of Kenan on the dirt floor.

Kenan pulled out his knife and dipped the tip of the blade into the potion. A current of energy raced up the blade and handle, throwing him across the cave. "Ah, yes," the witch said. "This is a good brew." She looked at the knife, standing upright in the bowl. "Pull it out now, I think it is done."

Kenan brushed himself off and walked over to the bowl. He gazed at the witch, who now had a small leather-bound notebook and a piece of coal in her hands. She peered over the top of the book at him. "Well, go on then," she said, "pull it out, it will not bite…*much*."

Kenan yanked out the blade. It looked no different.

"Of course it still looks the same," the witch said. "Now, come here, and I will cast a spell over the blade so your maker does not get a whiff of his impending demise." She chuckled to herself.

Kenan did as he was told, and listened to the witch as she whispered words he did not understand over his knife.

"What do I owe you?" Kenan asked.

The witch stared up at him. "Three drops of your blood."

"My blood?"

"You do not get to ask me any more questions." The witch walked over to the workbench, and picked up a small glass vial. She took out the stopper, picked up a small knife, and placed the vial under Kenan's wrist. He took the knife and used it to slice his skin, then turned his arm over and counted out three drops of blood as they fell into the vial. The witch's mouth broke into an unnerving smile. "You do know that for a vam*pir* to kill another in anything other than war or self-defense, is considered an offense?"

Kenan returned his knife to its sheath. "Yes, I know this," he said, "I consider every moment of my life a prisoner of my maker. His death will be seen as an act of self-defense. You need not be concerned about me."

The witch nodded. Kenan noted that she had tucked the vial somewhere in the layers of clothing that covered her body. He turned to leave. "Thank you," he said.

"Farewell, young Kenan," she said. "Remember, you only get one chance." The witch's words lay hidden in the place in Kenan's mind next to the memory of Ravinka.

O

Domenico's temper flared when Kenan retold the story of the men who had abducted him on the outskirts of Bologna. He took the satchel from Kenan, tipped it upside down, and counted out each coin. When he was done, he tossed Kenan a few of them. Kenan stared at the coins sitting in the palm of his hand. "Is this all I get for the work I have done for you?" he asked.

Domenico's nostrils flared as he sneered at Kenan. "Do you think you are worth more?" he asked. When Kenan didn't answer, he threw the satchel on the table, and turned to face Kenan. "Answer me!"

Kenan stood firm. "Yes, I do think I am worthy of more money," he said. He knew that he would need to rile Domenico, and then make his move. "I cannot build up my own cache if you do not pay me!" The slight stench of sulfur wafted from Domenico's body. Kenan had to attack him before he changed completely. He played into the game. "I am sorry," Kenan said, "I have no right to complain." He hung his head like a helpless puppy.

Domenico ran a hand over Kenan's head, and down the side of his neck. "I give you what you deserve," Domenico said, "but tonight perhaps I will give you a little more." He slapped Kenan hard across the face, and threw him to the floor. Before Kenan could do anything, Domenico was taking him from behind, thrusting deeply. Kenan ignored the pain, just as he always did. At the height of Domenico's orgasm, Kenan pushed back with all his strength. This caught Domenico off guard, and at that moment Kenan turned and thrust his blade into his maker's heart.

Domenico's eyes bulged in surprise, and then he began to laugh. Kenan held Domenico by his shoulders and shook him. "Why do you laugh in the face of death?"

Domenico smiled at Kenan. "You went to the witch, didn't you? We all do at some time or another."

Kenan grabbed Domenico's collar and yanked him forward. "What are you talking about? Tell me!"

"I used to be like you," Domenico said, "and like the one before me, I went to the old witch. I dipped my blade into the potion she made. I killed my maker too. But you see, by killing me, I am free. Now you will become the devil. Vinicio was the first to be claimed..." Domenico choked on blood. "The devil took him on the sands of the beach at Lazio."

Kenan's body trembled with anger. "You lie!"

Domenico was fading fast, and as he did, his face and body changed into human form. His skin was flush with color and his eyes shone green. "Read the diaries...they are here," he whispered.

Kenan looked at his own hands, something was happening to him. He jumped up. "No! I do not want this, I want to be free..." He fell to the ground writhing in agony. Sulfur filled his nostrils. His fingers were lengthening and his nails were becoming twisted and yellowed. "Please, no!" he begged. Kenan reached out to Domenico but all that was left of his body was dust. Unable to resist the inevitable, Kenan gave in to the pain as it took over his body, mind, and soul.

○

Ravinka stood at the edge of the cliffs. She stared out at the white-capped waves rising across the ocean, and watched as they gained momentum and crashed against the jagged rocks below. The strength of the ocean reminded her of the pale one she had fallen in love with. Both had the violent capability of taking away life.

She had known all along that eventually Kenan would break her heart; she had foreseen it. And even now, after a year of waiting at the cliffs every day, hoping for him to come to her as they had planned and escaping to another place, in truth, she knew their love was not to be. He would not come to her, not now. She would return to her homeland, pick up the pieces of her broken heart, and somehow meld it back together.

Thoughts of leaving this place, where the sunlight reached across the land for more than just a few hours each day, giving sweet fruits full of juice, and market stalls filled with bright flowers, made her sad. "What a fool I have become...a lovesick fool. Full of the melancholia of doomed love."

She wandered further along the cliffs, hoping for a miracle she knew could not be. Tears swam in her eyes and fell in rivulets of sadness over her cheeks. The last piece of hope for Kenan to return to her had shattered. She wiped her tears aside with the palms of her hands, and then turned away. But the wind called her name and she stumbled. Grief clotted her thoughts. She stood, took one step, and another, but the cruel wind caught hold of the hem of her cape. Tendrils of air snarled around her, pulling her this way and that.

"Kenan," she cried.

She knew then that the wind had heard her, because for a single, short moment there was silence, and she wondered if her cries had awakened her lover. But the moment passed and her sadness deepened. The wind blew by her one last time, and Ravinka's body fell. She heard the sea roar, as if angry with the wind. And then all became silent.

Ravinka lay on the jagged rocks. Her tears mixed with the saltwater. A large wave crashed over her shattered body, and carried her gently to the depths of tranquility. She heard the ocean speak to her: *You are home, my beautiful black-haired raven. You are home.*

Kenan forced himself out of a nightmare, where wind howled and Ravinka called out to him. She was falling, but he could not move to help her, his body wracked with pain and his mind spinning in a whirlpool of emotion. A glove of hatred had reached into his body, and yanked out every last morsel of goodness from his soul.

Ravinka was falling...

He called out to her, but all he sensed was a cold and empty silence.

As if the hatred wished to torture him, it left one small wisp of a memory of Ravinka's love for him floating in his mind. She held a kitten against her face. Her gaze met Kenan's, and then the darkness fell. The memory was lost.

Gradually, Kenan grew into his new frame. The day he awoke, his body was exponentially stronger, his mind more alert but tinged with a darkness that reeked with hatred. He looked around, and recognized at once that he was in Domenico's underground chamber. A memory rose... he had fought his maker, wanting only his freedom, so he could...

He inhaled, hoping to catch a plume of a forgotten memory. Why did freedom seem so important? Freedom from what...?

As thoughts rushed to the forefront of his mind, he remembered three things...

A blade.

A witch.

And a curse.

# 40

*Svalbard Islands, Arctic Ocean*

THE WIND WHISTLED as it ripped around a tall turret jutting up from the ocean. Waves smashed onto the ancient rocks beneath the fortified castle, which for eons had served as Freyja's bastion. Hidden behind a mass of swirling clouds stood looming cliffs. And at the northern side of the island, a long jetty reached out past the breaking swells, to the unforgiving waters of the River Styx that melded with the Arctic Ocean. Within the fortified walls of the turret, the flame of a single candle flickered. A woman sat beside a vampire, catching snippets of his dreams and patching the fragments of his life together.

Freyja twisted a lock of Kenan's ebony hair around her fingers. The soft sensation calmed her, and allowed her to concentrate. Her plan had worked. When Prudence had first seen Louisa's dead body, she had recognized Freyja's scent on the woman's skin. Knowing that she could not enter the dark realm without the help of her father, Prudence had sought out her parents to help her find the fragile human's soul.

Freyja's dreams often took her to a cliff face, where she could smell the salt air as waves crashed onto rocks below. When she awoke, her breath came in short gasps, her eyes appeared red and puffy, and a tightness grabbed hold of her chest. She wondered if this dream was related to a bargain she had made with Hakon over a thousand years ago.

Freyja first heard of Kenan when he had kidnapped the Creative, Chantal, from under the Allegiance's protection. She had watched him from afar, like a voyeur, waiting to introduce herself until Kenan was out of his depth and in need of her services. Had Freyja not entered Kenan's life when she did, Alessandro would have found his hiding place in the north and slaughtered Kenan upon sight. She knew of the perils attached to playing with an immortal like Kenan, whose thirst for life solely revolved around revenge, greed, and power. But after all, she smiled, was this not a reflection of her own manner of late?

She wondered if Kenan's thirst for revenge against the Allegiance stemmed from his maker, Domenico. For at times, when the horrors of Kenan's youth slithered from his dreams, Freyja had caught threads of images. She had witnessed the pivotal night in Florence when Savonarola ordered the Bonfire of the Vanities, and the moment when young Kenan encountered the vision of *his angel* appear between two flames. The angel, he would later discover, was Prudence, head of the Allegiance, and protector of everything he despised.

Freyja did not comprehend the hatred Kenan held in his heart toward Creatives and the Allegiance, and his malice for women reminded her of the evil human men of the dark years. The somber times, when the unrestrained power of kings and queens turned the story of a carpenter's son into a thriving religious business, and killed those who did not bow to their commands.

The mag*ik* Freyja had shared with her earthbound sisters for centuries—the healing potions, ceremonies to awaken the earth, and the rituals for childbirth—became slander, until gradually the wisdom of the feminine, once honored as the mother of the earth, was cruelly beaten down.

The lock of hair fell from Freyja's fingers. "Men were consumed with the need for power, many still are. I lost many beloved sisters to the cruelty of men." She gazed upon Kenan's sleeping face. "And you, once an innocent little boy, dragged unknowingly into the cesspool of greed, have become one such man. What happened to make you full of such evil?" Freyja whispered. She leaned in close to Kenan's lips. "And am I no better?"

Kenan stirred.

The wind screeched.

Hakon was near.

Freyja rose, and sprinkled strands of sleeping magic over Kenan's inanimate body, and left the room. She stood atop a landing where a spiral staircase led deep underground. She picked up two black kittens that had followed her from Kenan's room, and then began the descent. She did not stop until she reached the solid floor hundreds of feet below her castle. She placed the kittens on the ground, and they affectionately circled her ankle, their paws leaving tiny imprints on the dirt floor.

The air was icy cold. Roots from ancient trees twisted together and formed a towering archway through the rock. Freyja made her way to the end of the tunnel and stared at the image before her. An area of limestone framed the figure of a woman. Her eyes were closed, but the slight curve of her red lips showed she had been captured in a moment of bliss. Her long dark hair caressed her pale face and draped over her shoulders and around her body.

"Your lover is close," Freyja whispered. "I sense his need for you. Strange that he does not carry anger, but rather an emotion I am not able to put into words." She ran a hand through Louisa's hair, over her breasts, her belly, and her mound of femininity, and then brushed her fingers over her lips. "Please understand my reason for stealing you. I believe something of mine was once stolen, and you are the key to restoring what is mine." Freyja kissed her, gently. "You are Hypatia, Boudica, and Botticelli's beloved, and the thousands of innocent women who died at the hands of men fueled by fear. You must be strong, Louisa, for there is a price you must pay for your life."

Freyja picked up the kittens and cradled them in her arms. "I shall return shortly," she said, "for your people are close and I must tend to Kenan. He is close to rising, and it would not be good for your mother if he was to awaken at this time." A gust of wind whirled around her body, and the fluttering of feathers filled the air. Freyja took flight, and her black wings brought her to rest at the landing that led to her quarters.

# 41

## *Realm of the Dead, Svalbard Islands, Arctic Ocean*

WITH HAKON IN the lead, the group of immortals continued their journey. The deeper they went into the cave, the temperature dropped, and the earthen floor grew colder beneath their feet. The tunnel they were following opened up to a platform with a spiral staircase, which twisted downward into a somber abyss. A dome-like ceiling rose two hundred feet above, and mournful cries of damned spirits echoed in the chamber. One by one, the immortals descended the staircase, deeper into Freyja's realm of the dead.

Prudence noted anxiety building in and around Caprecia. She was a young vampire, and her twenty-eight years of living under Kenan's rule and captivity had not given her enough experience to control her emotions in chaotic environments. To Prudence, the air around Caprecia seemed to prickle, like static electricity. She hoped Kenan was not near.

The stairs ended, and another tunnel stood before them. They walked in silence, until the tunnel opened up to reveal a pool of slate-gray water with a narrow ledge along one side. The area resembled an abandoned underground railway, and beams of blue light, shaped in the form of human arms, could be seen emerging intermittently from the water. Hakon stepped onto the ledge. "These souls cannot be saved," he said. "We have entered the Hall of Contemplation."

Ignacio stared across the water, and then turned to Hakon. "How is it that you know this place?"

"I was once the prince of my kind; the fae," Hakon answered," but a few millennia have passed since that time, and we have lost many. When the earth cried out in pain from abuses hurled at her by mankind, the fae were also in peril, and were forced into hiding. Like humans, we depend upon nature, but the difference between us is that *we* have always lived in harmony with the Great Mother."

Ignacio frowned. "Why did your kind not ask others for help?"

"We did," Hakon replied. He looked out over the vast area before him. "Do not allow your thoughts to be drawn into the tragic deaths these souls experienced. It is best not to look into the water. Focus on each step you take, that is all."

They moved forward in silence. As soon as her feet touched the ledge, Prudence sensed the sadness of the souls who floated there beside her. Tendrils of pain, guilt, and lost hope beckoned to her, clinging to her dress, and inching up her body to her shoulders. She wanted to push them away but their shrill calls of desperation tore at her heart.

"Prudence…"

A voice called to her.

"Prudence!"

Her father's voice rang in her mind. The tendrils of despair descended down her dress, and she gasped when she realized Hakon had sensed her being drawn toward the dead. She shivered, and focused on the moment with pure intention until she knew for certain the creatures had slid back into the water.

As they approached the end of the tunnel, the water subsided, and they stepped onto a path of sand. The tunnel tapered off into a hallway of sorts, where tree roots twisted down the walls on either side. Curtains of filament fell from above, and shimmered in light that radiated from candles embedded into rocks. Every so often, faces, frozen in moments of pain, emerged from the walls, their expressions twisted and elongated. The contorted visages sunk back into the rocks, retreating to their personal asylums of insanity.

At the end of the passageway stood a thick wall of limestone.

"Louisa is behind this wall," Hakon said.

Prudence felt Caprecia's hand. "We must be wary," she said. Caprecia nodded.

Hakon placed a palm on the limestone, and the wall slowly receded into the sides of the tunnel. A shaft of blue light revealed Louisa, standing like Venus, her dark hair wrapped around her body, her eyes closed, a slight curve to her lips.

Ignacio looked to Hakon for approval to move forward, and when he nodded, the Englishman approached his beloved. Ignacio removed his long coat and wrapped it around Louisa's body while Caprecia held on to her daughter.

"Dearest Louisa," Caprecia whispered. "I love you with all my heart."

The flapping of wings broke the eerie silence, and the figure of Freyja stepped out of the shadows. "Leaving so soon?" she asked. "Did you really think I would allow you to take your human without payment?"

Hakon stepped forward. "What payment do you require?"

Freyja circled around the group and then faced Hakon. "Do not play games with me," she said, her voice drenched in contempt. "I want what is mine, what you stole from me centuries ago. Give me the memory!"

Hakon stared at her. "There is a reason I took the memory away from you," he said. "I was not sure your heart could bear such pain."

Freyja reached for Sonja, but Hakon was too quick for her. Stefan, Hakon, and Ignacio shielded the women. Freyja chuckled. "Such devotion, such humanity," she said. "What makes you think Louisa will be able to live as a human once her soul is returned to her body?" She shifted her gaze to Ignacio. "Once she leaves my realm, she will have one day and one night to live in her human form." Her face drew closer to Ignacio's. "After that, the only life she can have is that of a vam*pir*."

Ignacio's anger flared, the psionic energy invading the cool air. He reached for his dagger, but it flew across the floor before his fingers even touched the grip. Freyja stepped back and laughed. Prudence noted Stefan's hand on Ignacio's arm.

"Why did you do that to her?" Hakon asked.

"I took her soul moments before her death," Freyja said. "I saved her. In order for her to live, she will need Ignacio's blood. Without it, and away from my realm, she will die."

"Does Kenan know you saved Louisa?" Stefan asked.

Freyja's expression did not waver. "No," she said. "Like you, Stefan, I am a negotiator. I choose to fight only when necessary." Her gaze returned to Hakon. "I am waiting."

"I will return the memory to you," Hakon said, "but understand that once you have it, I cannot take it back. I only ask that you allow the others to leave safely."

"Agreed," Freyja said, and gestured dismissively toward the Hall of Contemplation. "Go!"

Prudence saw Sonja step forward, but Hakon gently pulled her back to him. "I will meet you at Charon's boat," he said.

Sonja shook her head. "No, my love…please let me stay here with you." She fell into his arms.

"You must look after our daughter," he said.

Prudence noticed Sonja and Hakon stare into each other's eyes, and sensed they whispered silent words to each other before they parted. Stefan reached for her arm and kissed her forehead. "We must trust and respect your father's wishes," he said.

Prudence laid a hand over his heart, and then withdrew. She approached Caprecia. "Perhaps it would be best if Ignacio carried Louisa," she said.

Caprecia nodded, and Ignacio lifted Louisa into his arms. When they were ready, Sonja and Prudence guided the others back along the tunnel. Prudence turned and saw Hakon place his palm against Freyja's forehead. A tiny thread of light appeared above his head, ran down the length of his arm, and disappeared into Freyja's forehead. Prudence whispered to Ignacio, "Whatever happens, you must continue forward and look after Louisa. Follow Sonja."

Ignacio frowned, and looked at Stefan. The Serbian's face was blank, but his hand rested on the hilt of his sword. Sonja proceeded along the sandy footpath, Ignacio followed along with Prudence, Caprecia, and Stefan.

Suddenly, Caprecia clutched her stomach, and shrieked in pain.

"Kenan must be near," Prudence said.

Stefan turned to Ignacio. "Go on ahead," he said. "Prudence and Sonja will lead you out of here. We will meet again at the jetty."

Caprecia looked up at Ignacio. "Keep her safe," she said through tears.

"You have my word, Caprecia," Ignacio said.

With a final look at Stefan, Prudence turned and led the others back the way they had come.

42

### Casa della Pietra

ARIANNA HAD FALLEN asleep in a comfy chair in the main kitchen. In her hands rested one of Katja's diaries, and the particular page she had been reading referred to the day Elion had given the carved wooden box to her as a gift. In her writing, Katja had explained that he had bequeathed the box to their daughter. Arianna stirred and opened her eyes. She heard a woman calling out to her.

*Arianna...*

Arianna's hands tightened around the diary, and she sat up. The voice called to her again, this time from beyond the kitchen. She stood and followed the voice, up the staircase and along the hallway to her suite. The door opened before she arrived, and for a moment she wondered if she was dreaming. Without hesitating, she entered, just in time to see the carved box Katja had given to her fall from the coffee table and onto the floor. She knelt and noticed that the box had fallen so that the underside was facing up.

She had an urge to run her fingers across the wood, and as she did, she touched a small indentation. She placed the box in her lap and again ran a finger over the wood, pausing for a moment. Once more, she heard the woman's voice call to her. Without thinking why, Arianna whispered her own name.

A clicking sound made her withdraw her hand, and as she did, a small drawer emerged from the wood. Nestled inside sat a tiny key. She put her hand under the drawer and tapped the underside. The key popped out and landed in her palm. She stared at the trinket, wondering what it opened.

Layla awoke from a nap, hearing her name being whispered. She sat up, and a flutter of the life inside her caused her to instinctively rest her hands upon her belly. She stood and listened as the familiar voice repeated her name, but this time it seemed to be resonating from the hallway. She opened the door and walked toward the voice as it called to her, leading her to Arianna's suite. She tapped her knuckles on the opened door and looked inside.

Arianna gazed back at Layla. "Did you hear a woman's voice too?" she asked. "Are we dreaming?"

Layla shook her head, entered the room, and sat on the floor next to Arianna. "No," she said. "This is not a dream. What did she say to you?"

"Just my name...she kept calling out to me," Arianna said, and explained the circumstances that led to her holding the tiny key.

Layla ran a hand over Arianna's hair, and smiled. "I think you may have inherited your father's genes," she said. "I know the woman's voice well, but not all can hear her."

Arianna looked down at the key. "So, what does this all mean?"

"That's a question for my mother," Layla said. She brought her hands to her belly as another flutter made her smile.

Arianna stared at Layla for a moment, and then a smile brushed over her face. "You're having a girl," she said.

Layla grinned. "Yes, but you, me, and my mother are the only ones who know, so keep her a secret."

"But how can I possibly know this?"

"Because my baby shares the same DNA that I have from my mother," Layla said. "Just as your biological father gave to you. The first night you were here, I woke up and heard a woman calling your name. I wondered what it meant, and now I know."

Arianna looked at the key. "What do you think this opens?"

"My guess is that it may have something to do with Callot's fairy statue," Layla said. "We'd best wait for Prudence to return, and perhaps my mother."

"Okay," Arianna said. "Have I met your mother?"

"No, and you'd remember her if you had," Layla said. "Her name is Antonia."

"Life's weird, isn't it?"

Layla nodded. "Yes, and it can be glorious."

# 43

## *Upper Manhattan*

THE STREET HAD been cordoned off. Neighbors stood behind yellow tape, their pajamas barely hidden under bulky jackets. Police cars and SUVs with darkened windows were parked randomly next to fire engines. Christopher pulled out his phone and sent off a text. Moments later, two men in dark suits walked up to him. One lifted the yellow tape and Alessandro, Coco, Sabine, Pelayo, and Christopher ducked under.

The two men led the group past parked vehicles to a set of heavy black metal gates. One of the men unlocked the gate and ushered the group through. When Coco looked back, both men had disappeared into the shadows. Pelayo placed a hand on her back and encouraged her forward. The short lane led to an underground parking garage. Sabine put an arm around Coco, and Alessandro did the same to Christopher. Using their vampire strength and agility, they easily leapt up three floors. Seconds later, they landed on the roof next to what was left of the destroyed brownstone where Sabine had last seen Gabriel.

Alessandro held onto Coco and guided her toward the edge of the roof. She peered down into the wreckage, and wished desperately that Gabriel were there to take away her concerns. She closed her eyes and blocked out the voices from the police radios drifting upward through the snow. The air around her pulsed with energy, but she pushed through until she found what she was searching for. The slither of silver thread that she'd seen back at *Casa della Pietra* glimmered in the distance. Coco welcomed the silence, and in her mind she walked toward the thread, but with every step she took, it floated away, as if guiding her somewhere.

She stood in the small studio off of Gabriel's bedroom. On the easel sat the painting she'd done months before: a female cloaked in a shadowed background, her eyes closed—and a man in the foreground poised in a defensive stance. The man, she now knew, was Gabriel. A hand rested on her shoulder, and she turned to see an image of the Lady and the Rose.

*"This painting will guide you to your beloved,"* the Lady said.

Coco nodded, and stepped closer to the painting. She raised a hand and pigments of paint lifted from the canvas and hovered at her fingertips, giving her access to a new and unfamiliar image.

*She walked beside a rusted iron fence, the top edged with waves of barbed wire. Behind the fence stood a church, neglected by time and disinterest. Coco approached a closed gate fastened with a large padlock. A second later she stood on the other side. She walked past the unloved building, its only sign of humanity beyond decay was a graffitti'd wall and boarded-up doors.*

*She followed a path where weeds grew through cracks in the broken cement, and then stepped through a gap in a low fence that bordered the path. Tall weeds brushed against her, a reminder that she was in a forgotten place. She looked up and noticed a woman leaning on a bench, crying. Coco approached, and as she neared the woman, her tears quieted.*

*When Coco reached her, she realized the woman was, in fact, a statue. She knew this image, she'd seen this woman painted many times, and Gabriel had said he would take her to the Uffizi Museum in Florence to see the statues exhibited there. This crying woman represented Niobe, a mother from Greek mythology, whose children were slaughtered by Artemis and Apollo. One daughter was spared, and became known as Chloris, the pale one...*

*A woman's breathy voice whispered to Coco: "Look at this life—all mystery and magic."*

Coco opened her eyes and realized she was no longer standing at the edge of the rooftop, but instead faced Central Park. She turned to Alessandro. "I saw a dilapidated church, with a fence and locks...and a woman's voice said: *'Look at this life—all mystery and magic.'* Does this make sense?"

Alessandro stared off into the distance, his furrowed brow caught deep in thought. "I know where he is."

"Is he close?" Coco asked.

"Yes," Alessandro replied. "That quote is one of Gabriel's favorites, and the one who said it is buried close by."

"Who?"

Alessandro placed an arm around Coco's waist. "Harry Houdini," he said, and leapt into the air.

O

They landed in an abandoned graveyard. Coco knew this place from her painting. She found the familiar path and sprinted off with the others behind her, not stopping until she stood a few feet away from the entrance to the Houdini family gravesite. A sudden wave of what could only be love struck her, as she stepped inside the bordered area.

The mist that hovered over the entire cemetery became a dense fog. She walked between gray headstones barely visible under ridges of snow, and past a planter filled with the remains of long-forgotten flowers. A rush of wind pushed past her, catching her in its wake as if guiding her forward.

She stopped at the foot of three steps that led to a granite exedra: a curved high wall surrounding a stone bench. Weather-beaten vines of ivy crept up from the earth and twisted their way over the wall. Poised on the ground in a sitting position, and leaning against the bench, was a statue of a weeping woman frozen in a moment of grief. A withered pink rose lay on the bench next to her, but it was the body resting beside the rose that caused Coco to cry out in horror, for she knew it was Gabriel.

Raw flesh glistened between patches of charred skin. Blood seeped from a wide and jagged gash across his chest and abdomen. Shreds of clothing melded into skin, and a bone protruded from his right thigh where fragments of metal lay embedded in his side. What was left of his hair was singed, his eyes were closed, and his entire face appeared bruised and bloodied. Coco noticed his right hand rested at the base of his throat.

In a flash, Sabine stood over Gabriel. She cut open a vein in her wrist and held it over what resembled his mouth. "We need to get him back to the fortress. Now!"

Coco's body trembled. She wanted to go to Gabriel but couldn't move. Christopher grabbed the painting from her bag and laid it on the ground. "We need you, Coco," he said. "Gabriel needs you. Coco!"

Coco snapped herself out of the shock. Alessandro stepped up to the exedra and picked up Gabriel's body as if he was picking up a newborn child.

"My blood will hold him until we get him home," Sabine said.

Coco lifted a hand toward the painting of Gabriel's study at *Casa della Pietra*. The pigments of paint lifted, and Sabine and Alessandro stepped through. Christopher grabbed Coco's other hand, and followed Pelayo. Coco looked back at the statue of the weeping lady, who once again became animated. She lifted her head and smiled at Coco. Petals swirled around the woman, and Coco recognized the scent of roses in the air, before she felt a tug on her hand and fell into the painting.

# 44

PRUDENCE GUIDED SONJA and Ignacio past the Hall of Contemplation and up the spiral staircase. Every so often, she looked back at Louisa, who lay still in Ignacio's arms. She thought of the choice the young woman would have to make upon her awakening, to either live as a vam*pir* or die. Prudence's heart ached for her own son whom she knew was fighting for his life, but it was another image she had seen that broke her heart and urged her forward.

At the top of the spiral staircase, Prudence paused and spoke to Ignacio. "We will not think less of you if you need to rest," she said. "We still have a ways to go and I have no idea if the succubi will attack us again."

Ignacio shook his head. "We need to keep going," he said. "Having Louisa in my arms gives me strength. I don't need rest, but thanks for your concern."

"The succubi will not bother us again," Sonja confirmed. "Freyja has absolute power here, and she gave us permission to leave. We shall have a safe journey to the ferryman."

Prudence noted that the mournful cries of tortured souls that had echoed earlier, under the dome-like ceiling, cried no more. Instead a ghostly silence hung in the ether.

Sonja cupped Prudence's chin, and saw the sadness in her daughter's eyes. "I know you have seen death in your family, for I have seen it too. However, remember, that as seers we only have the foresight to see one probable outcome. You must hold faith in your son and his beloved, for just as you and Stefan had uncharted territory to discover, so have Gabriel and Colombina." She closed her eyes for a moment, and then caught Prudence's hand in hers. "We must hurry, as our loved ones will soon be on their way."

Sonja led Prudence and Ignacio onward through the tunnels. They hurried past limestone walls mixed with gray rock, until the sound of waves crashing against the rocky shoreline broke the eerie stillness. They began the long walk along the aged wooden planks of the lengthy jetty, where they would wait for the others.

O

Caprecia had watched as Ignacio walked away with Louisa nestled in his arms. She had purposefully waited until Prudence and Sonja had faded into the distance before she doubled over again in pain. She looked up at Stefan. "Thank you," she said. Another wave of pain crossed over her face.

"Are you sure this is what you want?" Stefan asked.

Caprecia nodded. "It'll buy them some time," she said. "I can hold the pain as long as Kenan doesn't fully wake up." Stefan lifted her into his arms, and carried her back along the tunnel toward Hakon and Freyja.

Hakon was on one knee, holding Freyja in his arms, as she wept. "Does Kenan remember any of this part of his life?" she asked.

Hakon shook his head. "No," he said, "I do not know what happened to him during that time, only that he seemed to be in hiding for centuries. Remember, Sonja and I have not lived in this reality for over a millennium. We relied extensively on our perception. Later, when Kenan surfaced, I searched his thoughts, but I did not sense anything of you, or love...nothing, only darkness. I wondered if that was due to me viewing life through visions and not feeling the reality of emotion."

"No," Freyja said. "Kenan has a dark soul. I see now that I was blinded by my own wish to feel needed. I refused to see his wrongdoings as evil, but now I see him for what he has become."

"You chose to see the two faces rather than the vase," Hakon said.

"Yes," Freyja said, "the Rubin vase."

"Perhaps this is why humans say that love is blind."

Freyja wept. "But in doing so, I have also been a part of his darkness."

Hakon helped her stand. Freyja looked over at Stefan approaching with Caprecia in his arms. She could tell the young woman was ravaged in pain. "You must take her away from here," Freyja said. "She has suffered from Kenan's violence enough."

Hakon noticed fear suddenly cross Freyja's face. "What is it, Freyja?" he asked. "What has happened?"

Freyja looked at Stefan. "I am so sorry," she said. "I…I guided Kenan's warriors to the boundary of *Casa della Pietra* and weakened Prudence's magic. The protective web at the main entrance will completely shatter upon Kenan's arrival. What have I done?"

"Can you get us to where the others are, quickly?" Stefan asked.

"Go," Freyja cut in. "I will clear a safe passage for you, and hold Kenan here as long as I am able."

Hakon grabbed ahold of Stefan, who held Caprecia, and the three immortals disappeared.

O

Hakon and Stefan appeared out of the mist beside Sonja. Caprecia rested in Stefan's arms, her face and body still twisted in pain.

"Kenan is here," Hakon said, as he placed an arm around Sonja's shoulders. "Freyja brought him to her sanctuary to heal his wound. But he is restless and close to rising."

Hakon called Ignacio's name and tossed him another coin. Moments later, the ferryman appeared from out of the mist. Ignacio flipped the coin and it landed in the ferryman's open hand. Once they were all on board, Charon guided the boat past the jetty and into the open sea. The boat pushed through the roaring wind, bobbing up and over the foam of cresting waves. Ice-cold sprays of saltwater landed on the pale faces of the immortal passengers.

Gradually, the roar of the ocean died and was replaced with the sound of waves breaking on a beach. Light from two crescent moons hanging in a charcoal sky exposed the glimmer of a thick fog bank. Charon guided the boat onward and allowed the waves to carry them onto the beach, then waited while his passengers disembarked. Hakon guided the group along the beach and through the mist until it dissipated, and they stood once more in Hakon and Sonja's crystalline cave.

Prudence stood before Hakon. She threw her arms around Hakon's neck. "Thank you, Father," she whispered.

Hakon's arms tightened around her. "Your fortress is under attack."

Prudence stepped away. "How is this possible? Was it Freyja?"

"She regrets what she has done," Hakon said.

Prudence nodded, and looked into his sad eyes. She sensed Sonja's presence as she rested a hand on Hakon's shoulder. Hakon turned to Sonja and they gazed into each other's eyes. "The world is a different place, my love," Sonja said. "We cannot hide from this truth anymore, and I would rather live with those I love than live another moment without them."

Hakon placed his hands on either side of Sonja's face. Prudence became aware once more of a silent conversation between her parents. Hakon kissed Sonja's forehead. He turned to Prudence. "Go to your son. Sonja and I shall take care of Louisa and Caprecia, and your fortress." He reached for Caprecia, and Stefan carefully laid her in Hakon's arms. "We will see you both soon."

Hakon whispered ancient words. Mist rose from the ground and encircled him, and then reached outward to encompass Ignacio, Louisa, Caprecia, and Sonja. After a few moments, the mist dissipated, leaving only Prudence and Stefan.

"Do you know where our son is?" Stefan asked.

Prudence turned to him, and opened a hand. The silver thread Sonja had given her now glowed. "I will find him," she said, her voice drenched in grief.

# 45

*Svalbard Islands, Arctic Ocean*

THE FEATHERY TOUCH of familiar fingers brushed across Kenan's forehead, and his gaze fell upon Freyja's face. "I was a fool," he said. "In my haste I left behind one of my tainted knives. The whore's consort used it against me. Having tasted my own poison, I pity Alessandro, for when I next meet him in battle he will pay for his sins."

"Alessandro did what you would have done," Freyja said.

Kenan sat up and glared at her. "He is the father of a Creative! I wish I'd killed the child when I held her in my hands."

"Yet you did not," Freyja said. "Why is that?"

Kenan stood, ignoring her question. "Where's my phone?"

Freyja pointed to a table, where the phone sat next to Kenan's knife and clothing. He dressed, and then picked up his phone and stared at the screen. "No reception?"

"This is my realm," Freyja said. "I had to bring you here in order to heal your wound. And the power I supply is of a different kind."

Kenan's lips curved upward. "I need to return to my realm and my men. We have work to be do."

Freyja walked across the room, and looked out at the ocean. "While you were healing, your past filled your thoughts and drifted to mine."

"My past is my business," he said.

"Lucky you were with me, and not with others who could have picked up your thoughts," she said. She turned to face him. "What do you know of Bernardo Gui?"

Kenan threw on his jacket, and slipped his knife into an inside pocket. "Only that he was an acquaintance of Domenico's," he said. "An inquisitor, who sought to bring heretics to justice."

"How can you speak of him with pride?" Freyja asked. "He killed many of my sisters, innocent women, all of them."

"They were heretics."

"They were innocent peasants!"

"Not so innocent," he said. "They killed him, remember?"

"Oh no," Freyja said. "It was I who gave the humans the strength to push his wagon over and crush his evil body." She turned to face Kenan. "Gui, and others like him, stole the feminine from the human world and replaced it with a pack of greedy barbarians. It was the women who nurtured the earth with their rituals, and kept the townspeople healthy. Without the feminine, people were forced to leave their villages, their social lives, and live in the poverty scared men like Gui created!"

Kenan moved quickly and pinned Freyja against a wall, his knife at her throat and his mouth close to the side of her face. "Every woman Domenico killed, I paid for through his torment. Yes, I killed seers, but that is what I was made to do. I had no choice. His blood runs through me! He would have killed you too if he'd had the chance."

"You are a fool!" Freyja said. "Domenico could never have killed me."

"You are the fool! You think your magic will protect you against me? I was made with blood from the devil. There was a time when I would have welcomed death, but that changed the day I killed my maker. Not even you can escape me now."

Freyja whispered in Kenan's ear. "I cannot help you anymore, I have seen your darkest moments, your moments of goodness, and your fears. I had hoped I could change you, but you are no different from other men who taste power and forget their humility. The only difference is I fell in love with you…I fell in love with the devil."

Kenan pressed his knife into Freyja's throat.

The walls of the room began to shake.

O

Kenan stared at dirt and weathered stones. The scent in the air told him where Freyja had sent him. He pulled himself to his feet, and looked at the remains of the altar where his uncle used to preach. He picked up a rotted piece of wood that had once been filled with coins, and breathed in deeply. He closed his eyes and leaned in closer, to draw in the sweet-smelling aroma of copper. The scent reminded him that he needed sustenance.

Kenan flung the rotted platter across the room, pulled out his phone and checked the long list of text messages. He scrolled through to the last one, read it, and then wrote a reply. He brushed himself off and walked outside. Low clouds hid the city of his youth, but not the scintillating aroma of a nearby virgin. A teenager's low moans led Kenan to a car parked close to the ruins of his childhood home. Through the vehicle's fogged-up windows, he saw naked bodies tangled in the throes of lust.

He ripped the car door open, and the smell of fear immediately flooded the interior. He allowed himself a moment to feast on the succulent scent of terror, and then yanked the teenagers out of the car. He pinned the male face down on the ground, while he drained the life from the virgin whore. He dropped her body, and then found sweet pleasure in the young man, drinking the last drop of his fear-filled blood. With his strength regained, Kenan quickly ascended into the sky.

# 46

FREDERICO DROVE THE Mercedes past the security gates and into Vatican City. He parked the car, and a guard opened the door for Antonia. She nodded her thanks, and waited for Frederico and their two vampire escorts to join her before they made their way into the gallery by a side door. This was a restricted area—no tourists, only people with high security clearance were allowed access to this part of the building. Once inside, the guard exited, and an elderly priest took over.

Antonia greeted him in Latin, remembering from previous visits that this was the preferred language the priests used in this section of the building. "Thank you for guiding us," she said, "your time is appreciated."

The priest bowed his head. "The Holy Father is waiting," he said. "Follow me."

The priest ushered them in hushed silence along wide hallways, decorated with frescoes on the walls and ceilings. Life-sized statues carved from marble stood guard along the way. At the end of the third hallway stood two shining suits of armor, and between them stood a thick wooden door. The priest turned to Frederico and nodded, urging him and the other two vampires to leave their weapons at the door. Once they were disarmed, the priest lifted the brass key tied to his waist and unlocked the door. He motioned everyone forward, closed the door behind them, and continued walking down a steep spiral walkway. Antonia and the others followed.

Noticing the sheer drop and lack of guardrail, Antonia stayed close to the wall with Frederico beside her. "This is the part I don't like," she whispered, "such a strain on my Louboutins."

Frederico stifled a laugh. "Would you like me to carry you?"

Antonio rested a hand on his forearm and stopped walking. "It will take me all day to get down there with these exquisite gems." She removed her shoes, opened her purse, and pulled out a pair of flats. "Ah, that's better," she smiled, once the sensible shoes were on her feet.

Frederico peered down at her. "I thought you were taller," he said.

"That, Frederico, is why I love stylish shoes," she said. "They completely distract from reality."

They were silent the rest of the way down the walkway, and around the narrow ridge that framed the rotting wood of an ancient oubliette; the horrors of the secret underground dungeon clung to the wood of its only entrance. The priest unlocked the gate that led to the maze of underground tunnels, and pulled it closed behind them.

Antonia nodded her head in thanks, and then turned to a font embedded in a wall. Frederico and the other two vampires watched as she dipped a finger in the holy water and made the sign of the cross. When she was done, they began the long descent under the Vatican to the library of the Holy Catholic Church. Antonia glanced at the briefcase Frederico carried. She did not look forward to viewing the photographs Sabine had sent Christopher. The state of the girls who had been abducted and kept by Kenan's offspring was appalling and heartbreaking. However, she knew the Allegiance would need every bit of evidence they had in order for the ancient vampire to agree to rein in Kenan.

At the entrance to the final tunnel, Antonia stopped briefly to again change her shoes. Minutes later, they stood in front of an iron gate. The Holy Father approached, unlocked the gate, and motioned them all into the library, where he sat at the head of a large rectangular wooden table. When they were all seated, he took a moment before he spoke. "I can only surmise by the urgency of this visit that you have valid concern for the Church, and our kind," he said.

Frederico opened the briefcase, and handed Antonia a folder. "I am here on behalf of the Allegiance, Holy Father," Antonia said, "and yes, this matter involves the Holy Catholic Church. Human lives have been taken, and others put at risk by the immortal named Kenan. Young Latina human girls have been kidnapped and abused, and in some cases killed by Kenan's men. I offer this information, which includes dates the victims were taken, the atrocities used on each girl, including rape, torture, the taking of blood without due cause and, sadly, the taking of lives."

She watched the Holy Father for a reaction, and thus far he had shown none. "The second matter, which has been taken up from a legal standpoint in the mortal world, is that of fraud involving a United States politician. Money was channeled, from state and federal educational funds, to Catholic charter schools. In some cases, young girls, who chose to turn away from the Catholic Church, were hand-picked to attend the aforementioned schools, in a deliberate ploy to torture them for their decision to leave the Church."

The Holy Father raised a long, thin index finger. "And how did the politician steal from the federal educational funds?" he asked.

Antonia leaned forward and brought her hands together on the table. "It is policy in the United States that each student be accounted for every day while at school," she said. "This is important, because funds are allocated for each student annually. If a student is shown as absent for a long period of time, then the funding for that individual student is pulled. But, in all of these cases, the girls were only marked as absent for a few days, and even though they did not return to school it was reported that they were in attendance."

The Holy Father nodded. "And how did the Allegiance find out about this?" he asked. "And let us call this what it is…fraud."

"Until we know our informant is safe, we choose to keep this information secret," she said. "I'm sure you can understand the sensitive nature of this matter." She slid the folder across the table, where it sat in front of the Holy Father.

He opened the folder and read the letter signed by Alessandro, in lieu of both Gabriel and Prudence's absence, outlining the events Antonia had just explained. When he had finished reading, he pushed the letter aside and looked at the photographs of the young girls Dr. Fiore had taken as evidence against Kenan.

Antonia sensed the shift in the Holy Father's emotions. Which, although subtle, was obvious to her. Sensing emotions was the gift of her birthright, and the reason Prudence had chosen her as head liaison for the Allegiance. To anyone else, it might have seemed as if the Holy Father was not moved at all by the images, but Antonia noticed the change in his aura. He was sickened by what he saw. She decided to move forward with the proceedings. "There is one more area of concern that you need to be aware of," she said. "One of the buildings where girls were being held against their will was destroyed by a bomb." She waited for her words to sink in, and the Holy Father's demeanor this time was almost tangible, for he knew there would be a need for explanations to mortals.

"Were there any human deaths?" he asked.

Antonia shook her head. "No, but one of our own is fighting for his life as we speak."

"May I ask who that is?" he asked.

"Gabriel," Antonia said. "Prudence and Stefan's son."

The Holy Father closed his eyes for a few moments as if in prayer. When he opened them, he regarded each of the photographs, until he came to the last one in the stack, an image of a severely burned body, unrecognizable to most. He ran a finger over the photograph. "Gabriel," he whispered. "Do Stefan and Prudence know of this?"

Antonia took a moment to control her own emotions. "I presume, through the connection of family, they are aware of his suffering," she said, "but they are on a journey of another sort, and as yet we have not been able to get in touch with them."

The Holy Father closed the file, pushed back his chair, and stood up from the table. "There was once goodness in Kenan," he said. "I sensed it a long time ago, and prayed he would choose the right path. But, it seems, like his maker, that he did not." He wandered the length of the floor-to-ceiling bookcase, searched for and retrieved a leather-bound book, and read aloud:

*'Is there not rain enough in the sweet heavens*
*To wash it white as snow? Whereto serves mercy*
*But to confront the visage of offence?*
*And what's in prayer but this twofold force,*
*To be forestalled ere we come to fall*
*Or pardoned being down? Then I'll look up.*

*My fault is past. But oh, what form of prayer*
*Can serve my turn, "Forgive me my foul murder"?'*


When the Holy Father had finished reading, he looked to Antonia. "Kenan has strayed from God's flock," he said, "what do you need from me?"

Antonia rose. "We need to know that you support the Allegiance," she said. "We cannot risk Kenan's behavior bringing attention to our world. We ask for your counsel and assistance in this matter."

The Holy Father lowered his head in contemplation while Antonia and the others waited in silence for his answer. After a few minutes, he looked up and brought the book he was holding to his heart. "Shakespeare's Claudius had somewhat of a conscience," he said. "I am not sure that Kenan has access to his, anymore." He returned the book to its place on the shelf. "Do you know how many young girls have been stolen in his name?"

"Dr. Sabine Fiore is in charge of finding the girls," Antonia said. "She has identified five locations on the East Coast of the United States alone, plus the two in the photographs in your folder, and another in Los Angeles, bringing the total, thus far, to eight. But we have heard there are many more. At this time, thirty-five girls have been found, and sadly, we were too late to save five of them."

The Holy Father walked back to the table and flicked once more through the photographs. "Sabine is an honorable immortal and I have no doubt seeing young girls treated in this way must bring the horror of her own mortal life back to her. She will not rest until every one of these places has been found and the girls accounted for." He looked up at Antonia. "I am not sure Kenan will listen to me, but you have my word that I will reach out to him. Acts such as these will not be tolerated. Thank you for bringing this to my attention." He reached for her hand, and held her palm against his forehead for a few moments. When he released his hold, he smiled up at her. "As always your heart is pure, Antonia," he said, "and I do appreciate your shoes, my dear." He bowed his head to show the meeting had ended.

In a show of respect, Antonia, Frederico, and the other two vampires knelt and gave the sign of the cross before they exited.

# 47

*Beverly Hills, California*

SABINE GATHERED HER tribe together. These were her sisters from different lands, born from different eras. Each woman, during their human lives, had in some form or another been subjected to the plundering of the essence of their femininity. Incarcerated women with their virtues stolen, their will to live crushed, and their communities destroyed by the cruelties of man.

Sabine had deployed her best trackers to search for the missing girls Jason and Jeremy had discovered. They focused on the larger cities in the United States: Los Angeles, New York, and D.C., where signs of unusual behavior had surfaced. When her warriors returned with proof that girls were being held against their will, Sabine meticulously swept through each hideout, uncovering dens of debauchery, and killing the vampires responsible. She held no mercy for anyone who abused women, whether through verbal or physical exploitation.

With her warriors strategically placed around the two-acre Beverly Hills fenced estate, Sabine gave the order to enter the property. With vampire speed, she raced across the manicured grounds, past the swimming pool, and outdoor kitchen. She yanked open a door that led into a sunroom, paved with earth-tone Mexican tiles.

She stopped and listened. At the sound of a girl's mournful cry for help, Sabine hurtled over furniture, ran up a flight of stairs, and ripped a door from its hinges. The sight before her was similar to the room of torture she had witnessed at the Georgetown mansion. Above the bed, and hanging from a chain attached to her wrists, a young girl was being raped by a vampire. By the time he realized he was not alone, it was too late for him. Sabine sheathed her sword, and watched the male vampire's head, rolling lifelessly on the bed. One of Sabine's warriors released the young girl, induced her to sleep, and then began healing her.

Sabine's fellow warriors swept through the rest of the Beverly Hills mansion. They worked in teams; while one group annihilated Kenan's men, others rescued the victims. Once the girls were brought back to health, and memories of their abduction and torture had been erased, they were returned to their families with varying stories.

The recent rise in bigotry and discrimination against women and minorities across the United States sickened Sabine. She had no respect for men who sat in glass towers, slinging derogatory memes via social media platforms, while masturbating their unbalanced egos. Sabine checked the photos on her phone, and sent the evidence of depravity to Christopher.

A familiar voice called out to her, one she had not heard in centuries, and one that others could not hear. She turned to her second-in-command. "Watch over the girls," she said. "I have business to take care of in the nation's capital."

# 48

THE HOLY FATHER entered a deserted, subterranean chapel. The pitted stone floor echoed the age of the ancient frescoes, framed with marble arches, that decorated the walls. Images of biblical stories displayed a simplistic style, similar to scenes found in Roman catacombs. He walked along the nave to the chancel where he knelt before the altar. He stared up at a life-sized statue depicting the Crucifixion.

The Holy Father closed his eyes and brought his hands together in prayer. Incense that he had lit earlier, drifted over him in a mix of frankincense and myrrh. It seemed to linger, as if waiting to carry his prayers to heaven. He lowered his head and recited the words of "Our Father" in Latin. When he was done, he removed a silver chalice and dish from the altar, and then pushed back the thick slab of stone.

In a receptacle hidden there lay a bundle, wrapped in animal skin. The Holy Father picked it up and kissed it, and then slid the altar stone back in place along with the sacred objects. He laid the bundle on the stone and unrolled the animal skin to reveal an intricately carved sheath engraved with the symbol Chi-Rho; the letters "X" and "P" denoting the first two letters of the word Christ as represented in the Greek alphabet.

The Holy Father pulled the knife out of the sheath, held it up to the candlelight, and read aloud the inscription along the side of the blade from Revelation 21:6.

"I am Alpha and Omega, the Beginning and the End. I will give unto him that is athirst of the fountain of the water of life freely."

He ran a finger along the Greek letters, and then flipped the knife and traced over the image of an anchor at the tip of the blade.

"Which hope we have as an anchor of the soul, both sure and stedfast, and which entereth into that within the veil."

He returned the knife to its sheath, wrapped it in the animal hide and tied it safely within the folds of his robes. He knelt on one knee and made the sign of the cross. *"In nomine Patris et Filii et Spiritus Sancti,"* he said, and then turned and exited the chapel.

O

Upon leaving his sanctuary beneath Vatican City, the Holy Father hurried along the underground passageways. When the path ended, he reached for a key that hung from a cord of leather around his neck. He put the key into a lock and turned it clockwise. A grinding noise told him the ancient entrance was opening. He slipped through, and then watched the bricked wall slide back into place. The Holy Father was greeted by the dappled glow of moonlight. He made his way through the curtain of roots and tree limbs into the outside world.

From this point, the Holy Father, ancient vampire, and protector of the secrets of the Holy Catholic Church, took to the skies. He flew across Umbria and into Tuscany, where he landed on the ground, surrounded by a forest of aged trees. His nostrils flared. When he caught the scent he needed, he continued on foot through the dense and verdant undergrowth.

As the ground began to rise, the Holy Father slowed his gait. He cocked his head and listened to the sounds around him: water spilling over rocks and fallen trees, the light footfalls of deer running in fear of the vampire's presence. When he knew he was alone, the Holy Father pushed back a thicket of brush and tree limbs, and disappeared into the copse toward a hidden grotto.

Once inside the cave, he brushed off his robes and stared into the darkness. A pile of dead coals lay unlit in a fire pit. He waved a hand and they began to glow, until flames licked at brittle wood, emitting an orange light throughout the cave. The Holy Father strode across the dirt floor to a bench, where three small glass vials stained with a dark substance stood in an orderly fashion.

He removed the stopper from the nearest vial, and sniffed at the contents before resealing it. He followed suit with the next one, but it was the third vial that caught his attention. He pushed the cork back into the container, and returned it to the bench. "Put on the whole armor of God, that ye may be able to stand against the wiles of the devil," he whispered. "For we wrestle not against flesh and blood, but against principalities, against powers, against the rulers of the darkness of this world, against spiritual wickedness in high places."

A bitter scent tinged the air. The Holy Father turned to see the ghost of a familiar figure materialize from the flames of the fire. The witch's silver hair, piled high above her head, had changed since the last time he had met with her, and the slight wrinkles that once lined the corners of her mouth, had spread like a road map, across her face. Her eyes had changed and were now entirely white, but he noted the pierce of her stare had not deteriorated.

"Ephesians 6:11 and 12," she said. She lifted an arm and pointed one of her broken fingernails in his direction. "What brings you here?" Her words came through staggered breath. "Does your God not give you what you need?"

The Holy Father began to walk in a circle around the fire pit. "I do not need for anything from God," he said.

The witch cackled. "That is not true, or you would not be here."

"I have a question for you," he said.

"You said the same words when last we met," she said. "What makes you think I would answer your question this time?"

"Because this time the stakes are much higher." He continued circling her, noting her movements were slow, but not doubting the strength of her magic. "I wonder, what did the devil give you in exchange for creating his presence on Earth?"

"You think I would tell you this secret?" she said.

"Ah, so I am correct, he did give you something."

The witch stepped out from the flames and drifted toward the bench, but the Holy Father blocked her way. She lifted her head, and her white eyes bored into him. "Is the blood in these vials worth your life?" he asked. "Look what your fall from Christ has done to you. Is this what you wished for? Loneliness, with no God to honor?"

"Do not speak His name to me," she said. "Where was He when I lay dying? Where was He when the Church turned their back on me because one of their kind raped me?" She spat at him. "You were one of them, or have you forgotten?"

"I asked for an audience with His Holiness," he said, "but was denied."

She leaned forward. "The devil came to me when God did not."

"He came to you at your weakest moment. Did he promise you vengeance?"

"The Church murdered my only child," she said.

"Your child lived," the Holy Father whispered. "I smuggled him out of the monastery. He was raised by peasants."

The air charged with electricity. The witch's hair floated around her body as she whirled around the fire. When she stilled, her appearance had completely altered. She stood tall and with grace. Her hair fell in red ringlets down to her waist, and her face was that of a young woman. "You lie," she said, "like all men."

"No," he said, "I speak the truth."

"If this is so, why have you waited until now to tell me this?"

"Until a few minutes ago, I did not know you were alive," he said. "But certain evil has entered this world once more, and I remembered your curse as they stole your child away from you."

"You heard my curse because you were there and did nothing!"

"That is what the devil wanted you to believe," the Holy Father said. "Your child lived. I saw to it." He stepped toward her. "I sought you out because now the world is in danger. Men with evil in their hearts use the name of God to spin lies and accomplish power. They use His name to form a dichotomy of evil against love." He hung his head. "I did not realize until I caught the scent in these vials that you were involved."

"How do I know you speak the truth about my child?"

The Holy Father gazed into her white eyes. "I will take you to his grave. You will know by the scent of the earth that it once held the blood of your son."

The witch turned toward the entrance to the cave, and shook her head. "I have not left this place in hundreds of years…I'm not sure I will survive."

"Then I will carry you, and protect you," he said. "The grave is not far from here. He was put to rest near a village at the foot of the mountains." He took another step toward her, and offered her a hand. Her hesitation was slight, but the Holy Father knew her curiosity would win out over her stubbornness. Together they walked through the entrance and into the stillness of night.

The Holy Father landed on the outskirts of a small town at the foot of the Dolomite Mountains. He placed the witch on the ground where he knew her son had been buried. She sank to her knees and rubbed at the crumbling headstone that marked a grave. She dug through snow, into the earth, and brought a handful of soil to her face and drew in a breath. As she exhaled, tears fell down her face and onto the dirt beneath her. The Holy Father knelt beside her and said a silent prayer to God.

"What was he like?" she asked.

"He was a good man," the Holy Father said. "More like you than his biological father."

She turned to him, and he sensed the question she wanted to ask. "His father's life came to an unfortunate end shortly after the child's birth. I did not become an immortal until years later, and as such I was not able to do more for you."

"The blood in the vials…" she whispered. "You must take a drop from each one and place the point of the sacred knife in each. Only a man of God can kill him, and his death must be on hallowed ground. The devil has inhabited three bodies in his time on Earth, and with each new birth he becomes stronger."

"And the one whose body he inhabits now?" the Holy Father asked. "What will become of him?"

"This is something that only your God can answer," she said. Her body convulsed and she hunched over the mound of snow and dirt. "Get me back to the cave, please," she said through gasps.

The Holy Father gathered her into his arms, along with a handful of dirt from her son's grave, and flew into the darkness.

# 49

*Washington, D.C.*

CONGRESSMAN ROSS THORTON picked up a framed photograph from his desk. He ran his fingers across the glass, stopping at the image of a woman with her arms around two children. He turned the frame over, unclipped the back plate, and a small photograph slid into his hands. A smile lingered over his lips as he lifted the photograph to his nose, and smelled it. He kissed the photograph of a woman with charcoal-lined eyes, and then returned it to its hiding place. He glanced at his crotch, made an adjustment, and then pushed his chair back from his desk. He had fifteen minutes to get to a meeting.

When he opened his office door, he noted his secretary, busy with a phone call. She looked up at him, pointed to a TV in the corner of the room, and turned up the volume with a remote. On the screen were two separate photos: one of a man, the other of a woman caught in a happy moment. A bead of sweat appeared on the congressman's forehead as the reporter's words sank in.

"...since the initial investigation the police are no closer to finding their murderer..."

The victims' names were familiar; the congressman had written both on a piece of paper recently. His contact had said he needed the names of anyone who had access to certain information regarding education funding. *Surely their deaths were coincidental.* The bead of sweat ran down his hairline.

His secretary ended the call and clicked off the TV. "It's just awful," she said. "They both worked in accounting, and the police are still searching for the murderer. You picked a good week to be out of town, it's been nuts around here. Didn't you hear about it?"

The congressman walked to the door. "No," he said. "Make sure to send flowers. I'll see you later."

She nodded. "Of course, and good luck today." Her phone rang again. He exited and began walking along the hallway, trying unsuccessfully to calm his quickening pulse. He pulled out his phone and sent a text to his wife, explaining he would be working late and not to wait up for him. He waited for her reply. When it came, her response was short and to the point: OK.

O

Thorton had chosen the Logan Circle townhouse purely for the remote access that led directly to the interior. He undid his seatbelt, and waited for the garage door to close before he exited the car. He made his way into the starkly decorated white and chrome kitchen, and stood for a moment while the stress of the day faded. He closed his eyes and listened to the haunting melody of Bach's Orchestral Suite No. 3 in D major, second movement, drifting down the stairs and beckoning him to the bedroom.

He walked over to the staircase, noting the order around him. No children's toys to step over, or dog hair gathered in the corners of the steps, this whole place smelled of cleanliness. From the landing at the top of the stairs, he saw the woman from the small photograph reflected in the mirrored walls of the bedroom. The top of her white stockings peeped out from beneath a lavish dress of white silk and taffeta that rose to a mini at the front, and flowed like rapids of decadence to the ground. She wore a white satin bustier with laces that accentuated her curves. Her bare shoulders were framed with long, white satin fingerless gloves, and in her right hand she held a short riding crop.

He could feel her gaze wandering over his body, stopping at the strain of fabric hiding his erection. She walked toward him, her strappy-white stilettos clicking on the marble floor. She placed the end of the whip under his chin and brought her lips to his. Her tongue filled his mouth, and he moaned with delight while she pushed his suit jacket from his shoulders, letting it fall to the floor. She loosened his tie and unbuttoned his shirt, while he kicked off his shoes and removed his suit pants and boxers. He watched as she folded his clothes and set them neatly on the bed.

He stood perfectly still as she circled him, tracing his muscles with the tip of the whip. She walked into the bathroom, and he followed. Steam from the shower filled the space. She opened the glass shower-door, and he entered. The hot water fell over his body; he soaped up, rinsed off and then turned off the taps.

He saw her bent over a chair; the white dress was gone and her bare ass was shiny with oil. He ran a hand over his erection, and then moved it over her white skin, before thrusting his sword between her cheeks. She cried out, and he thrust harder and deeper, soon finding bliss through ejaculation. He pulled out, and dropped to his knees just as she turned around. He reached for her hard cock. This is what he wanted, to take her into his mouth.

Sabine met the Holy Father at the Logan Circle address. She stood beside him as they witnessed Thorton act out his sexual fantasies. Sabine filmed the entire performance. It hadn't taken long to uncover the dark side of the clean-living congressman. He had spent his life running on a platform of so-called Christian morals: anti-abortion, anti-gay marriage, anti-women's rights and, ironically, against anything transgender. But in a few moments, the facade of his morality would crumble, Sabine would make sure of it.

She sensed the breath of fear rise in the congressman. His eyes darted to the door. "What was that?" he asked.

His lover shook her head. "I didn't hear anything," she said.

The Holy Father flicked on the light.

"What the fuck?" Thorton sputtered. He shoved his lover away and reached for a towel.

In an instant, the Holy Father had Thorton by the throat and against a wall, with a towel shoved partly in his mouth. "You bring shame to God," he said, "to the Holy Catholic Church and everything we stand for.

You have desecrated the union of marriage, and betrayed your wife and children. Your bigotry and racism are intolerable. And let me remind you that God loves all children, no matter the color of their skin. You will no longer call yourself a Christian."

Thorton's face turned red as he snorted breath in and out of his nose like a rabid dog. The Holy Father turned to Sabine, and nodded. She grabbed clothes from a closet, and threw them at Thorton's lover.

"Get dressed," she said.

The woman warily took the clothes, and did as Sabine ordered. "Please, don't hurt me," she cried. "I never said I was religious…I needed the money."

"It is not you we are concerned with," Sabine said. She stared into the woman's eyes, and she sensed her body and mind relax. "You will go home to your partner and forget you ever saw the congressman. You'll return to your regular job and support those who need help." She found Thorton's wallet, took out all of the cash, handed it to the woman, and exited the room with her.

The Holy Father dragged Thorton into the bedroom and threw him onto the bed. He stared down at the man before him. A man stripped of his lies, his bravado, and his perfect suit complete with a lapel pin of the United States flag, Thorton reeked of fear, an emotion he preferred to heap upon others. The Holy Father sensed his mind darting in and out of alternate scenarios, to be with his wife and children, anywhere but here.

"And yet," the Holy Father said, "you chose to be here."

Thorton shied away, inching across the bed and toward a door.

"This time," the Holy Father said, "there is no escape. There is no one to call in to cover up your immoral behavior. No one else to blame, you are alone. This is your time for penitence. What say you?"

Thorton shook his head. "I will say nothing to you. I demand to speak to my lawyer!"

The Holy Father pointed a finger at Thorton. "You will speak to God!" he said. "You will be punished for your sins. For the pain you have brought to others, the innocent, the poor, your wife and children."

"Who are you?"

"A messenger of God," the Holy Father said. He glared at Thorton.

"You stink of fear and dishonesty. Confess your sins." He stepped closer and intensified his stare. He sensed the man's resistance snap.

"I used my wealth...p-p-paid for lobbyists to buy policy outcomes."

"You cheated children of the right to a decent education," the Holy Father said. "Children suffered because of you! Society suffered because of your betrayal, your greed, your need for power!"

"Not all deserve to be educated..."

Thorton was thrown across the room by an unseen force and he fell in a heap onto the marble floor.

"You are impervious to what life is like for those less fortunate," the Holy Father said. "Can you not see that education is the only chance these children have of rising above poverty? You took that chance away from them."

"I saved them from failure..."

"You took away their chance of a better life!"

Thorton lunged forward. Once more the Holy Father picked him up, and sent him flying across the room. The force of hitting the wall, caused blood to run from his mouth and nose. He touched his face and saw the blood on his fingers. "I gave them what they know, what their parents and grandparents had before them."

"You crave an uneducated society," the Holy Father said, "one that follows your rules, one that does not question your morality or your ideals. A society steeped in fear. Education is not a privilege meant only for the wealthy. Education is a moral right for all." He placed the tip of a finger underneath Thorton's chin, and pulled him up to a standing position. "As I speak, your office is being raided. Your homes are being torn apart, and all evidence will be brought against you and those who follow on your path."

Thorton slowly lifted his head. "I know others...like you," he whispered.

"Oh, I know whose cup you drink from," the Holy Father said, "I know him well. You are just a pawn in his scheme, a nothing. But I will flush him out, and I will bring those who support your ideals to justice." He tossed Thorton his clothes. "Get dressed, you have work to do!"

O

When Sabine returned upstairs, Thorton was dressed and on the telephone with his secretary, asking her to arrange an urgent meeting with the press. The Holy Father looked at Sabine, and she noticed his eyes were filled with sadness. She knew that he did not often enter the world above his sanctuary, and that what he had seen tonight bared a likeness to the depravity of times past, when such immorality was common behavior among the Church.

"I am not sure this world will ever be free of pain," Sabine said.

"You and I have seen humanity at its best and worst," the Holy Father said. "Have your people watch over his wife and family."

"Of course, Holy Father," Sabine said, " but what of him?"

"He will announce that he is stepping down from his current position," the Holy Father replied. "His next call will be to his wife. Make sure to send her a copy of the extramarital affair, and that the face of the prostitute is hidden. Once he has confessed his sins to members of the press, he will excuse himself for a moment of sanctuary. During this time he will die of natural causes," he looked up at Sabine. "He knows too many secrets, and his peers will all be running scared in about an hour. I must leave, dear Sabine, for I have unfinished business to attend to."

Sabine bowed her head in respect. When she looked up, the flutter of curtains, and slamming of the front door, told her the Holy Father was gone. She grabbed Thorton's smart phone, and forwarded the incriminating evidence to his number, and then on to his wife. A few minutes later the smart phone rang, and she handed it to Thorton just as he ended the call with his secretary.

He checked the screen, and when he saw his wife's name, he looked up at Sabine. "Please, I beg your forgiveness."

"The time for your forgiveness has long passed," Sabine said.

Sabine answered the phone herself, yanked Thorton to his feet, and shoved the phone to his ear. A woman's cries could be heard, but all Thorton could mutter was that he was ruined. Sabine took the phone and spoke kindly to his wife. When she had calmed her down, Sabine ended the call.

She stared into Thorton's eyes. "Give me the names of every person involved with the missing girls, the lobbyists who supported your educational scheme, and the amount of money you have stolen from the government...taxpayer's money. I want the names of everyone in your plan to sabotage the democracy of this country."

Thorton shook his head, but was unable to stop himself. He spewed out a long list of names, that Sabine captured on her smart phone. When he was done, she immediately forwarded the clip to Christopher.

## Casa della Pietra

Christopher clicked on an email from Sabine. The title read: Here's your solid evidence. He opened the attachment. When he saw the first few seconds of Thorton's sexual encounter, he saved it, and went directly to the next video. Realizing it was a full confession, he reached for the television remote, switched on the screen, and streamed the video.

He turned to Jeremy and Jason. "You both need to watch this."

When it was over, Jason leaned back in his chair. "Jeez," he said. "This is going to bring down half of D.C."

Christopher nodded. "He's called a press conference."

"He's going public with this?" Jason asked.

Christopher pulled up Sabine's text on his phone. "Yeah," he said, "full confession." He heard footsteps, and looked up to see Chantal and Arianna enter the room.

"Christopher," Chantal said. "You need to take Layla and Jason to the inner sanctum."

"What's happened?" Christopher asked.

"Kenan's men are gathering around the entrance to the grounds. Your father is concerned the barrier has been compromised," she said. "We're going to move the twins and Coco away from here. It's customary when we're under attack to separate the Creatives. In this case, Alessandro feels Prudence would not want to keep the twins here either."

"What about Gabriel and Kishu?" Christopher asked.

"Gabriel is still healing," Chantal said. "Kishu wants to stay with him to monitor his progress."

Layla entered the room and went directly to Christopher. He embraced her, and then grabbed his laptop and power cord. He noticed Jason hadn't moved. "Come on, we need to get out of here."

"I'm not going anywhere," Jason said. "Take Layla, I'll see what I can do to help."

"I can't let you do that, Jason," Christopher said. "Come on!"

"Chris," Jason said, "I'm not a member of the Allegiance and I'm choosing to stay here."

Arianna tossed her brother a jacket. "Let's go."

Jeremy followed Arianna to the door, and then turned to Christopher. "See you soon," he said.

Christopher nodded. "Take care of each other."

Chantal hugged Christopher and Layla, and then addressed Jason. "We could do with your help."

Jason picked up his laptop and headed out the door with Chantal. He turned to Christopher. "Talk soon, buddy, and make sure to save that last attachment, and forward it to me."

Layla placed a hand on Christopher's shoulder. "I know you want to be there for your parents," she said. "But what were Prudence's wishes?"

"For me to stay with you and the others in the inner sanctum." He unlocked the drawer of his desk and pulled out Prudence's book. "And, for the record, as much as my warrior side wants to go and fight alongside my parents, I'm choosing to be with you and our child," he said. He guided Layla out of the room toward the lower part of the fortress.

# 50

THE REALITY OF what was going on around Coco snapped her out of her sadness and longing for Gabriel. She kissed his lips, and then turned, and walked briskly to the only place where she thought an answer might be hidden.

Coco entered the main living area and closed the door, leaving the chaos of what was transpiring around the fortress behind her. She crossed the room and stared up at the Botticelli portrait of Prudence. With a deep sigh, she stretched a hand toward the painting, and instantly the pigment lifted and rested at her fingertips.

*Coco, Jeremy, Arianna, and Pelayo stood in a bedroom. The walls were made of stone and a rough-hewed beam supported the ceiling. Set into a wall was a window with a view that looked out over an ocean. Coco heard footsteps, and looked toward the door. Above the keystone, a ledge protruded, with a statue of the Lady and the Rose. The door burst open, and in its frame stood Kenan.*

No sooner had the image faded, and another appeared. Coco watched in dismay as an alternate fate played out before her. As the pigments of paint returned to the portrait, Coco grabbed onto the mantelpiece and caught her breath. Her heart pounded, as she remembered the nightmare she'd had where men had held her down with the intent of cutting off her fingers. She thought of Prudence's words when she had explained the significance behind the nightmare: *The blackness of the room and clothing*

*the men wore represents nigredo, the mortification...death in the metaphorical*
*sense, and a vivid reminder to be true to yourself and to do what is right.*

Coco raced out of the room and called out to her feline protector,
Thalia, and Max, the German shepherd that Gabriel had pulled from his
pack of rescued dogs to guard her. Both animals appeared at one end of
the hallway along with the rest of the pack, and caught up with her at
the top of the stairs. She ran through Gabriel's rooms, to her studio off
the bedroom, and quickly searched through the stack of paintings she'd
recently completed. When she found the three she needed, she ripped
each canvas from its frame, and laid one of the paintings on the ground.
She held a hand toward the image, and beckoned Max to step forward.
The rest of the pack followed. Thalia nudged Coco's legs and looked up to
her, and meowed.

"Go, Thalia," Coco said, "you have a job to do." Thalia lowered her
head, and then turned and walked through the image. Coco folded the
other two canvases, stuffed one into a back pocket of her jeans and held
the other in her hands. She took one last look around the room before she
ran back to Gabriel to say goodbye.

# 51

GRADUALLY, SOUNDS BECAME words. Not all were clear, but more importantly, Gabriel could sense Colombina's presence. Each time he drifted into darkness, the pull of her essence drew him back. This is what he focused on during the excruciating healing process while muscles, tendons, bone, and skin slowly returned.

The scent of roses was also a constant, and the figure of the Lady and the Rose wove her way in and out of his dreams. On other occasions, he would sense Prudence beside him, not in a physical way, but in the magical realm where they were most strongly connected. Sorrow swirled around her, as if she had lost something dear, but whenever Gabriel came close enough to discover what ailed her, her image faded and he surrendered to his unconscious mind.

The pain spiked. From previous experience, Gabriel knew this meant the healing had neared its peak. Not long now, and he would be completely healed. He willed his mind through a sudden rush of pain, and then he heard her again. Colombina was talking to him, but he still could not make out what she was saying. The emotion in her tone had changed. He fought against the distraction of torment as the last of his bones regenerated, and in that instant he comprehended her words.

*"The barrier around Casa della Pietra is falling. Pelayo and I are moving the twins to safety. Please, Gabriel, come back to me…I need you."*

Her soft lips touched his, and then something wet hit his cheek…a tear from his beloved. His mind screamed out to her to stay, to tell her that soon he would be able to hold her and protect her. He heard Alessandro's voice.

*"Gabriel would want you to be safe, Coco, as do Chantal and I. He'll find you as soon as he awakens, there will be no stopping him. I promise you this."*

Gabriel sensed her anxiety, and then she whispered two words that tore at his heart. *"Find me."* Her footsteps faded, and a few minutes later the essence of magic fluttered over him. She was gone.

○

Coco and Alessandro entered the main living area where Pelayo, the twins, and Chantal had gathered. On the floor was a fresh painting Chantal had completed. Coco looked at the painting of a bedroom with stone walls, and the familiar symbol above the window.

"This was Prudence's wish, should anything happen," Chantal said. "She said you would all be safe there."

Coco shook her head. "I had a vision too, Mom. We can't go there." She unrolled the canvas in her hand. "This is my most recent painting. This is where I have to take the twins. This is where they'll be safe."

The intensity of Alessandro's stare caught her by surprise. "Do you know this location?" he asked. "It's called the Island of the Crescent Moon."

"No," Coco replied, "but please trust me, Dad, I know the twins will be safe there."

Alessandro's stare deepened. "Pelayo knows the island." He turned away but the intensity of his glare left Coco slightly shaken. She hoped he had not seen past her lie. She laid the painting on the ground and then gazed at Chantal's face.

"I love you Mom," Coco said.

"And I love you," replied Chantal.

Coco willed her bottom lip to stop shaking. She clung to her parents as they hugged her, and whispered the phrase, *"Sine virtute omnia sunt perdita."*

Alessandro released her, and Coco noticed he clutched Chantal's hand in his. They stepped away and Coco stretched a hand toward the painting. She watched the image of a rowboat moving through water, and an island in the distance. Pelayo stepped through first, followed by Jeremy and Arianna. The last thing Coco saw before she stepped into the painting were her mother's eyes filled with tears.

# 52

*Outskirts of Florence*

KENAN STOOD AMONG gnarled trees. He smelled the air and frowned when a scent he could not discern caught his attention. Recognition of sorts tugged at his memory, but in an instant was gone. He scanned the area to ensure his privacy, and then ducked through the thicket and into the mouth of a cave.

He sensed the witch's presence immediately. Before she had time to cast him away, he had one hand around her throat and with the other had caught her hands. Kenan's breath brushed against the side of her face and he heard her blood rise with fear. He stared into her eyes. "You will come with me and give me the information I desire."

She shook her head, but Kenan knew she was unable to escape the pull of his demands. He dragged her out of the cave and leapt into the sky with her gripped tightly against his body. Towns soon became fewer, replaced by the occasional chalet dotted among the highest peaks of the Dolomite Mountains of Northern Italy. Kenan sensed his men close by. They came into view moments later on a mountainside white with ice and snow.

Kenan landed, and strode among his men, dragging the witch behind him. His men were gathered in an area where Freyja had weakened the barriers protecting Prudence's fortress. As Kenan approached, the air before him glimmered, and a web of magic appeared. Gradually, a small space in the web disintegrated, leaving a tear large enough for men to enter the grounds of *Casa della Pietra*. Kenan ordered a group of his strongest warriors inside, and then waited for the second ripple of magic he hoped would soon come. When it did, he yanked the seer to her feet and stared into her white eyes.

"Where did they go?" Kenan demanded.

She pursed her lips.

He grabbed a bunch of her hair and leaned close to her face. "You are not immune to my will," he said. "Tell me where they are headed!"

The seer's white eyes rolled back, and taut veins strained over the bulging membranes. Her pursed lips moved to shape a word.

"Tell me!"

Blood ran from her eyes, down her cheeks, and over her lips. Her body shuddered as she fought against the words that spilled from her mouth. "Island of the Crescent Moon..."

Kenan tossed her aside and leapt into the sky.

# 53

THE STEADY PULSE of a heartbeat told Gabriel a human sat close by. He tested his intuitive skills, stretching out beyond his own mind to the person beside him. He clung to the essence, and then smiled inwardly. He recognized Kishu. Willing his lips to move, he managed to speak just a single word.

"Colombina," he whispered.

Exhausted, he summoned his strength again. A bolt of dark magic from somewhere close by reminded him that time was of the essence. He recognized the movement to his right as that of someone standing. Kishu's heartbeat calmed, just as it did whenever he took a defensive stance. Panic rushed over Gabriel. He needed his body to harmonize with his mind. He focused on connecting the two, and the moment they linked he spoke Kishu's name.

He heard Kishu take in a breath. "Gabriel?" he asked.

"Yes," Gabriel said. "What's happening?"

"Kenan's men have entered the grounds," Kishu said. "Pelayo has taken Coco and the twins to safety, but I fear for their lives. If Kenan has found this area, then perhaps he has access to our other sacred places, or worse, he could be waiting to flush us out. Alessandro has ordered Maria, Isabel, Eduardo, Layla, and Christopher to the inner sanctum."

"Prudence and Stefan?" Gabriel asked.

"They have not yet returned," Kishu said.

Kishu's words stung Gabriel, and for a moment he wondered if the sadness he had sensed around his mother was because Stefan had been injured, but he could not allow that thought to grow. He returned his focus back to healing. Soon he would be able to move. He thought of his runes, and immediately the fingers on his right hand were wrapped around the familiar smooth stones. Suddenly every cell in his body connected to his lifeline of magic. He tossed a rune into the air and rose to his feet. At the same moment, his clothes and knives found their place on his body.

He gripped Kishu's forearm, and then together they strode from his study to the main area of the fortress. When they arrived, Alessandro held Chantal in his arms and Gabriel could tell she was recovering from intense pain.

"Kenan was close," Alessandro said.

Chantal stood up. "He's gone now," she said, "but I'm worried about Coco."

Alessandro firmly clasped Gabriel's forearm. "Prudence asked they go to your coastal villa, but Coco said she'd had a vision, and insisted they go instead to the Island of the Crescent Moon."

Gabriel strode to the window. "How did Kenan find us?"

"I'll take a guess and say Freyja," Alessandro said. He strode over to a cabinet, opened it, and began arming himself with weapons.

"Any word from Prudence or Stefan?" Gabriel asked.

"Nothing," Alessandro said. He turned to Gabriel. "Leave Kenan's men to me."

"I'll strengthen the barrier," Gabriel said, "and then I'll find Colombina." He turned and disappeared.

Gabriel stood on top of the tallest tower at *Casa della Pietra,* and searched for the tear in the magic barrier that protected the fortress. When he located the damaged area, he held out a hand and blew across his palm. A faint cloud of dust appeared and spread outward around him to the forests and valley below. He heard a slight ping in the air alerting him that his magic held in place, and the damage was repaired. He swirled around and reappeared in the main living room, in front of Botticelli's portrait of Prudence.

# 54

## *Island of the Crescent Moon*

PELAYO GUIDED THE boat through dark water. Coco looked up at tall cliffs of white and gray rock, glinting in the semi-darkness. As they approached the mouth of a cave, Pelayo cut the motor, picked up the oars, and guided the boat through the entrance.

Coco noted that the frescoes adorning the cave walls bore witness to an ancient time. In measured areas, archways chiseled from rock opened to pathways. Pelayo steered the boat toward one of the arches, pulled in the oars, and jumped out. He beckoned for Coco, Jeremy, and Arianna to follow, and then pointed to a set of two smaller archways about ten feet above where they were standing.

"That's where we need to be," Pelayo said. "It leads to the ancient underground tunnel…the one in your painting."

Coco gazed up to where Pelayo was pointing. "Okay," she said, doing her best to quell the sense of dread brewing in her chest.

"I'll take you ladies up first," Pelayo said, "and then come back for you, Jeremy."

Coco placed her arms around his waist, Arianna did the same, and in one swift leap Pelayo landed on the stone ledge, and returned for Jeremy. He guided them along a narrow pathway with oval-shaped windows that overlooked a pool of water. The pathway ended at a solid wall of rock. Pelayo placed both hands upon the rock and took a deep breath. He blew onto the rock wall, and a door magically appeared. He pushed the door open, and ushered Coco and the twins through. As soon as he entered, the door closed and then vanished.

They were encased in darkness.

"Where are we?" Arianna asked.

"The tunnel runs underneath what was once the Temple of Juno, on the Island of the Crescent Moon," Pelayo said. "This place is ancient." He pulled out a flashlight from his coat, turned it on, and handed it to Jeremy, and then led them on through a twisting tunnel of rock.

They continued walking in silence. A few minutes passed, and Pelayo suddenly came to a halt. He tilted his head, as if distracted by a sound. A shiver crept up Coco's spine. She instinctively grabbed Arianna's hand. Pelayo pulled Jeremy close to him, and rested his hand protectively on the young man's forearm. "Take Coco and Arianna, and head to the end of the tunnel," he whispered to Jeremy. "I'll meet up with you."

Jeremy's gaze met Pelayo's. "Come with us, please—"

"I'll be with you soon," Pelayo said. "Take care of each other."

Coco noticed Pelayo's grip tighten on Jeremy's arm.

"This is what I do, Jeremy," Pelayo said. "Go!"

With a final glance at Pelayo, Jeremy turned away and yanked his sister's arm forward. They hurried off along the tunnel, and Coco followed.

Seconds later, Pelayo's voice erupted into a series of angry Spanish curses. "Come on, Coco," Jeremy said. "Pelayo knows what he's doing— to go against his order would dishonor him."

Coco kept on running, but couldn't shake the feeling of déjà vu from her mind: the darkness of the tunnel, the pungent smell of earth, and the innate sense of urgency to escape. Suddenly, something grabbed her arm. She screamed, and instinctively reached for the weapon she never thought she'd have to use. She spun around and stabbed her attacker with the jewel-encrusted knife Gabriel had given her.

She shivered, as liquid spurted over the hilt and onto her hand. The figure staggered back. At the same time, Coco pulled the knife out and thrust the blade once more into her attacker's chest. From somewhere in her mind she remembered her father's words: *A sharp silver blade stabbed directly into a vampire's heart slows it down.*

Arianna stood frozen. Jeremy's gaze went from Coco's eyes to the man who lay gasping on the ground. "Jeez," he said. "Come on, we need to keep moving."

Coco knew she only had a minute at most before the fallen vampire would start to heal. She grabbed hold of Arianna, and with Jeremy's help she dragged her away from the injured vampire. Further along the tunnel she stopped, and so did Arianna and Jeremy. Coco pulled out a folded piece of canvas from the pocket of her jeans, and laid it on the ground. She reached toward the image. Through the semi-darkness, glimmers of light flickered from the canvas.

"Hold onto each other and step forward," Coco said. "It's the only safe way out of here."

"Not without you," Arianna said.

"I need to hold the image... go through, I'll follow. The moment you arrive, hit 1 on your phone—it will alert Pelayo to your whereabouts." Coco glared at Jeremy. "Do you understand?"

Jeremy nodded.

"But, Coco—" Arianna pleaded.

"Go! Now!" Coco screamed. "I can't hold the image for long...I'll be right behind you."

Jeremy pulled Arianna with him as he stepped into the flickering lights, and disappeared into the painting. Just as Coco was about to step through to safety, a sharp gust of wind rushed past her. She was thrown backwards against the rock wall. Pain gripped her chest. She looked down and reached for the place where the handle of a knife protruded. Her eyes drifted over the dark stain seeping through her t-shirt.

She fell to the ground and witnessed the final flickers of pigment from her painting dissolve. All evidence of the location disintegrated. She gagged, and her head fell back against the solid rock wall. A burning sensation rippled throughout her body. She looked up as a shadow passed over her.

"Colombina, we meet again." The Italian-accented voice came from a dark figure. He crouched in front of her. Coco looked at him through tear-filled eyes. She saw a scar across the man's forehead.

O

Gabriel closed his eyes and replayed in his head the conversation he'd had with Prudence prior to her leaving.

*"When you were a little boy, you asked so many questions," Prudence said. "Some I could answer, others I could not. Do you remember what I used to tell you?"*

*"You told me to search where before I had not found answers."*

*"Yes," Prudence said, "that is correct." She had turned her gaze back to the portrait. "Perhaps one day, this painting will speak to us, not just of my journey, but of yours too."*

Gabriel opened his eyes, and reached a hand toward the painting. The pigments flowed to his fingers, and an image appeared.

*Light from a flashlight flickered in the darkness. He saw Coco's hand outstretched toward a piece of canvas that lay on the ground. Jeremy stepped forward with Arianna and then disappeared. Coco gasped, and her hands flew to her chest. She staggered and slid down a rock wall. A dark stain spread across her t-shirt.*

Gabriel knew this place. Prudence had taken him there many times over the years when she had told him the story of her birth. Only a few members of the Allegiance knew of its existence. He tossed a rune before him and vanished.

O

Prudence and Stefan appeared out of the fog that surrounded the Houdini family gravesite. Prudence walked up to the granite exedra and knelt beside the statue of Niobe. She picked up the withered pink rose, and spoke the words: "Look at this life—all mystery and magic." She looked up at Stefan. "They found him," she said. "He is healed, and has gone to find his beloved."

Stefan held out a hand to her. "Where are they?" he asked.

"The Island of the Crescent Moon," Prudence said. She replaced the rose, accepted Stefan's hand, and together they stepped back into the mist.

# 55

THE MOMENT THE group appeared in the inner sanctum, Ignacio could feel Louisa's essence reaching out toward her body that lay on the bed. He heard Eduardo and Christopher speaking, but shut out their voices and pulled his focus to his beloved.

With help from Hakon, he lowered Louisa onto the bed next to her mirror image, and watched in awe as the two figures became one. He sat next to her, and witnessed color return to her cheeks and lips. When Louisa's eyes fluttered open, she looked up at Ignacio. "My love," she whispered. "What took you so long?" Her lips turned into a smile, as tears ran down her cheeks.

Ignacio leaned forward and kissed her lips. "Let's just say, it was one hell of a journey."

"I heard my mother's voice," Louisa said. "Is she here?"

Ignacio nodded. "Yes, sweetheart," he said, "she's standing right next to you. She's somewhat of an overprotective mother."

Louisa's bottom lip trembled as she turned toward her parents. She reached out to Caprecia. "I knew you'd come back one day."

Caprecia nodded, and clutched Louisa's hand in hers. "I'm so sorry I left you," she said. "I…"

"I understand what you were going through," Louisa said. "But you're here now, and that's all that matters." She smiled at her father. "Are you okay, Dad?"

Eduardo pushed a lock of her hair away from her face. "Yes."

Ignacio overheard Christopher talking to Hakon. "What's happened?" he asked.

Christopher turned to him. "The fortress is under attack."

Ignacio was stunned. He knew he was bound to fight alongside his comrades, as he had sworn to do for the Allegiance. As if reading his mind, Christopher shook his head. "No, you're not going anywhere," he said. "We'll figure this out."

Caprecia leaned forward, and kissed Louisa's cheeks. "I love you," she said. She looked up at Ignacio. "You must stay together, always." She turned to Eduardo and kissed him. "Be happy."

Ignacio sensed Louisa's pulse elevate.

"Mom, where are you going?" she asked.

"Chantal is like a sister to me," she said, "and I won't let her fight Kenan's men without me. I must go to her." She placed Louisa's hand in Ignacio's, and held them over her heart for a few moments before letting go. Then with one last look at her daughter, she walked over to Christopher and Hakon. "I want to fight alongside my friends."

Hakon gazed into her eyes. "Are you sure that's what you want?"

"Absolutely," Caprecia said.

Christopher stepped forward. "The magic Prudence cast over this room is strong. I'm not sure it can be broken."

Hakon closed his eyes for a moment. "I can break the spell," he said. "And I shall join you in battle, Caprecia."

Christopher shook his head. "No, that's not possible. Prudence made it clear that you are to stay here." He sensed Hakon's reluctance. "They were her instructions, Hakon. Protecting everyone here is imperative."

Hakon gave a nod to Christopher, and then guided Caprecia to the door. "You will only have a moment to go through," he said.

Caprecia nodded to Hakon. "I'm ready."

Hakon stepped back, and as he raised his arms, an intricately woven web appeared around the walls of the sanctum. Light fluctuated around each skein, pulsing, like a beating heart. A small gap appeared, and grew until it framed the entrance. Caprecia ran forward, pulled the door open, and exited. Immediately the door slammed shut and the web sprang back.

Hakon lowered his arms and the web diffused into the walls. He appeared frail, and Sonja guided him to a lounge chair by the fire.

Ignacio wiped the tears from Louisa's face. "I need to explain something," he said.

Louisa gazed into his eyes. "No, you don't need to explain anything," she said. "I heard Freyja's words, and my answer is yes. Mother was correct, we must stay together...always."

"Are you sure the life of an immortal is what you want?" Ignacio asked.

Louisa nodded. "If it is the only way I can be with you, then yes, I choose to be an immortal."

Ignacio kissed her, but then he remembered Eduardo was standing near, and there was a part of him that was somewhat fearful of the human. He was Louisa's father, after all. He took a deep breath, and looked directly into Eduardo's eyes.

"In truth," Eduardo said, "I'm a little sad for myself. This means I won't have grandchildren."

Ignacio nodded. "That's true."

Layla, who had been sitting near the fireplace with Maria and Isabel, walked over to Eduardo. "You will have grandparent rights with our children," she said, giving Eduardo a hug.

Eduardo smiled. "Thank you."

Louisa reached out to Layla. "You and Christopher...you're having a baby?"

Layla nodded.

"How long have I been gone?" Louisa asked.

"Too long," Ignacio said.

Eduardo kissed Louisa's forehead. He rested a hand on Ignacio's shoulder, gave it a slight squeeze, and then escorted Layla to a sofa by the fireplace.

"What can I do to make you comfortable?" Ignacio asked.

Louisa eased herself up to a sitting position. "Is Maria here?"

"Of course I'm here," Maria said. She walked over to Louisa and hugged her. "What would you like?"

"Chocolate," Louisa said. "Do you have any?"

Maria winked, and walked over to the small kitchen area. She came back with three bars of assorted dark chocolate. "How's this for starters, *passerotta?*"

Louisa smiled and took a bite. "Mmm...*perfetto, grazie.*"

Maria sighed. "I'll never understand why anyone would exchange the taste of chocolate for blood!"

# 56

## *Island of the Crescent Moon*

GABRIEL STOOD IN an underground tunnel carved into the rock. The walls whispered his name in acknowledgement of his presence.

"Where is she?" he asked.

The tunnel was illuminated with a dim light. In the distance, he saw Pelayo throw a dagger into the heart of an attacker. Pelayo yelled to Gabriel. "Go to her!"

Gabriel leapt over Pelayo and raced through the tunnel. One of Kenan's men tried to get up, but in one clean stroke of his blade Gabriel sliced off his head. A surge of adrenalin urged him onward. The only sound he heard was Coco whispering his name. Her voice echoed along the cave walls. A strong gust of wind rushed at him and threw him to the ground. When he looked up, he saw Kenan bent over Coco, weaving his fingers around her hair and pulling back her head. Suddenly, a knife landed in Kenan's back. He fell forward and then staggered back, blood seeping from his mouth as he gasped for air.

Gabriel sprang up just in time to see a dark figure disappear with Coco. A young woman stepped out from behind Kenan, and Gabriel instantly knew what she was by her striking amethyst-colored eyes.

The young woman glowered at Kenan. "Hello, Father," she said.

Kenan returned her stare. "I know your face…"

"Yes, I'm told I resemble my mother," she said. "She was raped one night in a Florentine alley."

Kenan stood and glared at her. "I would never fuck a Creative!"

"Mother's eyes were hidden so that she would be safe from men like you," she said.

Gabriel wielded his sword, and charged at Kenan. "You will die for hurting Colombina."

Kenan raised his yellowed eyes. "Go on, kill me."

Gabriel brought his sword down hard, but just before the blade made contact with Kenan's flesh, a force much stronger than his own stopped it.

"Let me kill him!" Gabriel screamed. He turned and looked into the eyes of an ancient vampire, dressed in the clothes of a holy man.

The smell of sulfur permeated the air. Kenan hissed at the holy man. "You are all damned!" Kenan said, and then disappeared in a cloud of darkness.

# 57

## Casa della Pietra

CAPRECIA RAN INTO the main room just as Alessandro, Chantal, and Kishu were arming themselves with weapons. Jason stood by the main window looking through a pair of binoculars. He turned when he heard her footsteps.

"Do you have any more knives?" Caprecia asked.

Alessandro gestured to a cabinet containing numerous swords and blades. "Did everyone make it home safely?" he asked.

"Yes," she said, "and Louisa has returned."

"What about Prudence and Stefan?"

Louisa shook her head. "They went to find Gabriel...Prudence said that's where they were needed most."

Chantal reached out to Alessandro. "It was the painting," she said. "I should have sensed something wasn't right. Coco must have had a vision..."

"What can I do?" Jason cut in.

"As soon as you hear from either Gabriel, Stefan, or Prudence, let us know," Alessandro said. He stepped forward, clasped Jason's forearm with a tight grip and nodded.

Caprecia strapped a sheath around her hips, placed a knife in her right boot, and went to grab another sword. Kishu strode over to her, took the weapon she held, and replaced it with a dueling rapier sword.

"This is lighter," he said. "Aim for the heart and be quick to slice through your opponent's neck."

She looked up. "Thank you."

"A warrior's mind is still in the midst of chaos," Kishu said. *"Chinkon-Kishin."*

"I understand," she replied.

When they were all armed, Alessandro opened a door that led out to a terrace. He grabbed Chantal's hand and leapt up to a ledge. Caprecia and Kishu followed. Alessandro pointed to an area in the distance, where Kenan's men had gathered in readiness to attack. "Can you fly, Caprecia?" he asked.

Caprecia shook her head. "I've never tried."

Alessandro motioned for Chantal to jump onto his back. He reached out to Kishu. "Take my hand," he said, and held his other hand toward Caprecia. "Don't let go until we've landed."

In unison they spoke the motto of the Allegiance. *"Sine virtute omnia sunt perdita."* Alessandro leapt into the air. Moments later they landed and immediately wielded their weapons.

○

Freyja looked out across the mountains until she found what she was searching for. Gabriel had sealed the magic bordering the fortress, but not before a few dozen of Kenan's warriors had entered the grounds.

She saw four figures battling to keep the fortress safe, but the two women were young vampires and not experienced at fighting battles. The male human fought with the fierce precision of a Japanese warrior. The older vampire, Alessandro, while known for his speed and tenacity, could not win this battle on his own, and now that she understood the depth of love he shared with Chantal, Freyja knew what she must do.

She leapt into the air, and her wings unfurled and carried her to the battleground. She landed close by and could hear the clashing of swords and the curses that came with war. Her wings retracted as she made her way past ribbons of gore and white snow freckled with blood. She picked up her pace, and as she ran toward Kenan's men, a double-edged sword magically appeared in her hands. She fought alongside Caprecia, who seemed to find a newfound vigor when she saw her fighting beside her.

Freyja slew Kenan's men quickly, decapitating any and all vampires who dared come near her sword. Ashes mixed with blood were strewn across the snow. She looked up and saw Alessandro, Chantal, and the human battling the last of the attackers. She ran through the snow and leapt onto the shoulders of an assailant and quickly sliced through his neck. She glanced up when she heard Caprecia scream Chantal's name, and watched in horror as Caprecia threw herself in front of Chantal. A sword meant for Chantal swept clean through Caprecia's neck.

Freyja flew up the hill and slammed her body into Caprecia's attacker stabbing him multiple times. A hand grabbed hers. She looked up into the human warrior's face. "Finish it quickly," he said.

With one clean slice she beheaded the vampire beneath her. She slumped over in despair. When she turned around, she saw Chantal and Alessandro kneeling beside the last of Caprecia's ashes as the wind and snow carried them away. Freyja stood up and screamed.

When at last she caught her breath, Freyja felt something wet drip down her face. She brushed it off with the back of a hand and fell to her knees. She felt a presence beside her, and looked into the eyes of the human who fought with the spirit of an ancient Japanese warrior. He gathered her into his arms. It was at that moment she remembered the greatest, and saddest, parts of humanity.

# 58

## *Island of the Crescent Moon*

THE ANCIENT VAMPIRE turned to Gabriel. "You cannot kill Kenan," he said.

"What?" Gabriel said, shaking with anger.

The vampire lowered his head. "The blade I carry must be the weapon that delivers Kenan's death blow."

"The Holy Father..." Gabriel said.

The ancient vampire nodded.

"Why now?" Gabriel demanded. "Why have you waited all these years to tell us that you have the only weapon to kill Kenan?"

The Holy Father looked up at Gabriel. "I was blinded by my faith in goodness," he said. "But now I must face the truth."

"And what is the truth, Father?" Gabriel asked. "What is this truth that has caused you to be blind to the deaths of hundreds of innocent people at the hands of Kenan?"

"The truth, Gabriel," the Holy Father said, "is that now I know that the devil is alive and lives in Kenan's body."

Gabriel sensed the arrival of his parents.

"Are you alright?" Prudence asked.

Gabriel stared into the tunnel where Kenan had fled. Unable to speak, instead he took hold of Prudence's hand and held it to his forehead so she could see into his mind. She closed her eyes for a few moments, and when she opened them Gabriel stepped back to reveal the young woman with the amethyst eyes. Prudence gasped. "Luciana?" she asked.

"No," the young woman replied. "I am her daughter, Flora."

"You are Kenan's child," Prudence said, "and a Creative." She took a step toward Flora and outstretched her hands to her, which flora accepted. "You have no idea how happy I am to see you," Prudence said.

Stefan turned to Gabriel. "We must go to Colombina."

Prudence spun around and stared at Stefan. "You know where she is?" she asked. "Did you know about this?"

"Yes, and no," Stefan said. "While we were away, I asked that Colombina be guarded. But I knew nothing of Flora. I am sorry I did not tell you, *tesoro*."

"Where is she?" Gabriel demanded.

"With my mother," Flora cut in.

Prudence placed a hand on Flora's forehead and closed her eyes for a moment. When her eyes opened, she shook her head. "Too many secrets," she said. She turned and spoke to the Holy Father. "The Allegiance will help you find Kenan, but you must give me your word that you will destroy him."

"You have my word, Prudence," the Holy Father said. "We shall work together."

"We will contact you shortly," Prudence said.

The Holy Father turned away, and in an instant they had all vanished.

○

Pelayo decapitated the last of Kenan's men. He sheathed his machete and then ran along the tunnel to the place where he sensed Gabriel had been. The tunnel was deserted. His phone rang and he answered the call. "Where are you?" he asked. He raised an eyebrow at Jeremy's answer, "I'll be there in a moment," he said, "stay exactly where you are."

Pelayo stared at his bloodstained hands. He reached into a pocket and pulled out a single weathered stone. He tossed it into the air and watched as it hovered before him. "Take me to the twins," he said. The stone didn't move and neither did Pelayo. He cursed and then froze. "I wonder," he said. "*Llévame a los gemelos.*"

# 59

## *Northern Alps of Slovenia*

LUCIANA STARED AT the beauty of the landscape before her. From the warmth of the chalet, she marveled at the changing light orchestrated by cushions of clouds floating across the dimly lit sky. A fresh layer of snow had drifted across the mountains, leaving a tidy border of snow-covered rocks framing the mirrored surface of a lake. Trees wore fluffy coats adorned with snow-trimmed collars, and the meadow beyond the lake settled beneath a quilt of virgin white.

She pulled at the tattered memories of when she was brought to this place centuries ago. She remembered seeing her friends beaten and lying dead in the alley, of not being able to run when Kenan had looked up and seen her staring at the horrific scene. His bloodied hands had ripped her clothes when he pulled her to the ground and stole her virginity. She had no recollection of returning to the Medici household, or of leaving Florence, only a vision of her parents. *"Sine virtute omnia sunt perdita,"* the ghost of her father, Sandro, had said. *"Be the light, not the shadow, our dearest Luciana".*

She had awakened to the voice of a man telling her she was safe and that he would look after her. At first she was wary of the pale-skinned immortal, but he was not the fierce creature of folklore, but a gentle soul. When the pain of childbirth took its hold, he had called for a seer whom he knew would help her. At his first sight of the child, the pale creature at once took on the role of her father. He taught her about music and art and philosophy, and of the mountains and animals that share their space. Through all of this he never asked for anything in return from Luciana, and perhaps this is what drew her to him. In reality, from the moment she woke up and saw his dark eyes smiling at her, she knew in her heart that she loved him. And so it was that the daughter of Sandro and Colombina, artist and dancer, fell in love with her immortal guardian, and he with her.

He had kept his word, and protected Flora and her from the rest of the world. Their secret was shared only by a few trusted friends and the seer who brought Flora into the world of light. Her beloved told her of his friendship with Prudence, how long ago he had agreed to her pleas and changed Stefan from his human form to a vampire. Stefan, was now his only living son. The two men met on occasion and it was on one such recent meeting that Stefan had asked his father to protect Gabriel, and the Creative, Coco.

Luciana had never met Stefan, but her beloved had told her of his great courage and kindness, traits that he honored above all else. A ping, like the sound of a violin string being plucked, alerted her to his arrival. She saw a young woman in his arms, and for a moment she panicked when she didn't see Flora.

"She will be here shortly," he said. "Coco is dying."

Luciana helped lay her on a sofa. She watched him gently tap her skin at the hollow of her neck. Two vials appeared. Another tap and the contents seeped into Coco's body.

Luciana peeled the bloodied shirt away from Coco's skin. She saw the deep wound the blade created, and smelled the bitter scent of poison. Her beloved opened a vein in his wrist and placed it over her mouth. Colombina gasped.

O

Coco's eyes fluttered open, long enough for her to see a woman whose amethyst eyes matched her own.

"Coco," the woman said. "Be still."

Coco noticed a man. His pale face and dark eyes seemed familiar. She tried to remember where she had seen them before, but she was so tired. She remembered Dr. Fiore had told her to do something, but the memory slipped away. A sudden pain jabbed at her heart and made her gasp. Drops of liquid quenched her thirst, but she retched at the taste of copper.

The woman with the amethyst eyes hummed a melody. The melody was familiar and Coco smiled as an image of herself floating in water drifted into her thoughts. She remembered the song now, and the words drifted by, as if guiding her on a journey.

*Catch my hand when I'm falling,*
*And my tears have left me blind,*
*Be my anchor when I'm drifting,*
*And bring me home, when life's unkind…*

For a moment, Coco remembered a thread of a memory, and one word escaped her lips.

"Gabriel…"

○

Gabriel, Prudence, Stefan, and Flora appeared in the chalet. Gabriel strode to where Coco lay. A woman sat with her, she turned to him and motioned that he take hold of Coco's hand. Gabriel fell to his knees and stared at Coco's face. "The vials…" he said.

The vampire who took Coco from the tunnel stood near. "I broke both," the vampire said, "and have given her my blood. The poison on the blade is strong and her human body is unable to resist its pull. Once the knife is removed, she will die. You have a decision to make."

Gabriel knew before he saw the folds of silver satin that Prudence stood beside him. "We never discussed this situation," he said. "We've not had time."

"There is never enough time to discuss death," Prudence said. "Give her your blood, and if that does not help, then you must do what your heart tells you."

Gabriel bit into his wrist and held the open vein over Coco's mouth. He waited for her lips to touch his skin and take in his blood, but nothing happened. He moved her hair away from her neck and placed a hand around the handle of the knife.

The sound of beating wings and a rush of air made Gabriel look up. In the middle of the room stood a tall woman. Black wings folded into her body and she stared at Coco. Gabriel grabbed hold of Coco and shook his head. "No," he screamed, "she is not yours to take, Freyja."

"I am not here to take Colombina," she said. "But to give her life. I can save her."

"Don't come near her!" Gabriel said.

"Freyja speaks the truth, Gabriel," Stefan said. "I have not had a chance to tell you what we have experienced. But I do know that if you want Colombina to live in her human form, then you must allow Freyja to help her before it is too late. I would not lie to you."

Freyja approached. Gabriel held Coco in his arms and watched as Freyja leaned over her. She brought her lips to Coco's and kissed her. She leaned in and pulled the knife from Coco's chest and then ran a hand over the wound. Gabriel watched as the skin healed and Coco gasped suddenly. Her eyes opened. She reached for Freyja's hand and squeezed.

"I once had what you two have," Freyja said. "Cherish your love." She kissed Coco's hand and then stepped away.

Unable to speak, Gabriel nodded his thanks to Freyja. He noticed her eyes swam with tears, and then she was gone. He hugged Coco and listened as she breathed in and out, each one stronger than the next. She brought a hand up to his face and he kissed her palm.

"Home..." she whispered.

Gabriel nodded. He glanced at the others standing in the room, stopping at the tall vampire who stood next to Stefan. "Thank you, Grandfather," he said.

His grandfather bowed his head, and Gabriel noted that he clasped the hand of the Creative who had helped him with Coco.

"Go now," his grandfather said. "We will join you at the fortress later."

Gabriel nodded. He stood with Coco in his arms. Prudence stepped forward and gazed into his eyes. "We shall speak soon," she said, and then stepped back into Stefan's waiting arms.

A weathered stone appeared before Gabriel. He stepped forward and vanished.

# 60

*Tuscany*

Pelayo appeared in Gabriel's office at *Casa della Luna Crescente*. His clothing was ripped and stained with blood, and the large wound in his chest had only just begun to heal. The twins were sitting on a sofa, with Thalia curled up on Arianna's lap and Max resting his head on Jeremy's knees. Gabriel's pack of rescue dogs sat on guard around the room and barked incessantly until they recognized Pelayo's scent.

He noticed a look of horror on Jeremy's face, and realized that to the twins he probably looked terrifying.

"It's alright," Pelayo said, "there was a fight, but my body heals quickly." He sensed the tension leave Jeremy.

"Where's Coco?" Arianna asked.

Pelayo shook his head. "I don't know. She was gone by the time I made it to where you were, and so was Gabriel."

Arianna tilted her head. "Gabriel was there too?"

"Yes," Pelayo said. "And I also heard Kenan's voice, and another I did not recognize. By the time I got to where you were last…"

"What?" Arianna asked. "What did you see?"

"I saw nothing," Pelayo said, "but the smell of fresh blood lingered." He decided not to tell the twins that the scent of Kenan and an ancient vampire seeped near the place where Coco had fallen. His phone rang, and when he saw it was Prudence he answered immediately. "Yes, they're safe," he said.

"Where are you?" Prudence asked.

"In Gabriel's office in Tuscany. But I'm going to need help transporting back to the fortress."

"I shall be there shortly," she said, and ended the call.

Pelayo returned his phone to a pocket and collapsed into a chair. "Prudence will be here soon," he said.

"What's wrong?" Jeremy asked.

A smile crossed Pelayo's face. "I used a lot of energy getting here."

"Where are we?" Arianna asked.

"Gabriel's villa in Tuscany," Pelayo said. "This is his study."

Arianna walked toward the door. "I'll go see if I can find the kitchen and get you water."

"Wait!" Jeremy yelled. He stared at Pelayo. "I don't think water's what you need, is it?"

Pelayo shook his head. "No, but Maria keeps a stock of blood in the refrigerator in the pantry."

Arianna opened the door and went in search of the kitchen.

Jeremy sat beside Pelayo. "Take my blood," he said. "It's the least I can do."

Pelayo's face grew stern. "Never say that to a vampire."

"I mean it," Jeremy said. He rolled up a sleeve and shoved his wrist under Pelayo's lips. "Drink."

Pelayo swallowed hard, inhaled, and then pushed Jeremy's hand away and shook his head. Jeremy walked over to Gabriel's desk, picked up a letter opener and stabbed his wrist. He turned to Pelayo. "Do it," he whispered, shaking in pain. "Please..."

Instantly, Pelayo stood by Jeremy's side. He took his wrist and brought it to his lips and listened to the rush of adrenalin surging through Jeremy's blood. He licked the blood seeping from the wound on Jeremy's skin, and savored the sensual connection between the two men. Jeremy's body relaxed as Pelayo latched on to his wrist and drank. His blood tasted sweet, of youth, and dreams, and passion. He did not take much, just enough to heal his wounds, just enough to confirm what he already knew. His tongue ran over Jeremy's skin and he watched as the gash healed immediately.

The two men stood together. Pelayo could hear Jeremy's rapid heartbeat. He released his hand from around the young man's wrist. "Thank you," he whispered. Jeremy grabbed his hand but Pelayo stepped away when he heard Arianna approach. She ran into the room with a bag of blood in her hands.

"This is all I could find," she said. She handed it to him. He turned away, ripped open the bag and drained the blood quickly. He had known his destiny from the moment he had reached for Jeremy's computer bag in Christopher's D.C. office, and now that he'd tasted Jeremy's blood, he knew the feeling was reciprocated.

He tossed the empty bag into a nearby trashcan. "*Gracias*," he said. He looked toward the center of the room, where moments later Prudence arrived. She closed her eyes for a moment, and when she opened them she smiled at him. "Dear Pelayo," she said. "You are a good student. Gabriel will be proud of you." She looked across at Jeremy. "Thank you for guiding your sister here."

"Is Coco okay?" Arianna asked.

"Yes, my dear," Prudence answered. "In need of rest, but she is safe and with Gabriel at the fortress." Her gaze traveled over the dogs and then to Thalia. "Let's all go home."

Pelayo saw Prudence dip her head toward the statue of the Lady and the Rose, and caught the lilting scent of roses flooding the air.

"I smell roses," Arianna said. She looked at Jeremy. "Do you?"

Jeremy sniffed the air. "No," he said. "I just smell dogs."

Pelayo raised an eyebrow at Prudence, and she winked at him, just as a mist fell over the room.

# 61

THE HOLY FATHER swooped over the mountains near *Casa della Pietra*. Kenan's men had fled the area, and the only sign of battle were the stains of blood on the snow-covered ground. He landed, and tracked the scent of the witch. When he found her, she was near death, and suffering from hypothermia. Kenan had dragged her from the safety of her cave without knowing she would die quickly, unless she had changed to her younger self before entering the outer world.

The Holy Father knelt beside her, and gathered her into his arms. She opened her eyes, and reached a hand toward the Holy Father's face.

"I see him," she said. "My son…he is waiting for me."

The corners of the Holy Father's mouth lifted into a soft smile. "Is it your wish to leave this life?"

"Yes, Holy Father," she said, her voice weakening in the throes of death. "You must take the seer, Prudence, into my cave…there are items there that must be destroyed upon my death." The Holy Father nodded, and took her hand in his. "I ask for forgiveness, Holy Father, for the evil I have created. I have not lived a righteous life." Her eyes flooded with tears, and the Holy Father watched as her aged face and body transformed into the beauty of her youth.

"You are forgiven in the name of God," he said.

The witch squeezed his hand. "You must end this evil…use the blade and kill Kenan. Remember…it must be done on hallowed ground…"

"It will be done," he said. "You have my word."

She breathed in short gasps of air, and the grip on the Holy Father's hand loosened. He leaned down and kissed her forehead. "Be with God," he whispered.

As she took her final breath, tears from the Holy Father fell upon her face. He said a prayer over her still body, clutched her tightly to his chest, and then leapt into the air.

The Holy Father took the witch's body to the chapel under Vatican City. He laid her on the altar, and prayed for her soul. He dressed her in the habit she had worn when she had taken her vows to live a life of poverty, obedience, and chastity in the name of God; before her love for God had been shattered by a man who wore the red robes of a cardinal. After completion of this ceremony, he left the sanctuary of his chapel and buried her deep in the earth, next to her beloved son.

# 62

## *Casa della Pietra*

GABRIEL WAVED A hand toward the fireplace, and flames sprung to life. He sat on a sofa in his bedroom with Coco in his arms, gathered a blanket around her and kissed her. Her body trembled from shock, reminding him of the elements of humanity that he had almost taken away from her. Placing a hand on her forehead, he sensed her body slip into the pull of sleep. Only then did Gabriel allow his own body and mind to relax.

The whisper of his own near-death surfaced, he pushed the agony of the pain away, and instead caught hold of the image of the Holy Father as he grabbed the blade Gabriel had aimed at Kenan's neck. The power the ancient vampire yielded was immense, similar to that of his grandfather. Two powerful immortals; one who chose a path of religion, the other a path of a warrior. Gabriel had only met his grandfather once before, and since that time the ancient vampire had chosen to live his life in peace, hoping to cast away the bloody battles of his past. He sensed a deep love between his grandfather and the Creative, Luciana, a story he looked forward to hearing later.

He had no doubt that Prudence had received a premonition of his own death, for he knew that without the care and guidance from the Lady and the Rose he would surely have died in the explosion. Prudence must have asked for her help. He wondered if his mother had also seen Coco's death, a question for another time, along with the reason behind Freyja's sudden fervor to do what was right. He stared into the flames until they became embers. Coco stirred; he kissed her eyelids and stroked her hair.

"Gabriel," she whispered.

"I'm here, *amore mio*." Her eyes opened, and a wash of tears made her amethyst eyes sparkle in the soft light.

"You were right," she said.

Gabriel frowned a little. "About what?"

"I would have chosen life as an immortal over death."

He stared into her eyes. "I was unsure of what to do."

"I floated in a pool of water," Coco said, "and it was so quiet…just the water lapping over my body, then absolute silence. A woman came to me…she laid one hand on my forehead and the other over my heart. I could see her clearly and yet she seemed ethereal. All pain left my body, but then I realized, this was death, and a pain much worse than any other tore at my heart. The pain mirrored my loneliness without you. The woman sang a familiar song…and gradually the water dissipated. And here I am…home, in your arms."

There followed a long silence, a silence that spoke much more than words. Gabriel clung to Coco and she to him. He sensed Coco had a question. "What is it?" he asked.

Coco closed her eyes, as if to recall a memory. "The woman who brought me back…who was she?"

Gabriel hesitated for a moment. "Freyja," he said. "At first I wouldn't allow her near you, but my father came forward and explained that if I wanted you to live in human form, then I had to let her help you. I sensed a deep sadness around her, but nothing to make me believe she would hurt you in any way. Something about her has changed…no doubt my parents will explain when we see them later."

Coco sat up.

"How do you feel?" Gabriel asked.

"I won't lie, I'm a little sore."

"What can I do for you?" he asked.

"I'd love a hot bath."

Gabriel raised an eyebrow. "I'm happy to oblige, but I'm going to wash your body in the shower first."

"Do I smell?"

He nodded. "Yes, of your own blood, and it's causing me some discomfort."

Coco's cheeks flooded with color.

He lifted her up and walked to the bathroom. A nod of his head brought the shower to life. He kicked off his boots, and stood with her under the hot water.

"Discomfort bad, or discomfort good," Coco asked.

He grinned. "Definitely good," he said. "Now, let's see if you can stand."

He lowered her feet slowly to the tiled floor, and then cupped her chin and kissed her deeply. When their lips parted she stood naked, and Gabriel watched the last of the merlot-colored water wash away from her body. He kissed the skin above Coco's left breast, where the symbol of the rune Dagaz pulsed with the beat of her heart.

# 63

THE DOOR TO the inner sanctum closed, leaving Ignacio and Louisa alone. News of Caprecia's death had brought with it a cloud of melancholia. Ignacio's heart ached for his beloved, knowing that after years of absence her mother had returned, only to be taken away forever. He sensed her need to talk, and chose wisely to give her space and time. He leaned against the mantle and stared at the flames as they flared and fell.

Louisa sat in a chair by the fireplace with a blanket around her. Her despondent voice tore at Ignacio's heart. "When I was younger, I traveled with friends to Spain, but after a few days I left and found my own way to Portugal. I went there to see if I could uncover anything about Mother's past and her family." She sniffed and ran a hand over her eyes. "My grandmother was a prostitute, and this became my mother's life too. From what I could find out, one of her admirers took her to Madrid and then left her there to fend for herself. I learned from records that she'd been brought in numerous times by the police for using and selling..." She paused for a moment. "She'd used money from a trick to buy heroin... that was the last time anyone saw her. It was also the night my father arrived in Madrid for a gallery opening. Somehow, he must have found her...or perhaps they found each other."

Ignacio tossed more wood onto the fire. "Did you tell Eduardo what you'd discovered?"

Louisa shook her head, and burst into tears. "I couldn't...when my mother disappeared, he was in so much pain," she said, "I was just a little girl...but I remember hearing him cry at night. He loved her so much."

Ignacio knelt on the floor before her, and took her hands in his. "In the short time I spent with Caprecia, I can tell you that her love for you was infinite. She gave her life protecting you, Chantal, and the Allegiance. Your mother rose from a cruel, harsh life and became a hero." He wiped her eyes with a handkerchief. "Talk to Eduardo, tell him what you know. This will help both of you."

Louisa leaned into Ignacio's chest, and sobbed. When her sadness eased, Ignacio handed her a glass of water. She peered up at him. "Thanks, but I'm not thirsty."

He pushed a stray lock of her hair away from her face. "It's time," he said. "Please, drink."

She accepted the glass and drank the water.

"Are you sure this is what you want?" he asked.

She placed a finger over his lips. "Is it what you want? Will you still love me when I'm immortal? Will you still want to make love to me, kiss me, let me take your photo?"

Ignacio grinned, took the glass from her, and set it on a table. He kissed her fingers, brought his lips to hers, and kissed her deeply. "I will want to make love to you twenty-four hours a day, every day, until our time is no longer ours. You are my breath, my strength, my passion...and yes, you may still take photos of me," he said. He picked her up in his arms and laid her on the bed. "Any other questions?"

Louisa nodded. "Tell me what happens...how will I feel?"

He kicked off his boots. "First, I'll make love to you," he said. His dark jeans fell to the floor along with the rest of his clothes. He straddled Louisa and began to undress her. "The bite will feel no different to what you've experienced with me before; however, this time you'll fall into a deep relaxed state. Silence follows, and then it's as if a switch is turned on. Every cell in your body awakens. Then comes the thirst." He kissed her forehead, eyes, lips, and neck, and then moved slowly down her body.

Louisa moaned. "Will I feed from you?" she asked.

"Yes, my love," Ignacio whispered. "*Sempre...*"

# 64

GABRIEL LED COCO along a passageway lined with portraits framed in gold gilt. Beneath her feet she saw, as if for the first time, images of dragons and peacocks woven into the fabric. Further along, a pair of egrets sprang to life and took to the air, and circled above Gabriel. He waved a hand and a thick wooden door opened. The egrets soared to freedom and disappeared into the light of the real world.

Coco's pace quickened. She stepped outside and peered up into the sky. She watched the sleek white birds dip and circle above her, encouraging her to follow. Gabriel tugged at her hand. "Come on," he said. "There's something I want to show you."

They walked away from the main grounds of the fortress, through an orchard whose trees stood in rows, barren and twisted. Coco noticed the snow melting and tufts of grass bursting up from the earth. The trees were now shedding their winter coats of white, and were donning shining necklaces of emerald green leaves.

Coco glanced across at Gabriel and he grinned back at her. He reached up and picked a ripe peach from a tree laden with gems. He stood still and sunk his teeth into the peach. She watched, as he chewed the fruit and closed his eyes, savoring each drop of sweetness. He held the peach in front of Coco. She took a bite. Her teeth broke through the skin and into the flesh. She smiled with delight as juice escaped her mouth and dripped down her chin, and onto Gabriel's fingers. A burst of sweetness flooded her mouth and awakened her taste buds. She wanted more. She reached up to take it but Gabriel's hand was suddenly empty.

"No more," he said.

"But the peach…it was so delicious."

Gabriel placed an arm around her shoulders. "Remember that sensation."

They walked on to the end of the orchard and entered a forest of tall evergreens. Warm, woody scents saturated the air with lemon, balsam, resin, and cedar. Coco breathed in deeply, and on her exhale she experienced a sense of freedom. Smiling, she turned to Gabriel, and then sprinted off through the trees, laughing, releasing the tension of what had been.

She slowed her run to a jog, and listened to the noises of the forest. Birds spoke in song, and somewhere near, water trickled and splashed over rocks, dancing and gurgling. Coco looked up and saw Gabriel ahead of her, naked, and standing waist-deep in the middle of a body of water. Clouds of steam wafted above the surface, and as Coco came closer, she could sense the warmth of the water drawing her near.

She kicked of her shoes, slipped out of her clothes, and walked into the crystal-clear warm water. She dove in, swam across to Gabriel, and wrapped her arms around his neck. He lifted her up and placed her legs around his body, and then kissed her. His mouth felt warm and comforting, like chamomile tea.

Coco broke the kiss and whispered against his lips. "I love this place."

Gabriel ran a finger down her spine, and cupped her breast, massaging gently. She pushed herself up and descended slowly, filling herself with the pleasure of having him inside her. He moaned in delicious delight as she moved her body slowly.

He grabbed the back of her head, and brought her lips to his and hungrily kissed her. Their rhythm slow and gentle, their kiss deep and hard. They gasped in unison at their joint release. They stood together for a time, exchanging silent vows of love. Gabriel walked over to a large flat rock where he laid Coco down, and then lay beside her.

"Is this all real?" Coco asked.

"For a short while," he said. "After what we've both been through, I thought we needed time alone, together…taking in the essence of nature."

"What happens next?"

Gabriel leaned on an elbow and gazed at her. "A meeting with the Holy Father has been arranged for tomorrow. We'll decide upon the best strategy to locate and destroy Kenan."

"Do you think he'll stay low for a while?" Coco asked. "Now that he doesn't have Freyja's power behind him?"

"No, I don't see Kenan as patient," Gabriel said, "and his own power has grown infinitely stronger. The devil does not sleep."

"And Luciana and Flora, will they stay with us now?"

"Yes," Gabriel said. "And my grandfather…well, actually, both of my grandfathers, and my grandmothers. I want to apologize for not keeping a promise to you. I left for New York without telling you, and without drinking your blood."

Coco went to speak, but he placed a finger over her lips. "And I forgive you for lying to Alessandro and Chantal."

Coco closed her eyes. "Who told you?" she asked.

"Chantal," he said, "and I saw behind the Botticelli painting. I'm guessing you saw that too."

"I didn't know what else to do," Coco whispered.

Gabriel lifted her so that she lay on top of him. "I forgive you," he repeated.

"And I'll forgive you on one condition," she said.

"And that is…"

She leaned forward, and whispered, "Drink from me now, and all will be forgiven." Coco knew from the sudden tension in Gabriel's body that her request excited him. A moment later, he'd flipped her over and straddled her, and sent her mind into a torment of lust as he kissed her, and then trailed kisses in a path to her neck. His bite brought her to an instant orgasm. She moaned as heat flooded throughout her body and gathered between her legs, causing her to call his name as her body peaked once more. His tongue ran over her neck, and she found herself lost in his mouth as he kissed her and made love to her. When he finally broke away, he grinned down at her.

"Am I forgiven?" he asked.

"For now…yes."

They lay together, listening to the stream spilling over rocks, and the sigh of leaves whispering to the wind, catching branches as it dipped and danced through the forest. In time, they swam back to the shoreline. Coco luxuriated in the caress of the warm water as it swept over her, and then dripped from her body, as she emerged onto the shore.

She tugged her jeans over her damp skin, giggling like a teenager as she hopped about, almost losing her balance. Gabriel caught her in his arms, and a familiar heat again surged through her. Gratitude flooded her heart, and Coco knew this moment was now etched in her soul.

When they were dressed, they headed back to the fortress arm-in-arm. Coco looked back, and noticed the green of the forest changing back into the magic of winter. She snuggled into Gabriel's body, knowing that being with him, meant being home.

# 65

CAPRECIA'S BLOOD HAD seeped beneath a layer of virgin snow, where her friends and family now had gathered to say farewell. Louisa had requested a particular song be played in memory of her mother. As a child, she remembered Caprecia reading poetry written by Amalia Rodrigues, and how it always brought tears to her mother's eyes. The song that drifted over the place that marked her mother's death mirrored the poet's words that spoke of fate, and the connection between the lament of a guitar and her beloved Portugal, the country of her birth.

The lyrics spoke of destiny, of pain and loss brought to life in the singer's voice; a sigh at the end of a line and twisting syllables over the glorious strings of a guitar. Deep sorrow landing in the midst of all that is the music of *Fado*.

Louisa, accompanied by Ignacio, stepped forward with Eduardo, and placed a bunch of lilacs on the ground. On her ring finger, Louisa wore her mother's wedding ring. A veil of enchanted black lace covered her face, keeping her sharp new sense of smell at bay so she could attend her mother's funeral. Chantal clung to Alessandro, who knew the tears she cried were not only for the loss of a friend, but also for her blood sister.

From a mountain in the distance, Freyja watched Caprecia's loved ones say goodbye. She had met earlier that day with Prudence, Stefan, Hakon,

Sonja, Gabriel, the Holy Father, and Gabriel's vampire grandfather, and had vowed to let them know if she discovered where Kenan was hiding.

Her wings spread wide, and she jumped off the peak and soared into the air, circling above the place where Caprecia had given up her life to save her friend. Freyja whispered Caprecia's name, and a plume of light grew up from the snow and reached into the sky. In a flash, it burst into a shower of gold, and dissipated into the air. Freyja, too, had disappeared.

# EPILOGUE

IN HIS CHAPEL, deep below the Vatican, the Holy Father unwraps a piece of animal hide and reveals a knife. He takes the sacrament, drinks the blood of God, and then recites the Lord's Prayer. He prays for hours, asking God to give him strength so that he may find and kill the devil.

On the outskirts of Rome, in a villa by the sea, evil seethes and plans his next move. With his fingers tightly laced through a young boy's head of golden curls, Kenan empties his seed into the boy's warm mouth. At the height of his orgasm, a memory tugs at Kenan's mind: a woman standing on a cliff. He reaches out, but the memory fades into a Florentine alley, and a daughter he must kill. He drains the boy of blood and drops his naked body to the floor.

And on a mountain, way in the distance, stands an immortal woman. She closes her dark wings and gazes out across the mortal world; a voyeur of human behavior, yearning for a love lost in time.

○

From high above *Casa della Pietra*, an observer might see tufts of pastel, reaching out in search of love, or the attraction between humans yet to be awakened. The icy touch of an immortal's hand brushes against the warmth of human flesh. Pelayo sighs. Jeremy moves closer, their lips meet, and their love is sealed.

Lovers whisper sonnets of love, and find communion within each other's bodies. There are now two pianos in the art studio, and Alessandro and Gabriel play for their beloved Creatives while they paint. The lilting music of Viktor Stepanovych Kosenko's Opus 19: No. 7, Gavotte in B minor, drifts down stairs and through the maze of hallways, under doors, igniting passion and joy along the way.

In the main living room, light from a fire casts shadows across a portrait full of secrets. Layla, Antonia, and Prudence watch with reverence, as a young woman places a tiny key into the folds of a dress worn by a fairy, and cast into plaster. A ripple of recognition stirs within Hakon, and an ancient secret draws him to Arianna and the story of her ancestors.

Others gather in the heart of the fortress to enjoy one another's company and find love in preparing food. A fire swells in the hearth in the kitchen, bringing warmth, and nurturing souls. Wine is consumed, tongues loosen and attractions rise. Outside, the snow is heavy. Dark clouds sweep in from the north, relentless in their power, and bringing forth the darkest depths of winter.

End of Book Two...

# ACKNOWLEDGEMENTS

Thanks to my beta readers, Trudie Town and Jennifer Webster, your time and notes are much appreciated. To Katherine Odesmith, MFT, thanks for your Jungian insight.

Thanks to Siobhan Daiko for checking the Italian translations, and Evan Graham for doing likewise with the Spanish translations. And to Damonza, thanks for the awesome book cover. Thanks also to John Hudspith.

An extra big thanks to my copy editor, Joshua Sindell; for ingesting, digesting, and regurgitating every word, line, and sentence in the manuscript, and for catching my Australian/American/English grammar slip-ups, and nudging me over my writing edge. You're a gem!

Thanks to all of the readers, book bloggers, and reviewers for taking the time to acknowledge my books. Your reviews and messages are much appreciated. Thanks to the creative team who made the fabulous book trailer for The Devil And The Muse: Brian Beverly and James McEachen. Thank you to our actress, Paloma Palau, and to Suesie Shaw for feeding us all on set, and after wrap.

And to my sons, Angus and Jack, and my husband, Brian: thank you for your patience and understanding, and for putting up with my compulsive daydreaming.

See you all in book three!

CPSIA information can be obtained
at www.ICGtesting.com
Printed in the USA
BVOW06*1034050617

485909BV00009B/3/P